PYRAMID STUNT

ALEX LA BRUYÈRE

To all my fellow feminists who love some noncon.
There's nothing wrong with taking your power back in
a fantasy that is a controlled setting. You have nothing
to be ashamed of and nothing to apologize for. Your
feminine rage is still valid in real life.

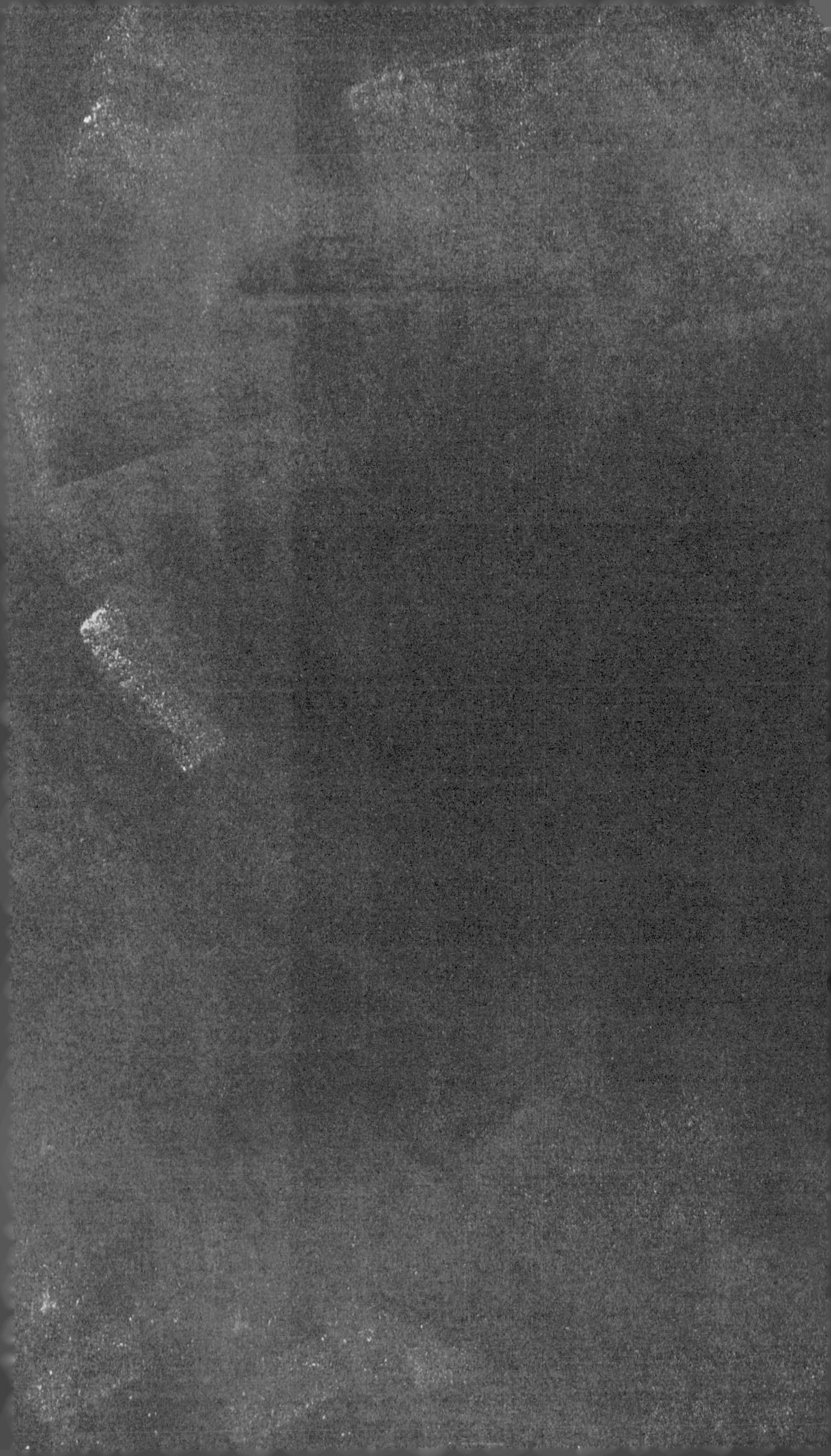

Here's what some of you know as Trigger Warnings and some of you know as the Grocery List:

Cheating between the main characters (with each other, and they will all end in an HEA, promise), face-slapping, non-con, dub-con, CNC, somnophilia, internalized homophobia, incest kink (but no actual incest. Two of the mains are stepsiblings), snowballing, praise and degradation, public play, fisting, edging, impact play, restraints, biting, hierarchical power exchange, strap-on, spit play, reverse Eiffel Tower, ass play, double penetration, choking and hand necklaces, primal play, D/s dynamics, cockwarming, and pegging.

All jokes aside, if you find any of this content objectionable, it's okay if this book isn't for you. Please listen to your intuition and refrain if you need to.

PEYTON'S BOOKLIST

A Midsummer Night's Dream- William Shakespeare
Babel- R.F. Kuang
Saint- Sierra Simone
Tomorrow, and Tomorrow, and Tomorrow- Gabrielle Zevin
King of Scars- Leigh Bardugo
The Woman in Me- Britney Spears

PLAYLIST

You should know I wrote this to the Barbie soundtrack.
Even the noncon scenes... especially the noncon scenes.

This Love (Taylor's Version)- Taylor Swift (Heather and Graham)
Physical- Dua Lipa (Graham and Peyton)
Stupid Love- Lady Gaga (Heather and Peyton)
Modern Girl- Sleater-Kinney
Girls Like Us- The Julie Ruin
Toxic- Britney Spears
Romance- Varials
PERRO NEGRO- Bad Bunny
Good Lookin'- Dixon Dallas
Rebel Girl- Bikini Kill
Still Into You- Paramore
Not My Fault (with Megan Thee Stallion)- Reneé Rapp

PROLOGUE

PEYTON

The bell is already ringing when I step into Wickersville High School. I sigh because, of course, Mama dropped me off in barely enough time to get my shit together before classes start. Now I'm going to get chastised when I go to pick up my schedule and told off again when I actually figure out what class I have for homeroom. I could complain about not being old enough to drive but it's not like it would matter. Will we even be able to afford a car for me when I turn sixteen anyway?

We've moved to this small town an hour outside Nashville because someone Mama knew in high school has opened a bar and wants her to manage it. I don't really want to leave Nashville proper but Mama says little towns like this drink more than you think, and regulars can give mighty good tips to live off of. Whatever. They don't deserve her. This town doesn't deserve me, either. I can tell there is some Pleasantville bullshit happening here and I don't. Have. Time.

I turn a corner and immediately knock into someone, promptly scattering their papers and books all over the floor. Fuck, I'm such a klutz. I panic for a second, and just fucking stand there like an asshole, taking in who I've bumped into. It's a sun-kissed girl, blonde, sapphire blue eyes, tall- like at least 5'10", showing a lot of leg in a cheerleading uniform in what I guess are the school colors of black and gold and proudly announcing "Hornettes" on the crop top. Seriously? I never can understand why team uniforms are never dress-coded in these stupid Southern states. They act as though if you are cheering for the patriarchy, it somehow nullifies how "distracting" you are to the male gaze.

"Did you hear me, bitch? I SAID pick it up," the blonde girl is saying.

"Um, fuck you. I would have helped you but not if you're going to be a cunt about it. It was an accident," I scoff in reply.

"Did this bitch just call you a cunt? Oh, she's about to have her shit rocked," A curly-haired brunette behind the blonde chortles. The blonde is a spectacle all on her own- I hadn't realized three more cheerleaders flank her. They're all much shorter than her- more like my 5'5" height- and they are all white like the blonde, all sun-kissed, and come in a variety pack of hair colors: red, blonde, and brunette.

"Listen," the blonde starts, saccharin-sweet. "I haven't seen you around, which obviously means you don't know how it works around here, but I'll let you in on a little secret. I'm the queen bee, and you have the fortune of being in my hive, so you're going to do everything I say or I'll ruin your life. Does that help?"

"Do girls like you seriously exist IRL? I don't give a shit who you are. I don't give a shit who thinks you're in charge of them. You're not in charge of me. Not now. Not ever." I start to move around her but she catches my wrist, turns me, and then shoves me hard back into the lockers.

The redhead gasps, "No one tells Heather no!"

"I guess she's gonna have to learn what it means. Sucks to suck," I retort.

"You little fucking peasant," Heather begins, but then she's cut off.

"Pretty girl, what's going on here? Is there a problem?" A shadow forms over me in the form of a huge fucking white guy- what are they feeding them in this backwater swamp of a school? He wears a football jersey in the same colors as the girls' cheerleading sets. The gold of the uniform brings out the emerald green of his eyes.

"This here is a new girl who just rained all over my parade, Graham, " Heather whines and pouts at him.

"Do you need help? You know I'd do anything for you, gorgeous," he winks at her. Then he turns toward me. "Listen, sugar, you probably don't know how it goes here, but you're going to want to listen to Heather if you don't want to commit social suicide. In fact, you should be kissing her ass."

"Are you trying to mansplain high school bullying to me right now? Both of you psychos can fuck right off. I can't believe I'm in a CW show right now. This is insanity and can't possibly be reality."

His gaze turns hard. "I'm trying to be welcoming to you right now, hun. But you're starting to get on my fucking nerves."

"Ugh. Keep your fake niceties to yourself. The 'Southern

gentleman' act doesn't really work when you're helping your girlfriend cage me against a locker." I raise my hands and push Heather back, then escape under her arm, only to feel a large hand on the nape of my neck, pulling me back toward the scene of my harassment.

"Ugh. Get off of me!" I try slapping Graham's hand away, but he just takes his other hand and pulls both of my arms behind me. Nothing left to do besides kick him, I raise my right leg and kick back. I hear a grunt.

"Jesus, Heather. Why'd it have to be a fighter? I have shit to do this morning."

"Lover, she ran into me. You think I should have just let her get away?"

I'm squirming around, trying to kick back at Graham and trying to get my neck and arms free while they just talk over me.

"Of course not, pretty girl," he sighs deeply. "I guess I'll throw her in the dumpster. How about that?"

"Thank you, baby. I love you so much," And then I swear to God, though I couldn't see them, they started making out while Graham is restraining me. These people are legitimately insane.

Graham tosses me over his shoulder and starts walking out of the school. I can see Heather blow him a kiss as he walks away with me.

I continue to kick and hiss at him the whole way outside and to the back of the school where the dumpster apparently is. The entire time I struggle, this asshole is just whistling "Somewhere Over the Rainbow." Imagine- such a wholesome song coming out of this guy's psycho mouth.

He sets me down, and I immediately turn to run away but he pulls me back into his hard body. He divests me of the backpack I'm wearing, smirks at me, then bends to grab my legs and hoists me into the dumpster. Unfortunately or fortunately, bags of trash break my fall when I land.

"Watch your back, new girl," I hear him laugh as his voice grows distant.

I try to stand up in the dumpster but keep falling over. I look up at the opening but it is higher than a typical dumpster. How am I going to get myself out of this? I pat my pockets but realize my phone is in my backpack's front pocket, which Graham had taken off me before relegating me to this smelly prison. Fuuuuuck. My first day is one for the books.

CHAPTER 1

PEYTON

2 YEARS LATER

I never thought Mama's love of football would be what ruined my life. Although I wouldn't say it's my deepest, darkest secret- that one's a doozy- I'm reticent to tell people that Peyton Manning is my namesake. As a die-hard Volunteer, my mama likes to remind everyone of his glory days at UT. I love that she has her passions, but we've never been able to bond over football.

The bullying didn't stop after the janitor found me in that dumpster and got me out using a ladder. It's been two years of clawing and scraping my way through school. Heather's locked me in a closet- this one is a repeat.

PYRAMID STUNT

Graham's stolen my textbooks. Heather's swapped out the copy of my play so that I memorized the wrong lines. Graham's shoved me into a locker. Heather's poured her drinks on me at lunch- that one is a repeat as well. Graham's put sugar in the gas tank of the car that I did manage to buy after I turned 16. The list could go on and on.

And now, I'm moving into Graham's house. Because of football.

It turns out Mama is a real hit of a bartender in town. On the day Graham's dad came in to watch the game, she made him the best old-fashioned he had ever had, they rooted for our favorite team in orange, and they hit it off. Now mama's eloped with Ashton and I'm supposed to share a wing- yep, this house is so huge there are wings- with one-half of my archnemesis duo.

I could be a pessimist but I ended up making a small group of friends at school, I'm slated to be Valedictorian, and I'm all set to audition for the lead in the fall play. And hell, it's my senior year. I'm almost out of here and into college. To major in what? It's freaking me out that I don't know. But I'll figure it out. Mama has always drilled into me that we will always find a way, and we always have.

I'm in my room- bare bones, beige walls, one king-sized bed empty of sheets, a wall of bookcases empty of books, and a desk empty of detritus. I'm trying to find the box that holds my bed linens when I hear footsteps in the hall and then hear my door opening. I turn around and see Graham leaning against my doorframe. It seems impossible, but he's gotten even bigger since I first saw him. He's easily 6'5" and 230 lbs by now and regularly uses all of that height and muscle to ensure I feel afraid of him. He's tried to dominate me. He's tried to bend me to his will. And the truth is that I'm petrified of him. I just don't let him know it. Like now. And I really don't want to deal with him right now. I know I'm going to have to get used to him pestering me at my house- this is not a home. It's frustrating that I have no safe place to go now, nowhere to hide from him. It's midnight. I've been moving boxes all day and the last thing I want to do is go through these boxes. But I need sheets, at minimum a blanket, to go to bed. Now I have to gear up and put on my tough girl façade when I just want to cry with how unfair it all is.

"What do you want, asshole?"

"Baby, don't be like that. I'm here to welcome you to the house."

"Oh, for fuck's sake. You're in "Southern gentleman" mode today. Got it. Well, you can take your posturing and fuck right the hell off, thanks very much. Or, actually, no thanks. Either way." I turn and give him my back.

"Darlin, we're going to have to start getting along. At least at home, for the parents. What would they think if they knew what a bad girl you were to me?"

I flip back around, "I'm sorry, what?! Like you're the one who suffers because of me? What a crock of shit!"

He smirks. "So you *do* suffer, then. That's what I like to hear. I'll pass it along to Heather. I know it'll make her so happy."

"Ugh. You are the worst. Can you just fuck off and die now? Buh-bye."

"I'm gonna help you unpack, baby girl. Let's find some sheets for that bed, huh?"

I raise an eyebrow. When Graham's giving me the sweet side of him that he shows to the rest of the world it's seriously difficult to say no to him. The fear is still there. The goosebumps on my arms are still present. My hackles don't totally calm down. But sometimes, I watch him do the "nice guy" routine and wish it were directed at me. And right now? He's giving it to me. I'm too tired to fight with him. Too tired to pretend I'm something I'm not, which is a strong woman who isn't afraid of anything. Maybe…maybe he can be nice tonight.

"Well, if you're here… fuck it. Sure." I hand him a box. "It's Friday. Shouldn't you have a football game or something?"

He chuckles. "Look who pays attention to her brother's schedule. Love that for us, sis."

"Ew. Fuck off with that. We are not brother and sister. So you can kill that shit real fuckin fast."

"First of all," he begins in a dark and honeyed drawl which I know not to trust, "I'll call you whatever the fuck I want." He sets the box down gingerly and walks toward me. And because I can't control my body, I step backward until he's cornered me against the wall. He looks down at me, green eyes darkening, dark brown curls falling over his forehead, and runs the back of his finger over my cheekbone. "Second of all, you should embrace our newfound roles. Maybe brother and sister will suit us better. Third, it's a bye week. I don't expect you to know-"

"I know what a fucking bye week is, you douchecanoe. Mama did teach me some shit."

"Such a smart little mouth. I'd love to show you what you should be doing with it."

I gasp. Graham has bullied me for two years but he's never been remotely sexual about it. And, in fact, I don't think we've ever been this close to each other for this long. But his breath is hitting me even from a foot higher than I am, his body is crowding me in, and his finger is still stroking my cheek.

What in the fuck is happening? I never can get a good read on Graham unless he's actively bullying me. That's the one time I know what I can expect from him. It's the one time he makes sense. Because he plays nice so often and without warning, especially around observers. He only really lets Heather see how dark and twisted he is.

"I- um… what?" My voice is coming out breathily, and I cringe at hearing what I sound like. Is…is my bully actually turning me on right now? If I don't want Graham to know he scares me, I definitely don't want Graham to realize he's getting me hot. My head is muddled from him crowding me in, making my mouth water with his pepper and bergamot scent that's overwhelming me.

"You heard me, little sister. I should fuck your mouth," he smirks at me and runs his hand down to my throat to hold it.

"Why am I "little" and you're "big"? We're the same age." Oh, God. This guy is giving me a hand necklace and I'm debating with him about semantics. But I'm grappling for control. Despite never having been turned on this much in my life, I need to come out on top. I'm used to my intellect carrying me through situations. But maybe I've been so used to dealing with boys. And he's not a boy- he's a man.

"I think it's pretty clear why you're 'little' and I'm 'big.' I'm a foot taller than you," he punctuates his words with a soft squeeze to my throat and moves closer. Now I can feel his whole body pressing up against mine. His hard muscles are pushing into the soft curves of my body. My palms are sweating and I think I'm starting to shake. I don't know what's scarier from this guy- violence or sexual intent. I begin to squirm under his touch and my body comes into contact with his pelvis and… holy mother of- he's hard. His dick is hard. And it's so big. Not that I know a lot about dicks because I've never had a boyfriend. The only experience I have is a lot of making out with friends when we play Spin the Bottle for funsies.

"You know what? We really need to find those sheets,"

I say in a panicked voice, wrapping my hand around his wrist and pulling his hand off my throat. He removes it easily and steps back from me.

He tilts his head and raises an eyebrow. "Mmhmm. Sheets."

Then he adjusts himself and I turn around so he can't see me blush.

I grab my phone to change the music to Paramore and he laughs. "Of course, you listen to this emo shit. Jesus, Peyton."

"Better than that weird misogynist pop you call country," I retort. "Ah! I found the sheets."

"Let me have the other side. I'll help put them on with you." He reaches out toward me and grabs the other side of the fitted sheet. "Are these little Eiffel Towers? How cute. Could you be any more basic?"

"I'm not afraid to be like other girls if that's what you're implying. There's nothing wrong with liking things the majority of girls like. There's nothing inherently wrong with being girly. Girls who are afraid to be girly buy that lemonade you sell that teaches them internal misogyny."

"I thought your whole thing was not fitting in? Isn't that why you wear all those goth clothes and hang out with that weirdo theatre kid crowd?" We finish the fitted sheet and he grabs for the top sheet.

"I'm just being myself. I like the goth aesthetic but I'm not afraid to like PSLs or pink or whatever. And aren't you being hypocritical? Your girlfriend is queen of the bimbos," he opens his mouth angrily at that, and I cut him off before he can start, "I'm not using bimbo derogatorily. Women have taken that back. I would have no problem with Heather, except she is a fucking terrible person. But her being what you would categorize as a basic bitch has nothing to do with that."

"You're so full of shit. You think you're better than her because you're all 'cultured,' 'non-conformist,' and 'alternative.'" He and I do a hospital corner simultaneously on each side of the bed.

"No, I'm an actual no-shit intersectional feminist. I would never put a woman down for being girly. You can keep that with your patriarchal trash outlook. That's all you."

"So, you'd be friends with Heather, then? If you're not too good for her?"

"Are you braindead? The two of you have bullied me incessantly for two whole fucking years. She's a bully, she's mean, she's catty, she's the girl with whom other girls are only superficial friends because she wields secrets like a weapon. I don't want to be friends with someone like that. No one wants to be friends with someone like that."

"You know what? You're such a little bitch."

"Graham. You literally fucking asked. And I answered. Don't be upset if I have some harsh words to say about your teenage sweetheart."

"Someone should really show you where you belong."

I roll my eyes, "Yeah, haven't you been trying to make that point for two years? I don't think it's working." It's totally working. I'm so afraid of him right now. We're trapped in this house, in my room, and I'm just going balls-out telling him off. It's like I can't shut my mouth.

"That's enough!" he yells, and then grabs me by the throat and squeezes.

"Graham... stop," I wheeze out.

"You just couldn't shut up. You can never just shut up. So I'll make you."

He picks me up under my arms and throws me on the bed. Then he unzips his jeans and pulls out his cock. It's long. Thick. Veiny. Purple at the tip. And so, so hard.

My stomach does a summersault. No way can he put that thing inside of me… anywhere. I shake my head and try to bolt for the door, but he blocks my way and then slaps me across my face.

Holy shit. No one has ever slapped me before. My face is warm and my ear rings for a second. Being degraded by Graham's words is one thing, but this feels even more degrading than the worst words he could say to me.

"Get on the bed, Peyton, or you won't like what happens next." He pushes me back toward the bed.

I stumble forward and grip the baseboard. I'm dizzy, and I need to get my bearings.

Graham takes advantage of my position, grasping my leggings and pulling them and my panties down my legs with one shot.

"Graham, no, please, please," I cry out. I turn, but I get tangled in my pants around my ankles and fall to my back onto the bed.

"Oh, perfect position. Let's just get these the rest of the way off, shall we?" He grabs my pants, pulls them the rest of the way off, and climbs on top of me. I start pushing at his chest.

"Fuck. You. I'm not going to fuck you. I don't want this. I'm saying no, Graham. Stop."

He pauses over me, body blotting out the ceiling light. I feel so caged in, so helpless.

"What will you give me instead, sugar?" He starts stroking my cheek again, and a shiver goes through me.

"Um… what do you want?"

He looks down at his dick. "Well, baby, I think it's pretty clear I want to come in your pussy. Wouldn't you agree?"

Fuck. Fuck. Fuck. "I'll do all your homework for the next month."

"Hm. That's a pretty good bargain. The Valedictorian

on call for my homework. Keep talking." He starts tracing my lips with his thumb, his hand big enough to wrap around my throat while he does so.

"For all of football season. Right? That's a good bargain. You can focus on football. I'll do your work. Just please, please, please, don't do this. Don't take- just don't. Please. Graham."

"What if you did my homework and you were a good girl for me?"

"What does... what does being a good girl for you mean?"

"It means you don't run that mouth at me or Heather. You keep to your place at school. You take your punishments without protest. Could you do that? Can you be a good girl?" He's drawing out the words good girl, and I don't know what's happening. It's making me all tingly to hear him call me that. Like, do I maybe actually want to be his good girl?

"Um. Okay. Okay, I can do that," I don't dare nod or move an inch. My heart is fluttering so hard. This man is terrifying and he's one move away from pushing his cock inside of me.

He nods to himself, and I can tell he's thinking. Then he pushes his thumb into my mouth, and I don't stop to think: I just lick out to taste him, making him groan.

"Nope. Not worth it. But keep that in mind for next time, won't you?" Then his dick is pushing, no- tearing, its way inside me, and I scream out.

"Oh, fuuuuck yes. Scream for me. That's making me so fucking hard," he says as he pumps in and out of me.

"Help! Help! Mama! Ashton!" I scream with all my might, but he just laughs and keeps going.

"Not that I don't love hearing you scream for mercy, Peyton, but our bedrooms are far away from our parents.

They'll never hear you scream for them. But keep it up. Maybe yell about how much I'm hurting you and how much you hate me."

I freeze for a second, then I rear back with a punch. Apparently, he's multitasking sex and survival because he catches my fist with one hand and slaps me again with the other.

"Bad, bad girl. I'm giving you all this dick, and you can't be grateful? Do you know how many women are dying to have me? You should be worshiping me right now, not screaming. But then again, I'm really into the screaming. That's never happened before," He grabs my discarded leggings and binds my wrists above my head with them while never slowing inside of me. "You know, I don't know why you're fighting this so hard, you're so fucking wet for me." He glances down at his dick and pauses. "Are you on the rag, sugar?"

"No," I sob, tears welling in my eyes.

"Are you a fucking virgin?" He's still paused, his dick filling me impossibly.

"Not... anymore," and I can't stop the tears now. They're streaming down my face.

"Oh, fucktoy... holy shit," he breathes and runs a hand over his face. "Oh, God, I can't believe I just took your virginity, and now I'm going to come inside your virgin cunt. Just when I thought you couldn't make me any harder- here we are with your blood on my dick."

I shut my eyes and start crying in earnest now. My thoughts are too jumbled to make sense of anything. I make him hard? He's glad he's my first? What in the absolute fuck is happening to me right now?

I feel a tongue lapping up my tears. "You're so gorgeous for me right now, fucktoy. Taking my cock, bleeding, and crying for me. I'm gonna reward you for how good you're doing. How about that, hmm?"

My eyes are still shut to block him out, but I feel him rub my clit and I whimper.

"Oh, that's a good girl. You're going to come on my cock, aren't you, fucktoy?"

"No, not for you. Never for you," I sob out.

But it's no use. To my absolute horror, this feels so good. I'm so full of him and it feels like little shocks are running through my veins. I've been a virgin up until now but I'm no stranger to orgasms. And I know from experience I'm coming up on one right now. Suddenly, I feel teeth sink into my shoulder and two things happen at once: Graham is coming inside of me, and electricity is flying through my veins as I come with him. I've never had an orgasm like this before. It simultaneously feels like I'm stepping into a warm bath, like I've just been flung upside down on a rollercoaster, and like fireworks are popping off inside my brain.

His teeth release my shoulder, and he returns to licking the new tears off my face.

"Hold that position, fucktoy," he whispers in my ear as he slides out of me. But he is sorely mistaken if he thinks I'm capable of movement right now. I feel like I'm high on the best strain of weed. I feel incandescent, like nothing in the world can touch me.

I open my eyes to see him standing over me with his phone pointed in my direction. I can only imagine what I look like. Spread eagle, hands tied above my head with my own clothes, cum and blood dripping out of my pussy. I'm not thinking clearly, but something niggles in the back of my mind that I should be upset about this.

"If you don't want this picture to go public, you'll shut the fuck up and never tell Heather about this. Got it?"

Ah. There it is. My bully just gave me the most intense

orgasm of my life. Now he's threatening me with my other bully, who just so happens to be his girlfriend. Who he just cheated on… with me. Fucking outstanding.

My hands may be tied up, but my fingers still work, so I give him two middle fingers. Fuck this guy.

Oh, wait, too late for that. I already did.

CHAPTER 2

GRAHAM

I'm so confused, but I know two things with absolute clarity: I'm deeply in love with Heather, and I just cheated on her with Peyton to have some of the hottest sex of my life. I didn't know sex could be like that. I just…let go with her.

Heather knows me best in this world. She knows the nice guy persona I give to the world, the loving boyfriend I am with her, and the dark and twisted guy I am when it comes to protecting those I love. In the beginning, Heather wanted to make Peyton a target for not adhering to the rules of our social structure. And I, being the supportive guy I am, helped Heather out with her little Peyton problem. The thing is, it started to become somewhat of an addiction. I can never decide if I love it more when Peyton fights me or when she crumbles because of whatever new torment I've concocted for her. Both versions of her are delicious. I don't know when I went from seeing her as the girl Heather hates to being obsessed with her tears.

And now? Now I'm lying in bed after cleaning her up and tucking her in. I can't stop thinking about corkscrew curly black hair and flawless amber skin covering a thick, luscious body. Heather and I have some hot sex, but I've never been like... whatever I was just like with Peyton. Her screams made me harder, her tears made me fuck her faster, and her blood on my cock was a revelation. I took Heather's virginity because we've just been together that long, and I liked it then, too, but I was as nervous as she was- although, of course, I didn't show it: I pretended to know what I was doing. I could barely take in what was happening until I thought about it later and realized breaking her hymen was hot. Then I was disappointed I hadn't been in the moment because I would never get to do that again.

It's not like I was planning on fucking Peyton. I have never seriously considered cheating on Heather. I know we're young, and it's our first relationship. But I want her to be my wife for fuck's sake. She does it for me.

I also know that I've been jerking off to Peyton- and still Heather; she's perfection, dear God- for longer than I'd care to admit. Sometime between throwing her into that dumpster on her first day and having her come on my cock today, I'd toyed with the idea of her crying as I pumped into her. I've gotta say... the reality was 100x better than the fantasy.

But the sex can't happen again. I'm loyal to Heather. I guess I've figured out I'm not so loyal as to tell her I fucked someone else- someone she hates- but let's be honest. I'm protecting Peyton by not telling Heather. If I tell her, she's liable to go full nuclear on Peyton. Until now, we've not done anything serious to Peyton; we just made her life inconvenient. I don't trust Heather not to do something utterly insane if she finds out I stepped out on her. And, okay, I'm a little worried for myself. Heather and I have had fights, but nothing so major as what this would cause. I'm not willing to sacrifice the rest of my life just so Heather can be worried about another woman. She shouldn't be worried. I'm hers forever.

The following morning I'm in the kitchen after a run. The housekeeper, Willow, hands me my protein shake-why do it myself when Dad has hired help?. I start downing it while I lean against the kitchen island and stare at Peyton eating at the breakfast nook. She looks up from her omelet and gazes back at me blankly. I can't stop eye-fucking her, even in her oversized black hoodie and skintight leggings. Her hair is still in a silk scarf, and she's wearing big black framed glasses. I've never seen her in glasses. I think I'd like to fuck her in them. Fuck. No. Bad, Graham. No more fucking your new stepsister.

Hm. But I can torture her a little.

I move close to her seat and shadow over her. "Good morning, fucktoy. How did you sleep?"

"Like I was dead, actually. Despite being sore," she glances up at Willow, who is in the beginning stages of what looks like lunch. "For some reason."

"Sore? What was sore? Do you need me to look at it?" I can't help myself. She looks so uncomfortable.

She shifts. "Um. Just…" She suddenly seems to find her strength because she straightens up. "You know damn well why I'm sore, and fuck you very much about all of it."

"That's my fucktoy. Always running her mouth," I smirk and bring my hand up to touch said mouth but she smacks my hand away.

I lean into her more, and she narrows her eyes. "I can't do anything to you in this kitchen right now. But you should know, I have a long memory."

"Graham. I say this with all the disrespect possible. Fuck. Off."

I'm just about to open my mouth when Heather walks into the kitchen, in a flurry of pink bathing suit cover-up, full makeup, and hair in braided pigtails.

"Baaaaaaaaby," she sashays across the kitchen to me and runs her hand down my bare chest. "Oh, Graham. On the one hand, you're clearly running late. On the other hand, you look so good, all sweaty after a workout."

I tug on both pigtails, and she squeals. "Stop, you big bully. You'll mess up my hair."

"Pretty girl, you love it when I mess you up," I smirk at her and then drop my hands to her waist and pull her into me. I move in for a kiss, and she immediately opens for me. I groan, licking into her mouth. This is what I need after last night. She is home. My tongue paints into her mouth, and she gives as well as she takes. After years together, we're a well-oiled duo. We're not just a power couple because I'm the quarterback, and she's the cheer captain. We just fit in all the ways. We make sense. I feel myself getting hard against her, and I bite her bottom lip before diving in again. She runs her hands from my shoulders down to my cock to squeeze my dick. I'm a little surprised she's doing this in the kitchen of all places because we're usually pretty well-behaved in the house's public spaces. But then I realize it must be for Peyton's benefit, and I can't find it in me to care. If she wants to stake her claim, I will gladly be her prop for the exhibition. I pick her up under her thighs, set her on the counter, and grind my bulge into her center. She whimpers. And Christ, I love that sound. She starts kissing from my jaw down my throat and to my shoulder while I tighten my grip on her compact hips, digging my thumbs into her. I look over at Peyton and stare into her eyes as Heather licks sweat off my nipple, and I hear as well as see Peyton throw her fork onto her plate.

"Just when I thought you two couldn't get more disgusting than you are at school. Now I have to live here and be present for all of this. Can't wait until I can hear you fucking while I try to sleep. *Ugh!*" She stands up from the table, grabs her plate and fork, and walks over to the sink to deposit them.

"Oh, Graham, I love your body so much," Heather drawls out while moving to my other nipple.

"Psychopathic freaks!" Peyton yells out as the door swings behind her.

Heather abruptly stops nibbling and licking my chest. "Oh, good. She's gone. Let's get you in a bathing suit. I guess since we're going to the lake, you can shower after. I honestly do love the way you smell when you're all freshly sweaty."

"What happened to us fucking in the kitchen? I liked where this was going," I run my hands up and down her back.

"Graham. We are not going to fuck in the kitchen. Willow is literally standing right there," she points to our housekeeper who is doing an excellent job of ignoring us entirely. If her earpods are any indication, I think she also might be listening to an audiobook. And those things get smutty, if it's any indication of the cover flashing on her phone.

"Then what was that about?"

"What?" she blinks her eyelashes up at me. "I'm not allowed to be a little territorial with my man? She's living here now, so I just thought she could use the extra reminder of who you belong to."

It's like this woman can read my mind. Fuck, fuck, fuck.

"Pretty girl," I kiss her forehead, eyelids, and finally peck her lips. "I know who I belong to. You don't have to worry." She doesn't. Because last night will never get a repeat.

We swim for a while out in the lake behind my house. We're splashing each other when a thought occurs to me. "Babe, what would you think if I hit you?"

"What the fuck, Graham?" She stops splashing and looks at me in puzzlement.

"Wow, that came out wrong. Not like… violently. Like… sexily?" I raise my eyebrows.

"I'll repeat myself. What the fuck, Graham?"

"Okay, like picture this: we're fucking, and I slap you across the face and call you a slut. Or I spank you before we start?" I've been thinking about this since last night. Maybe if Heather can do what Peyton does for me, I won't want to fuck Peyton anymore.

"What is going on with you?"

I sigh, "Never mind. I… I don't know." How can I tell my girlfriend I want to pretend I'm raping her? God, I'm so fucked up. What was I thinking? What am I thinking? I run a hand down my face.

She suddenly makes a face. "Are you… are you bored with sex?"

"Oh, pretty girl, no, no, no," Oh, fuck. What have I done? "I love sex with you. I love you. You are perfect to me. I'm sorry. I'll shut up."

She tilts her head. "You would tell me?"

"I tell you everything. You know that," You know, except the one thing I absolutely can never ever tell you. Maybe it can be a funny story when we're old and gray. Hey, wife of mine for the past 50 years, remember that girl we bullied? Yeah, my stepsister. I took her virginity. Oops! Another drink?

She nods. "I love you, too." She splashes me again, and it gets me right in the face.

I swim over to her and dunk her in the water. Not long. Not as long as I would if it were Peyton instead of Heather. I've never made Heather cry, and I don't plan on starting now.

I let her pop back up, and she gasps in air. "Oh, you're fucking getting it now!" she screeches at me, and suddenly she's tickling me in all my sensitive spots.

I grab her legs under the water and pull her into me until she wraps her legs around my hips. I move in for a kiss, and her mouth opens under me. I palm her ass and grind into her as well as I can while I tread us in the water. I lick into her over and over until she's moaning into my mouth, and then I reach around to her back to untie her suit top. I fling it over to land on the dock, leaning down to take a nipple into my mouth while I use my hand to pinch her other one. Her short nails dig into my back, and I love the sting as she scratches me. I bite a nipple just this side of hard, and she groans loudly.

"Graham. Baby. Please. I need your thick cock in me," she moans and pushes her center into me. We're in the water, so I can't feel how wet she is, but I feel her heat against me.

"Anything and everything you want, my love," I softly bite into her neck as I swim us over to the ladder on the side of the dock.

I smack her ass as she goes up the ladder, and she turns to wink back at me. She's a vision: up above me, pink suit bottom climbing up to showcase that little but juicy ass, blonde hair braided and lying against her tanned skin, laughter on her face because of me, long legs that I can't wait to feel wrapped around me.

I climb up behind her while she takes her bottoms off and spreads out a towel. She looks up at me. "Because splinters in my ass is not a look I want to try," she explains as she lays atop it.

"Are you wet for me?" I prowl over and stand above her, dripping lake water onto her body.

"I think you should use your tongue to check," she replies, putting her arms behind her head in a picture of laziness and arrogance.

I salute her and then get on my knees between her thighs. I can see her glistening, and I don't actually know that it's from her body's lubrication and not the lake, but if I know my girl- and I do, fuck you very much- it's because she wants me.

I don't need to be told twice to eat her pussy so I lean down and plunge my tongue into her hole. She giggles and clamps her legs around my head like my favorite pair of earmuffs. I slide my hands under her thighs and grip tight as I plunge my tongue in and out of her while her gasps increase in frequency and volume. Then I run the flat of my tongue up her slit until I reach her engorged clit and make circles with my tongue. One of her hands fists my hair as she starts to pull, and the other grabs onto my shoulder, her nails digging in to make what I suspect are very distinct crescent shapes. The pain spurs me on, and

I groan against her mound. I bite her clit lightly and then suck it into my mouth, causing her to buck underneath me. Her thighs are starting to shake around my head, and I know I've got her close. So close. Her thighs are locked around me, so I release my grip on them and move my hands up to her nipples, toying with them while I suck on her clit. I suck a little harder at the same time I pinch both of her nipples, and she screams. I feel her gush against my chin as I suck her clit through her orgasm. When her thighs relax their hold around my head, I lick down to her hole to taste her sweetness and lap up her cream. I lift my head and crawl up her body.

"You are my favorite taste in the world," I tell her.

"Mmm. Better than Willow's grilled cheeses?"

"Yep."

"Better than… Ben & Jerry's?"

"You know it."

"Better than… carne asada?"

"100%."

"Mmm… well, I guess I'll have to try. Give me a taste, baby," I spit in her mouth, and she smacks her lips.

"Hmmm… it's good. Give me more?"

Then I dip down and cover her mouth with mine. She moans and opens for me. This is not the first time we have had this conversation. It's a repeated one we have wherein I tell her she's my favorite flavor, and then I push her own juices into her mouth. We love it.

She arches into me and grabs my dick, pulling it to her entrance.

"Mmm, pretty girl. You ready for this dick?"

"Graham, I'm vibrating with how much I need you to fill me up. Make me whole, baby," she moans out to me.

I grip her tits and shove my cock inside of her, and she growls out.

"Oh, God, Graham. Only you can fuck me like this," she runs her fingernails down my abs, leaving a red trail.

I start pumping in and out of her. "You will only ever know this cock, isn't that right, pretty girl?"

"Only you, only ever you. God, the way you fill me," she bites out as I start fucking her harder.

God damn, does she feel good. She's so fucking wet from coming for me, and she's always so fucking tight. Like a vise on my dick. I toss her legs onto my shoulders and keep plowing into her. She grabs me by my hair and pulls me down to her lips, tongues tangling. I love how flexible she is that we don't even have to think about the positions I put her in when we're fucking. I pull away from her.

"How close are you?"

"Close. Keep going. Maybe lift my hips a little to hit my cervix the way you know I like, yeah?"

I peck her lips and do as she says. The lake water has dried off of me, replaced with the sweat Heather says she likes. I'm dripping so much it's starting to drip onto her body like a drizzle. She opens her mouth, and some of my sweat dribbles into her mouth. Heather may not be whatever I'm beginning to think I'm into, but that doesn't mean she's not a filthy little freak. She leans up and licks my throat, humming.

"Come on, pretty girl. Come with me," I demand and then bite those gorgeous collarbones of hers.

She squeals as I feel her pussy tightening around me, warmth gushing around my dick. I wrap my hands around her lean torso and pump twice more, making sure the last pump is to the hilt as I come deep inside her, groaning.

I slip out of her and slide back down her body to reach her pussy. I groan as I watch the cum dribble out of her body, then I lean forward and suck my deposit out of her.

I hold my cum in my mouth as I crawl back up her body. She's lying there in a daze, so I tap my fingers on her lips, and she opens her mouth so I can kiss her and push my cum into her mouth. She hums into my mouth as her tongue lazily strokes mine. Then I flip onto my back and pull her into my side, my arm underneath her head.

"You know I'll love you forever, right?" I ask her, shutting my eyes.

"Of course, baby. I'll love you forever, too. Even if you think our sex is boring."

"Heather Abigail Lovelace. That is not what I said. And that sex was so hot. It hasn't been that hot in a while."

"Top 5?"

"Top 5," I agree and raise my arm for a high-five. She smacks it and then bites into my pec.

"We're gonna get stale sometimes. But we will find our way back to each other."

"Yeah, pretty girl. I hear you." I tuck her further into my side and start stroking her lower back.

That's what I've gotta do. Just find my way back to Heather... and only Heather. So, how do I stop wanting Peyton?

CHAPTER 3

I lower the binoculars and drop back onto the chaise lounge on the balcony of my bedroom. I feel hot and tingly all over. I can't believe I just watched Graham and Heather fuck on the dock like their lives depended upon it. It started out as curiosity, how Graham acted with Heather. Like, what was their dynamic when they weren't making my life hell or trying to prove to everyone that they were Barbie and Ken? When Graham dunked her under the water I thought for sure he would get weirdly violent with her like he had with me. And it's not like their sex was vanilla. No, definitely not. It was raw and animalistic but also, even from far away, I could tell it was loving. I can't understand how anyone could love either of those monsters. But maybe that's just it. They are both monsters and it takes a monster to love a monster. When they finished and they snuggled up together I could feel the devotion between them. And honestly? Not only did watching them turn me on but it made me jealous. I want someone to love me the way they so clearly love each other. And if those two could find their other half then I could certainly find mine.

I do wonder, though. What is Graham feeling now that he has cheated on Heather? It's not like he wants to break up with her and it's not like he actually wants me. I just watched his adoration of Heather play out- as though this morning in the kitchen wasn't enough for me. Surely I'm safe from his sexual advances now that he has had me... right?

One thing I'm sure of is that I need emergency contraception and fast. I love Mama, but neither of us want my future's trajectory to follow hers, even if hers had worked out and she claims to love her life. I don't want kids at all. I want a career and maybe a partner if they can get on board with my ambition.

I open the French doors and walk inside, immediately being accosted by all the boxes I have yet to unpack. Sighing, I move past them. I don't have time to think about that. Fertilization is imminent. I have shit to do besides worry about making my room aesthetically pleasing.

I find Mama in the living room merging some of the things from our old house into the atmosphere here. She's listening to some Britney Spears and singing at the top of her lungs, her dark brown skin sheened with sweat and her locs tied up on top of her head.

"Mama!" I yell.

She keeps dancing around the living room, "'Too high, can't come doooown.'"

"*Mama!*" I yell louder.

"'Can ya feel me now?'" She sings and pops her ass.

I search around the room until I find her phone, going

over and pausing the music. She notices me, finally.

"Hey, baby! Whatcha doin?"

"Um… can we talk? It's pretty important."

"Anything you want, my heart." She wipes some sweat off her sepia forehead and looks around for a second. Humming, she grabs her sweet tea and sits on the couch, patting the cushion next to her.

"Um. Okay. So I know I tell you everything…" And by that I mean almost everything. I have certainly not told her about Graham and Heather's bullying. When it started we had just moved here and I didn't want to stress her out. The longer it went on, the more I felt ridiculous about telling her how long it had gone on and admitting that I hadn't told her. So it is the big secret between us now, not that she has a clue that it is there. And this is another secret I'm going to be keeping from her. "I… well, there's no good way to say this. I lost my virginity last night. And we weren't safe. And I know that I should have been, but please just don't harangue me for this. I'm coming to you because I need plan B and I want to get an IUD so if I have another slipup like this I can stay safe." I breathe out in a rush.

"Ooookay. Wow. This is me being a cool mom, not a regular mom and trying to sit with this while I unpack it. Let's start with step one: thank you for telling me. I love you no matter what you do. And you know your virginity has nothing to do with how wonderful you are as a person and is largely a social construct anyway. I just thought we talked about this and how you needed to be safe when you did start having sex. I don't want to be that parent that's all 'kid, you're smarter than this,' but like, baby girl, you are smarter than this."

"It… wow. I guess it happened so fast that it got away from us?" I cringe. Because yes, it did happen so fast. But I didn't want it to happen in the slightest at all anyway so it's not like I could have controlled Graham and gotten him to wear prophylactics.

"Okay. Do you think having sex is something you can handle if it got away from you? You're the smartest teenager I know but this doesn't sound like you. I didn't even know you liked someone." She lays a hand on my shoulder.

"I don't even like him," I mumble.

"What? I didn't catch that."

"Nothing. I mean. I'm good, Mama. I just need help for the next step, please." I lean my head onto her hand.

"Getting you plan B, right. That's easy enough. I guess we can make an appointment with a gynecologist for an IUD." She pulls her phone to her and starts typing.

I panic. Because what if... what if Graham comes back before I get the IUD? I can play off one mistake to Mama but our trust would start to erode if it was more than one time that I needed plan B. Thank goodness I planned for this conversation.

"Actually, I looked it up, and if you go to the ER, they'll do emergency contraception, to include IUD placement. It's a thing."

"Trust you to do your homework. But seriously, can I trust you to know how big a deal sex is? It's not just pregnancy you have to be aware of. STIs are serious too."

"We don't need to make it a thing. Please believe me when I say I know how serious this all is. Please. Please. Please. Just buy the lemonade without hearing the pitch for once, Mama."

"Okay, kid. Let's go to the hospital." She stands up and I follow after her. She begins to walk away then turns back to me and wraps me up in a hug. "I love that you feel safe enough with me to come to me with these things. We're gonna make it okay. I love you infinity."

"I love you infinity and beyond."

"That's my girl," she soothes my nerves. And I take a beat to be thankful for her. At least I have one parent that hasn't phoned it in.

After driving in Mama's car the 15 minutes it takes to get to the local ER, we check in and wait what seems like forever. Not like we're on a time crunch here. It's just the rest of my life on the line, right? We're led back to a curtained room and I'm told to take off everything below the waist and change into a hospital gown. Then we wait another 45 minutes for someone to come in and see me.

"Hi there, I'll be your nurse practitioner today. It says here you are in need of emergency contraception."

"Yes. I had sex last night but we didn't use any form of birth control. So I'm here to get plan B and an IUD for future... mishaps."

"What was the start date of your last period?"

"Ummm. Two Mondays ago."

"Right. Well. If you get the hormonal IUD inserted it's not going to be immediately effective. We recommend 7 days for full efficacy if it's not inserted within 7 days of your last period. But if you get the nonhormonal IUD, it starts working immediately and you don't even need to suffer the side effects of the pill. Have you ever had birth control before?"

"No, never."

"And how are your periods? Are they pretty light? The good news with a hormonal IUD is that within 6 months to 1 year, your period vanishes. Nonhormonal doesn't usually affect the period after the first couple of days, in which you can experience spotting after insertion."

"I pretty much don't even notice my periods because they're so light." I think about it for a second. I don't have 7 days if Graham gets a hair up his ass again. "I think I'll take the nonhormonal so it starts acting immediately."

"That's a great choice. We can do that in an outpatient procedure. Let me just get some forms for you to fill out. Just so you're aware, there is some pain associated with the procedure and you'll experience light to moderate spotting for a couple days as well as some cramping after insertion. Is that okay?"

"Will it prevent me from getting knocked up?"

"There is a less than 1% chance of pregnancy."

"Great. Hook it up. I'd rather have the aches and pains of this than the pain of pushing out a watermelon through a straw. I'm cool."

"Before I go get that started, I just want to check in. Was the sex consensual?"

"I… what?"

"Because we are the ED, we see a lot of sexual assault victims come in for emergency contraception. We can offer a rape kit as well. I know it seems scary, but if you're interested-"

My heart is pounding like a jackhammer but I manage to cut her off, "No, no. Um… totally consensual." It was not consensual. But I also liked it. Fuck. I can't deal with this. "Just the IUD, thanks."

"Of course. You let me know if you change your mind."

I have changed my mind in the last 24 hours. Because not only is Graham petrifying he's also thrilling… intoxicating… and I can't deny that he's starting to make me wet. But that doesn't mean I want him to fuck me again.

CHAPTER 4

HEATHER

Graham has always been the light to my darkness. Don't get me wrong, that man can match my twisted mind if he wants to. We get told we're the golden child duo all the time, but I don't think I would measure up if it weren't for Graham. We both grew up with money, but his dad loves him… something I would be envious of him for if Ashton hadn't basically adopted me as a daughter years ago. The truth is, I'm such a cliche: poor spoiled rich girl. I have every material object I could ever want, but my parents are so absent as to be called negligent. Graham may have lost his mother to cancer when he was a baby, but he grew up in a loving household. Without Graham, I'd be a terrible person. He's the one who showed me what love was, that I could let down my walls to love and be loved.

It was my first day in kindergarten, and despite how cheerful my outfit looked: me in a pretty fuschia dress with a matching bow in my hair, I was scowling at everyone who glanced my way. I had sat through the morning counting lessons- I could get up to 20- and the alphabet- I could never remember what came after "K"- but I was sooooo bored. I just wanted to go home and play with my Barbies. Mama had given them to me and told me she played with them when she was my age. She even played with me once, and I have played with them ever since- hoping for a chance she would play with me again. She hadn't, but now I loved changing their outfits and secretly making the girls smooch- I never had enough Ken dolls, so they had no other options. I also knew that this was dirty so I didn't let anyone know. Not like they would understand. Some of the girls had come up to me to tell me my dress was pretty, but I couldn't figure out what to say to them back. My dress was definitely the prettiest one in the room, so it's not like I could compliment them on their outfits, which were, frankly, yucky. I would have thrown a fit if someone tried to dress me like them. A lot of them were wearing pants, but I was a proper Southern lady, obviously unlike them. I couldn't conceive of making friends with any of these girls.

Then it was recess and I was excited to play on the monkey bars because no one was around to tell me it wasn't ladylike. But I wanted to hang high above the ground so bad.

I was just about to climb the ladder, teeth biting my bottom lip in anticipation, when someone tapped me on the shoulder. I turned.

"Hey, you're real pretty. You're the prettiest girl in the class." A boy said to me. He had on a red and blue plaid shirt and khaki shorts.

"Yeah. I know." I said, and started to turn back around.

"I thought girls were supposed to pretend they didn't know

stuff like that?" He said behind me and I turned, sighing.

"Who told you that?"

"I dunno. My mama always acts so surprised when someone pays her a compliment." He squinted at me.

"Weird. Well. I mean. I have eyes. So I know I'm the prettiest girl. Why would I act surprised about you telling me what I already know?" I popped a hip out and put my hand on it.

"Oh. Okay. You should be my girlfriend." He grinned brightly at me.

"But you're not the prettiest boy in class," I told him in puzzlement.

"You're mean and I don't like you unless you agree to be my girlfriend," his hands were curled into fists at his side and his face was getting red.

"I'm not being mean. I'm being honest. And I'm not gonna do that. Bye now," I went to turn but he caught my arm and turned me back around.

Before I knew what he was doing, he took my arm in both of his hands and twisted, giving me a rope burn. I screeched. No one had ever hurt me before. My response was immediate. I hauled back and punched him in the face. Blood spurted from his nose and tears started streaming from his eyes.

He ran off crying and I was pleased with myself. I got up on the monkey bars and started my way across, feeling my tummy soar with excited butterflies. I was having a great time up there until our teacher came over to stand under me.

"Miss Lovelace! Get down from there right now!" She was a prim woman, with her hair up in a bun and a pencil shoved into it.

"I'm having fun. Can it wait?"

"No, it absolutely cannot wait. You're in big trouble." She pointed to the ground.

I jumped from the height, and that was fun too. The monkey bars were my new favorite thing.

"What did I do?" I asked.

"You know very well what you did. You punched Zachary in the face! There is a no tolerance policy for violence at this school. We never hit!" She shook her finger at me.

"What about when someone hurts you first?" I held up my arm with its red burn marks.

"Then you come find someone and tell us you're hurt. It's not ladylike to hit, Heather," She grabbed my arm and started dragging me inside.

"I'm very ladylike. I don't hit people unless they deserve it," I said. I hadn't hit anyone else before today but this seemed like a good idea to me now that I had said it.

"You're going to the principal's office," she towed me inside.

"Is he going too, then?" I asked.

She ignored me and sat me down on the benches outside the principal's office. I waited there forever. I was wondering if I had been forgotten- I was used to that with my parents- and if I should just sneak out but then a boy walked into the office with a folded letter. He stopped at the secretary's desk but she couldn't see him because he was so short, so he waved the letter above his head until she noticed him.

"What's this?" She asked.

"This is from my teacher. She said it's for the principal. I don't know that it says not to believe Heather that she's lying about why she hit Zachary. I didn't read it because I was told not to."

The secretary sighed and took the letter.

The boy turned and grinned at me.

"You're Heather. You're the girl who punched that kid. I saw it."

"Yeah. And?" I scowled at him and folded my arms.

"I saw him being mean to you. No one wants to believe he hurt you first but I do."

"This is not helpful to me."

"I'm Graham!" He held out a hand.

I eyed him up and down. He had short, curly brown hair and green eyes, and he was wearing a gold polo with pressed black pants. This one, my brain said. This one is the prettiest, especially when he smiles.

No one had ever shaken my hand before. But I knew in old movies, ladies let a gentleman take their hand and kiss their knuckles. So I did that instead.

"No, no, Heather. You're supposed to put your palm against my palm," He tried to move my hand.

"This is how gentlemen do it. You bend down and kiss my hand because I'm a lady," I refused to let him move my hand.

He smiled at me again, grinning big. "I'll do whatever you tell me to do. You're so pretty you make my eyes hurt. Oh! I think that's what I'll call you. Pretty girl." He bent down and kissed my hand sloppily.

When he called me pretty something tingled in my tummy. Not like when that other boy did it. I liked it when Graham called me that. But I just stood there and watched him, not knowing how to respond.

"Does your arm hurt?" He pushed himself up on the bench and sat next to me, taking my arm in his hands.

"Not really," I said, not wanting him to think me a wimpy girl.

"Oh. Do you want me to kiss it anyway?" He looked up into my eyes and I saw flecks of gold in them. I wanted to crawl inside his eyes forever. He was soooo pretty. What could I do to make him smile at me again?

"Yeah. Do that," I breathed out.

Then he very seriously leaned down and pecked the reddest part of my arm.

"I think my lips hurt too," I whispered.

His eyes widened. "Really?"

"Yep."

Then he leaned into me, and I leaned into him. He smelled like Skittles and I liked that. It was no green apple Jolly Rancher but it was still good. His lips brushed mine and suddenly I felt like I had a fever. He leaned back and tapped his mouth with a finger.

"Wait. Does this mean you're my girlfriend now that we kissed?"

"Oh. Oops. Yep." I didn't know what he was talking about but I did know I wanted to lay claim to this boy. Probably forever.

"Okay. If someone hurts you again, then it's my job to protect you," he said, straightening up and puffing out his chest.

"I can protect myself!" I folded my arms across my chest again.

"Oh. Well. Can I help at least?" he titled his head at me.

"Yeah. I guess that would be okay. Then I won't be alone all the time," I told him.

"You're alone all the time? Ick. Well, you'll never be alone again," he beamed at me.

I think about that first day we met and smile. I really have never been alone again after that day. Graham has loved me through it all.

I finish my run around the track during PE and slow to a halt. Stretching my calves against the bleacher foundation, I spy Peyton up in the stands lying down on her back with her eyes closed. She is one of those girls who think they are too good to get sweaty. Girls like that astound me- how do they pass these classes? And I know she is passing because she is in line to be Valedictorian. It makes no sense to me. Just go for a light jog for heaven's sake. It is good for the body. I keep my body in peak physical condition for cheer. I would love to be a flyer but I am too tall, so I am a base. I weightlift, run, swim, and dance on the regular. I am svelte but muscular: I can pick up Graham and pin him against a wall if I want to.

Peyton yawns from her place on the bleachers and pulls her hoodie over her eyes to block out the sun, drawing my attention. Fuck that bitch. When she came to this school two years ago and didn't give me the respect I deserved, I decided to make her my new plaything. In all that time she still hasn't learned her lesson. But at this point even if she had I'd probably still fuck with her. It gives me great joy to plan out her little punishments and see her rail against me. It's not like anyone but her weird little group of theatre outcasts gives her any attention, so she isn't hurting my popularity. I think my reminding everyone how powerful I am by my treatment of her is actually helping keep me aloft, anyway.

Today's grievance with Peyton is that I didn't like how Graham was looking at her when I came into the kitchen on Saturday morning. He was leaning in close to her and it looked less intimidating and more seductive. If they are going to be living together, I will have no opportunity missed to show her what she is in for. The only thing that will save her is graduating and going to a college outside the state.

Today's torture suddenly occurs to me and I jog inside to the locker room. I sneak inside coach's office and find her bolt cutters. Then I take the quickest shower possible and wait for Peyton to come in to take hers.

It's a hygiene policy that everyone is required to shower after PE and coach is strict about monitoring it, so even though Peyton had done fuck-all during class she's still going to shower. And that's when I'll strike.

I watch her open her locker and pull out her toiletry kit. Then I watch as she strips, revealing more of that light brown skin. She is my opposite. Thick where I'm lean, soft where I have muscle. I narrow my eyes. She puts all her clothes- PE and street- back in her locker and walks back to the showers.

Cutting the lock, I open her locker and pull out her clothes. Peyton always wears black- what a drag. We get it. You're "alternative." I catch a whiff of sage and rain and bring the material closer to my nose to make sure I'm categorizing her scent more accurately. She smells like a Goddamn forest after a rainstorm. My eyes float closed for a moment before I get my bearings. Angrily, I ball the black jeans and trademark oversized hoodie up. Of course she always wears baggy clothes. She wouldn't want anyone getting an eyeful of her massive tits, hula hoop hips, dump truck ass, and thick thighs. Not... that I'm thinking of those things. Anyway. I leave her bra and panties- which are lacy and cute... who the fuck is she wearing those for? I grab her PE clothes too, and stuff them all in my locker. I'll deal with those later.

Then, I leave the locker room and go to lunch to enjoy the show I've orchestrated.

I don't have to wait long. I'm sitting with the girls and eating chicken and rice when I hear a wolf whistle and look up.

And there she is in all her nearly naked glory. Peyton looks murderous as she stomps up to my table and slams her palms down onto it.

"I think you have something that belongs to me," she bites out.

"Yeah, your dignity," Amber chortles.

"Oh my God, I would be so embarrassed if I were you," Hannah joins in.

"I didn't know the diet situation was this bad under all those baggy clothes," Molly laughs.

But me? I just can't stop staring at her. All that smooth leg, soft belly, deep cleavage encased in frills and lace. Why can't I speak? This is exactly what I had wanted but now she's in front of me decked out in lingerie and my brain has shorted out.

Peyton screams and her hand flies out to dash our lunches to the floor. She turns and walks away, leaving me to watch her hips sway, ass and thighs jiggling. I bite my bottom lip.

"Ugh, that bitch!" Molly screeches. "My lunch!"

I finally come back to the conversation as I realize my rice is all over the floor. The whole encounter with Peyton is intensely dissatisfying. Every time I think I have figured out the best way to get under her skin, it's never enough for me. I guess I had better start plotting my next attack…

CHAPTER 5

GRAHAM

I am waltzing into the dining room when my phone vibrates with a text message. Opening it up, one of the boys has sent a picture from earlier today when Heather had stolen all Peyton's clothes and Peyton had stomped into the lunchroom. I wasn't there because lunch is "for the girls" as Heather tells me. So I usually sun out on the quad with my teammates. I am regretting that lunch choice now. The picture is great but I can't imagine seeing her in lingerie in real time. Now that I have seen her in lingerie via viral text message, I can admit what I couldn't before: Peyton is a fucking smokeshow and she doesn't even know it. Salivating over her curves in the photo, I don't hear anyone come up behind me until I see a hand reaching for my phone.

"Give me that!" Peyton screeches.

I pull my phone toward my chest. "You mean, give you my phone, which is my property? I think not," I pat her on her head.

"Delete that fucking picture of me!"

"But then what would be my phone wallpaper?" I grin at her.

"I don't know, your fucking GIRLFRIEND, you psycho?" She tries to reach for my phone but I tuck it into my back pocket and grab her wrists with one of my hands.

"There's a lock screen and a home screen for a reason. You both could feature," I tell her.

"Ugh! Let me go!" She starts squirming against me, and oh, here we go... Now I'm getting hard right before family dinner- inconvenient timing, to say the least.

"Maybe we should go upstairs so I can teach you a lesson before dinner," I wink at her while I back her up against the nearest wall.

"You know what? Fuck you for that. Did you know I had to get plan B after Friday night? Yeah, wouldn't that be a kick in the balls. You getting me knocked up. Well, fuck you, Graham." She's still wiggling against my hold, inadvertently- or dare I hope on purpose- rubbing herself against my length and causing me to thicken in my pants. Then her words sink in.

"What? You aren't on birth control?" My grip on her tightens because I hadn't thought of that. Heather and I have been going raw for years since she got on something, and stupidly I hadn't even thought about that when I had fucked Peyton. What a fucking oversight.

"What part of *virgin* didn't you understand when you had my blood all over your cock, Graham?" she spits out.

I let her go, back away, and run a hand over my face.

"Fuck, fuck, fuck," I start chanting.

"Yeah. Weird how actions have consequences, right? Your life would be pretty fucking derailed if I was carrying your baby in my belly right now."

"But you fixed it? You took something?" I panic.

"Yeah I fucking fixed it. I'm not going to be tied to the likes of you for the rest of my life. You can fuck off with that." She narrows her eyes at me.

"Oh, thank God. Wait… I told you not to tell anyone. Did you tell your mother?" I move forward, backing her into the wall again.

"And ruin her fresh newlywed bliss knowing her stepson is a rapist piece of shit? No, Graham. I did not."

I cringe at her words but focus on the important parts of what she just relayed.

"And you're not going to? Remember that I have pretty damning evidence of you now." I smirk at her.

"Ugh, you fuckboy. Not like it matters when I have a lingerie photo floating around but I remember. She's not going to know. I won't ruin your pristine image with her. Everyone but me will continue to think of you as the perfect little golden boy. Too bad they don't know how fucked up you are."

I roughly grab her chin and tilt it toward me, locking our eyes. "Fucktoy… you have no idea."

She swats my hand away and steps around me, walking away briskly and saying, "And I hope not to know, fuck you very much."

I follow her into the dining room, where Willow is pouring wine into our glasses, and Regina and Dad are already sitting beside each other. It sounds like they were talking about- what else- college football, and I roll my eyes. I like Regina just fine, but I'm really curious about what Peyton's mom and my dad have in common besides a love of Volunteer football. Peyton Manning is my idol but even I have other interests besides the sport.

I sit across from my father and wait for Peyton to take her seat next to me. She slides in and folds her linen napkin across her lap.

The dining table is large, but we are intimately seated in the middle of it- so close that I reach out and run my hand over Peyton's upper thigh, tucking my hand between her legs. She gasps and stiffens, then tries to push my hand away, but I dig my fingers into her thigh until she whimpers and sits back in her chair.

"I'm so happy we're all living together now. I know the weekend was a whirlwind, but I want to do family dinners together every night during the weekdays so we can catch up. Graham and I have been doing this since he was a boy, and now we'll continue it with the four of us." Dad raises a glass and straightens the glasses on his face.

"Cheers to that," Regina co-signs and raises a glass.

"Um, Mama, there's wine in my glass. Since when am I allowed to have that?" Peyton raises her glass, and I watch as she sloshes the wine around in her cup.

"Yes, baby. Ashton lets Graham have a glass at dinner, and I've decided we will do the same with you. You're eighteen now, and I'd rather you have a respectful relationship with alcohol," Regina explains.

"Oh. Um. Okay." Peyton takes a sip of the red and then immediately makes a face. "That's... a bold flavor," she summarizes.

"This one does have a particularly bold bouquet, and it's full-bodied. Is this your first time trying red wine?" I ask.

She mumbles under her breath, and I catch snippets including, "he would" and "arrogant son of a bitch."

"You'll have to repeat that. I don't believe I heard you, Peyton," I drawl out politely but then raise my hand on her thigh, pinky grazing her covered cunt.

"Yep. First time," she glares at me as she gulps wine.

"Now, now, Peyton. This wine is to be sipped. It's been paired with dinner for a palatable experience," I chide her.

She grunts in reply, and I smile at her.

"I know you'll walk her through it," Dad says to me, and then turns to Regina, saying, "I told you he's always been such a helper. I know he'll take his responsibility as brother seriously."

Regina looks both her daughter and me up and down before laying a hand on Dad's arm. "I'm sure he will, Ash."

Willow serves our food, a lamb loin with yogurt sauce complimented by basmati rice mixed with green peas.

"How are your college applications coming, kids?" Regina asks as she swirls a bite of lamb into her sauce.

Peyton ducks her head down and focuses on her food.

"I'm sure Dad has told you, Regina. But I'm going to UT." I smile at her.

"I guess that question was more for my daughter, Graham, but thanks for answering," Regina responds with a gentle smile.

Peyton tries to become smaller in her seat, and I confusedly look at her. She removes her arms from the table and tucks her hands under her thighs, refusing to make eye contact with anyone. Seeing her distress, I move my hand from her thigh to her wrist, caressing her and moving my thumb in soothing circles.

Regina clears her throat, and Peyton sighs, collapsing back onto her chair but not removing her hand from my hold.

"Mama. I'm working on it. But… I… I don't…" Peyton's pulse is going wild under my thumb.

"Baby, you can tell me anything. What is it?" Regina puts her utensils down and focuses all her attention on her daughter.

Peyton breathes in hard, lets out a breath, and then bursts out, "I don't want to go to UT!"

Regina's eyes widen, Dad coughs into his fist, and I turn fully toward Peyton.

"Is there... a reason you don't want to go to state?" Regina inquires.

"Yes. I mean no. I mean... I don't know. I just don't. Can we just drop it? I'm working on applications, and I'll get into a school that's good, and I'll go, and I'll figure out what I want to do, and it'll be fine. Yeah. It'll be fine. Okay?" She doesn't take a breath until she's finished, and then she lets out a growl.

"Wow. Okay. I just thought your dream was to go to Rocky Top," Regina says carefully.

"No, *mother*. Your dream was for me to go to Rocky Top. You never bothered to ask me where I wanted to go. Maybe I'll go to Vanderbilt." Peyton is still stiff in my hold, her pulse fluttering wildly.

"*Vanderbilt?!*" Regina looks to my dad for saving.

Dad suddenly realizes he's needed and pats Regina's shoulder. "Now, now, dear. That's a great school. It's not like she's saying she'd go to Alabama."

Regina pales and raises her fingers to press into the corners of her eyes.

"You will never hear 'roll tide' come out of my mouth, Mama. I can promise you that," Peyton tries to joke.

Regina laughs weakly. "Okay, well, do you know what you want to study yet?"

I feel Peyton's pulse rise under my thumb.

"No, Mama... I'm still not sure," Peyton mutters.

Regina looks at my dad searchingly. "What about drama? You love that. Or literature? You're always in the middle of a book."

"I do love drama. It's my favorite thing. And I could see that being a minor or something, but I'm not cut out to be a professional actress. That's just way too much everyday rejection. Plus, I'm not cookie-cutter enough to be an actress. That's never going to be my life. But that's okay because I can enjoy something without it bringing me income."

"Baby girl, you're beautiful!" Regina starts.

"Mama. Please stop. That's not for me. Let me just enjoy something for the sake of enjoyment. Didn't your generation start that?"

"Yeah, all right. What about literature, then?"

"It's the same sort of thing. Books are my escape. I don't know that I want it to be work. But I can't decide what I want work to be like."

Regina's eyes go wide, and then she's crushing my dad's arm with her hand. "You do… want to go to college, don't you?"

"Yes, Mama. I'm going to college. The first two years are general education, anyway. I can explore and see where I want to go from there." Peyton is putting up a good front, but her pulse is still going haywire. I keep rubbing soothing circles into her wrist to calm her.

Regina visibly deflates. "Okay, good, good."

My dad pipes up, "How's the fall play coming anyway? What will we see you as?"

"*A Midsummer Night's Dream*, actually. I'm hoping to be Titania," Peyton's pulse begins calming.

"Sounds great. Do you have to try out?" Dad asks.

"When it's theatre, it's called 'audition,' but yes. I have to audition for the role."

Dad nods. He knows fuck-all about plays but it is nice he is trying. Hell, I don't know anything either. But we will all go to see her in it when it is time.

PYRAMID STUNT

The rest of the dinner goes by in a stilted sort of way after that. I find that I can't keep my hands to myself and have one hand on Peyton the whole dinner. I can't fuck her again but I can at least give myself this. Touching her, caressing her, letting her know that I'm a presence she isn't liable to shake.

But when I find myself in bed that night tossing and turning, I'm thinking of that picture that my boy Andy had sent to me earlier. I can't sleep, so what is the harm?

I shift and pull out my phone, opening my saved photos- of course I saved that shit. Bet. Just looking at her picture, my cock is filling in my boxer briefs. I slip a hand inside my bottoms and palm my cock. God, she is a luscious creature. She spills out over her bra and panties, her body too thick to be contained by little slips of fabric. The picture captures her with her hands slammed down on the table, eyes narrowed in anger. It's not as good as when she cried, but I love when she's so riled up in anger. I could swear that when she's angry at me, her herby rainwater scent is stronger and it gets my dick hard.

I turn to my bedside table and reach for my lotion, pumping some into my hand to spread on my cock. I stroke my cock a couple times but then a thought occurs to me: she is right across the hall. Instead of beating off to her, I could have her right fucking now. I could crawl into her bed and pump into her pussy. I just have to keep my wits about me so I don't come inside her again and create a… situation.

Resolved, I tuck my dick away and grab my phone. I stealthily walk to her door and slowly open it, thanking heaven for WD-40. The moonlight shining in through her window illuminates her body underneath her covers. I take a moment to admire how she looks sleeping: her hands tucked under her head while she lays on her side, blanket underneath her chin, mouth set at a relaxed upwards tilt. I positively have to have her.

I walk toward her bed softly, placing my phone next to the bed on the table and slipping my underwear down my legs. Lifting the blanket, I slide in behind her, my erect cock pressing into her. In her sleep she presses back toward me and I stifle a groan. What a fucking cocktease this bitch is. I run my hand up her leg feeling only skin until I reach a pair of panties, then slowly remove them. She twitches and tries to slap my hand away but it is sleepy and half-hearted so I keep going. I tangle my legs in hers, grabbing a thigh to hitch over my hip. Then I place my dick at her entrance and slowly slide inside her.

She's less wet than the other day when I fucked her, but the lotion is good enough that I know I won't tear her and wake her up. She is just as tight, though, and I have to turn and bite the pillow to stop from moaning in her ear. She bucks against me and whimpers. I thank heaven that she's a heavy sleeper. I push inside her to the hilt and pause. I can feel something familiar inside her pussy. This little bitch. She may not have had birth control the last time I fucked her but I can feel the string of an IUD inside her now. Fuuuuuuck. All bets are off. I had been planning on pulling out but now I am 100% gonna come in my fucktoy.

She whines and squirms against me, and I can feel her waking up now. I push a hand under her sleepshirt to palm one of those heavy breasts and whisper in her ear, "Shh. It's just me. Go back to sleep."

"Graham?" she whines sleepily.

"Yeah, fucktoy."

Suddenly I feel her slicken and get hotter around my cock. Well, well, well. It's official. I turn my little fucktoy on, even if only on a subconscious level.

I keep pumping in and out of her, slowly, softly, torturously. God, this feels so fucking good. She's moaning louder, grinding back onto my dick so I decide to take a chance. I lick the pads of my index and middle fingers and start rubbing circles into her clit. Her hand wraps around my wrist, pushing me closer and her nails dig into me. I grind my teeth together instead of leaning forward and biting into her shoulder. Instead I circle my pelvis and she seizes up. I feel her come hard around me and it incites me to follow her. When I've fucked her through our orgasms, I keep my dick inside her even while I soften. I snuggle into her, with our legs still tangled, my hand on her breast, the other on her belly and tuck her head under mine.

I sleep hard with her entangled in my arms until my alarm goes off the following morning. I reach behind me to turn it off, but it's too late. Peyton has woken up. I know immediately when she awakens because she stiffens.

"What the fuck!" she yells, and pushes her arms behind her to move away from me. She flips around, pulls her shirt down over her body, glares at me, then slaps me in the face.

CHAPTER 6

PEYTON

"Good morning to you, too," Graham says and massages his jaw.

"Get… out… of… my… bed," I bite off slowly as I rush so fast out of bed I trip over my own legs.

"Yeah, all right. Not like we have time for a quickie before school," he pouts and reaches down to palm his hard dick, looking down at it. "Sorry big guy. Later."

"Later had better be with your Goddamn girlfriend. Later most certainly will not be with me," I pull at my shirt's hem to better cover my legs.

He smirks and crawls over to my side of the bed, pulling me into him by my waist. He scrunches my shirt up over my tits and starts biting into my waist while he tweaks my nipples, which have traitorously peaked. He leaves a particularly brutal bite into my side and I throw my head back moaning while I slide my fingers into his hair. Then I realize what I'm doing.

I step backward out of his reach and fling him away by his hair.

"No, Graham! This is not going to become a thing," I say as I pull my shirt back down to cover myself.

He swings his legs around and hops off the bed to come toward me, backing me up against a wall. I forget how terrifying he can be until he's towering over me like this, using his size as another weapon in his arsenal. He's got an arm resting on the wall above me, leaning into me. He looks totally at ease while I'm afraid to move.

"Listen, fucktoy. Last night was the best night of sleep I've ever had except for when Heather's in my bed. Now that you're conveniently located across the hall from me, we're going to do this every single night she's not here."

I realize with alarm that I'm trembling, so I try to hide my hands by placing them against the wall behind me. His green eyes are boring into me and I'm frozen, unable to speak. I watch in horror as he reaches down to untie my scarf and lets my curly locks free. When he plunges a hand into my hair, I finally find my strength.

I push my hands into his chest, but he's as unmoving as a tree, "Get the fuck out, Graham."

He quirks an eyebrow at me and laughs. "Yeah, all right. I'll see you later," he agrees and in a flash, he's leaning down to bite and then suck at my neck. I tense at the bite and then I feel my pussy flood with heat at the way he's lavishing attention on such an erogenous zone. I bite my bottom lip so I don't make the mistake I did earlier when I moaned for him. I think I moaned when he fucked me last night, too. I couldn't help it. It's a hazy memory but he felt so good moving inside of me while I was asleep. I was weighed down by sleep in the most pleasant way, and the way he fucked me slowly while he rubbed my clit was rapturous. But no. I am afraid of this man. I can't keep fucking him, but who am I kidding? It's not as though he's taking my permission into account.

He finishes sucking what I imagine will be a blatant hickey into my neck and ends with a big lick up my neck.

"Bye, little sister," he croons as he leaves me and my pussy, which by now has a heartbeat.

After I finish getting ready for school, I go out to the driveway to get in my car but Graham has me blocked in. I roll my eyes, but I figure that he's got to get to school too, so I'll just get in my car. I unlock my car and go to open the door but suddenly, all six and a half feet of him are sliding between me and the door.

"I'm driving you to school today," he tells me and turns me by my arm and then guides me by the nape of my neck to his passenger door, where he opens the door for me and hoists me into the seat of his cherry red Black Widow Dodge Ram 2500. I throw my head back on the headrest and groan.

"Graham, are you just going to take over my life now? I can't have some spare moments throughout the day without you in them?" This just figures. I can't get my dad to be a consistent part of my life, but I've managed to snag the attention of the second least-desirable asshole I know.

He stands on the running board and leans over me with the seatbelt and, I wish I was making this up, buckles me in like I'm a toddler.

"Don't tempt me. I have football practice, but you have drama club so we will finish at roughly the same time. You can meet me by the car when you're done, and I'll drive you back home." He pats my cheek.

"You know my schedule?" I ask him.

His eyes widen. "Fucktoy, I know everything about you." Then he moves out of my space and closes the door. A beat later, the driver's side door opens, and he's hopping up into the cab. He starts the truck, and we're off.

"Don't think I didn't notice you covered up the mark I left on your neck," he growls out darkly.

"Yeah. It's this little thing I like to call being discreet since the man who gave it to me is practically betrothed," I retort.

"You don't have to tell people who gave it to you. In fact, I'm sure it would add to your mystery if you didn't. But you're going to leave it uncovered from here on out."

I loll my head toward him lazily, "And if I don't listen to you?"

"I'm sure my punishments can start getting more creative." He turns briefly at a stop sign and winks at me. "Actually, keep covering it up. I think next time we can add some spankings into the mix."

"There is no next time, Graham."

"Fucktoy, I don't know what I need to do to get it through your head that this is going to be a repeat affair."

"And you mean affair literally because you're cheating on Heather."

He scowls. "I don't need to explain myself to you, Peyton. That's not how this works between us."

I laugh, "You don't have to explain yourself to me anyway. You want to have your cake and eat it, too. You know, you're a bigger piece of shit than I originally thought you were. You've always treated me like shit but at the end of the day, I thought you worshiped Heather. Turns out you can't even be a loyal boyfriend. I don't even know why I'm shocked."

He abruptly pulls over onto the side of the road, turns

towards me, and then my chin is roughly grasped in his fingers while he glares down at me.

"I don't need your thoughts on Heather. Do you want to be punished today, fucktoy? Because that can be arranged. Your torture is my delight."

I gulp and close my eyes, trying to slow my racing pulse.

"No... no thank you," I breathe out, still keeping my eyes closed.

"You're going to be a good girl for me?"

My mind races. What does that even mean? Does that mean if I don't mouth off he won't come into my room again, or does it just mean he'll fuck me sweetly instead of roughly when he does? I'm so confused by this man.

I feel a thumb brush my lips and suddenly I wonder why he's fucked me, marked me, but not kissed me. What does that mean? And why am I wondering? Do I actually want this guy to kiss me? Do I want to feel like I mean something to him?

"Peyton? Are you going to be good?"

I nod, not really knowing what I'm agreeing to. I just want him to stop touching me and setting off this conflict between my body and my mind.

Instead of getting him to remove his hand from my chin, he keeps hold and I feel his other hand stroke my cheekbone. I tremble in his hold.

"I can't tell if you're scared right now or if you're turned on," he whispers.

That makes two of us.

He pulls away from me, his warmth leaving my skin, and begins driving again.

I leave my eyes closed for the rest of the ride. Like a cat, I'm convinced if I can't see him, he can't see me. Keeping still and quiet in the passenger seat will keep him from talking to or touching me again. My illogical thought process seems to pay off because after a while we come to a stop and he turns the car off.

I unbuckle as fast as I can and move to open the door but Graham plunges a hand into my hair and pulls me back toward him. He leans into my ear and whispers, "Remember what I said about being good." Then he flings me forward and I have to put my hands up on the window to keep my face from smashing into the glass. No one can give me whiplash like Graham.

As I get out of the truck, I see Heather walking up to Graham. At first when she sees me she looks wary, but then her eyes narrow at me before she turns to Graham and nuzzles into his neck as she winds her arms around his torso and tucks her body into his. That's definitely my cue to scurry away.

I manage to complete a day of school with no Graham or Heather run-ins- which is fair, when you think about how much Graham I've had in the past 12 hours: I think I'm due for a break. I do well at school but it's all background when you consider how in love with drama club I am. That's where I truly feel like myself. I get lost in the characters and their motivations, in bringing someone's vision to life. I know it's just high school but even our little renditions of plays and musicals make me so happy. I love reading a play and then watching it be brought to life. Our fall play is Shakespeare's *A Midsummer Night's Dream*, and I'm dying to play Titania, queen of the fairies.

I'm in the drama room cuddled into the floor pillows and I'm studying my lines with who my friends and I like to call "The Triad": Adrian, Sam, and me. They've been my besties ever since I walked into my first drama club meeting and found my people. Adrian is white with blond hair and hazel eyes, clad in what I like to call one of his "preppy chic" outfits: he's got ankle jeans on with loafers, a button-up, and he's even got the country club Ken sweatshirt tied around his neck. Sam, who is Cuban with black hair and brown eyes framed by bisected eyebrows, is dressed more like me in tattered jeans and a vintage Bikini Kill tee- because third wave feminism rockers, hello. Adrian has been sighing over and over- but this is usual so I've been focused on my script. Finally he throws his copy down and I look up at him.

"Okay, enough of this. Why haven't you spilled the tea on who gave you that hickey?" he pouts at me.

"What hickey?" I try to avoid and go back to my book, flipping a page.

He groans and falls over onto the floor. "Samaraaaaaaa. Why is she like this?"

Sam grabs a bookmark and places it into her script, gently placing it down. She winks at me and continues, "Whatever do you mean, my beloved?"

Adrian kicks his legs. "I meeeeeean why does she not tell us all her secrets like a normal best friend? There are *rules*," he huffs and crosses his arms.

Sam looks over at me. "Yeah, actually, as much as I love leaning into Adrian's queen tantrums, I am invested in hearing about this too."

"In hearing about what?" I ask dumbly, and blink my eyelashes.

"You're real cute when you do that. You know I want to give you whatever you want, but Adrian has a point," Sam points out.

Adrian sits up and excitedly says, "I do? I mean, yeah! I do!"

I sigh and admit, "Well, there's obviously a guy."

"Well, that takes all the wind out of my sails." Sam picks her book back up.

Adrian smacks her arm three times. "There's a

guyyyyyyyy." He doesn't just drawl it out; he full-on sings it.

"Yeah, this officially interests you more than it does me. If it were a girl, I'd be ravenous for info, but this is your department," Sam licks a finger and turns a page.

"Puh-lease. If the love interest in question were of the lady variety, you'd be green with envy and fight to the death for Peyton's honor," Adrian returns.

"Well, that's only because leaving a hickey is so juvenile and smacks of heteronormative patriarchy. A woman is not property. That's basically putting everyone else on notice that they should not touch what is already owned," Sam argues.

I cover the mark with my hand and duck my head to hide my flushing face.

"Sam, you sound lecturey right now. Get off your high fucking horse so Peyton can explain her mystery lover to us. I need deets." He turns to me, "Come on, sug, you can tell us anything. You know that."

Usually, I would 100% agree with that statement. But right now, I am petrified. How am I going to explain to my best friends what had occurred- what is occurring- with Graham and me? Just like with Mama, I decide to keep my cards close to my chest. Adrian will drag me to the police station, and Sam is liable to burn down Graham's house- never mind that I am living in it. I love them, but they are rash and impetuous and will not understand this situation at all.

"Just a guy… you wouldn't know him. He goes to another school. And he might have… taken my virginity but it's not going to happen again," I blush again, deciding to share half of the story with them.

"Ew, Peyton. Don't say a guy 'took your virginity.' In fact-"

"Can you not, Sam? Can you seriously not? I know all your thoughts on virginity already," I roll my eyes.

"I'm just saying that as a culture, men are expected to dispense with their 'virginity,'" here she makes air quotes, "as soon as possible and with little fanfare, but a woman is supposed to make it a big to-do-"

"You're literally making it a bigger deal than it needs to be right this second," I harrumph.

"Okay, fine, but there's a mystery guy who you can't even name, and he's marking you like a caveman? Did you just let him do whatever he wanted? Did you even have agency in this coupling?" Sam raises an eyebrow at me and waits.

"I..." I start, but I realize I can't explain any of this away, and I'm getting more embarrassed by the moment.

"That's what I thought. My Pey would never let some alphahole suck a hickey into her neck, despite how good the D or puss was. So why are you letting this guy walk all over you?" Sam finishes and looks awfully pleased with herself.

Her words leave me feeling defensive. "Maybe I would let someone do that if I'm freshly fucked. It's not like you know what I'm like in bed."

Adrian gasps at the low blow, and Sam's cheeks flush with what I can only assume is indignation and embarrassment. Which, great, now we are both embarrassed and on the defensive.

"Maybe you should be a little more careful about who you let into your bed, Pey," she responds hotly.

"Wow, slut-shaming much? Because my partner does something you're not into in your own sexual life it's not okay when it happens to me?"

"I don't think you're ready to have sex if this is how you're reacting to this conversation. You may have the book smarts, but you're lacking the street smarts to be sexually active." She gives me a cold smile.

"I was prepared to blow the whole thing off, but you can't stand it when I do something you don't like. You have to go into this superior teaching mode you do and lecture me about all my fucking life choices." I gather up my books and stuff them into my backpack. "And fuck you, Adrian, for sitting there and silently co-signing. You know what? I'm so over this. I'll see you all later."

I can hear Sam and Adrian arguing as I walk out of the room.. My plan to get a ride from Sam or Adrian has quickly fizzled out, and I can't believe I'm choosing Graham over either of them. Honestly, it's a lose-lose situation, but at least he doesn't make me feel like I'm doing something wrong. I have plenty of time before Graham is done with football practice, so I take a detour to the bathroom by the field. I realize my mistake as soon as I step inside and am met with blue eyes that turn angrier the longer I hold their gaze.

CHAPTER 7

HEATHER

Peyton's brown eyes go wide and she turns to leave, but I'm faster than she is. Slamming my hand against the door so she can't open it, I grab her arm and turn her toward me. The five extra inches of height I have makes it so I am looking down at her. She looks behind me as though to escape, but I box her in with my other arm.

"I think we have things we need to discuss, little freak." I move closer to her so that she has to strain to look up at me. She's so soft against me, my tiny tits pressing into her big ones.

"I know you're starving for a conversation with some depth, but I'm afraid now isn't a good time for me. Things to do, people to meet," she says offhandedly, and I don't like that she doesn't seem to be afraid right now. She's trapped at my whims. She should be shaking. Then I reflect on what she has just said.

"People to meet like Graham?" I ask.

"Actually, yes. Only because he's taking me home. To our home. You know, the one I'm forced to live with him in. Against my will. Despite my complaints and reservations." She is babbling now, and that relaxes me. Of course, I make her nervous.

"Let's talk about that. How's that been going?"

"Why do you care?" She retorts.

"I don't. But you need to stay away from him. If you think your life is hellish now, just cozy up to my boyfriend and see how feral I can be, bitch," I smile at her, but I know it's cold.

She scoffs. "I don't want anything to do with him, I can promise you that. You two psychopaths are made for each other."

I stare into the depths of her eyes, noting the golden flecks in her brown gaze. I take in what she's saying. I have always felt secure in Graham and my relationship. On the one hand, we truly are made for each other, and I don't believe anyone has the power to come between us. But on the other hand, I still feel some type of way about Graham's body language in the kitchen the other day, and I certainly don't like that he has decided he's driving her to and from school now. We had a brief conversation about it when I saw them together this morning, but he just told me it made sense since they were going to the same place.

"If you think you're going to get in good with him and be friends with us or something unhinged-" I start but she cuts me off.

"Oh, fuck off, Heather. There is no part of me that wants anything to do with your plastic world. You don't even have real friends."

"What are you talking about? I have three great friends." I raise an eyebrow at her.

"Who? Your very own version of the plastics? Those bitches don't give a shit about you.

You have the most superficial friendships I've ever seen."

"Watch what you say to me, Peyton," I narrow my eyes at her but she's on a roll.

"People are just either afraid of you or they want some part of your limelight. But

otherwise, you wouldn't know a real friendship if it bit you on your cheerleading ass. I don't even know if you're capable of it. Maybe you're one of those women who hate other women."

"That's ridiculous. I don't hate other women."

She laughs at me. "Yeah, okay. I'd say prove it, but I don't know how you could possibly-"

I lunge at her, molding her mouth to mine and shoving my tongue into her mouth. My hands leave the door behind her, and one plunges into all that dark hair while the other grabs her fat ass and palms it, but it overflows out of my hand. She feels so good against me, so plush and thick. I kiss her deeply, loving how sweet her tongue is on mine. Kissing her is nothing like kissing Graham, whose stubble I could feel against my cheeks, or how he meets my roughness with his own. This is rough- of course it is, I'm the one doing the kissing- but has an undercurrent of sweetness I imagine is only possible because I'm kissing a woman.

Wait. I'm kissing a woman. Not only a woman but Peyton. I'm kissing the girl who has been a thorn in my side for the last two years. The stain on my pristine high school record. What am I thinking? But then she moans into my mouth and grabs my hips to twist her pelvis into mine, and I stop thinking. My brain blanks out, and I lean down to grip her under her thighs and hoist her into my arms, using the door to brace her weight. We are pressed so tightly together I clock her pulse rise at that move, and I congratulate myself on keeping her off balance. Yeah, that's what I'm doing. This can be another maneuver. I can get her to let her guard down and then hit her in a weak spot.

My fingers are digging into her thighs, and I hope I'm leaving bruises so that whoever is leaving marks on her neck will see them and think she's cheating on them. I mean, I guess she's cheating on them by kissing me. Which means, fuck, I'm also cheating on Graham by kissing her. Somehow, that makes this hotter. I have never had a secret from Graham. He knows me inside and out. But now I have this minor- tiny, really- indiscretion, and he can obviously never know that I have kissed his stepsister.

I bite her bottom lip, and she rucks up my top to scratch her nails down my back in reply. Fuck, she's a good kisser. I want to just lay in bed with her and make out with her all day... I could trace my fingers over her soft brown skin and maybe get a better look at those tits she keeps hidden under all those hoodies. The day in the cafeteria wasn't enough. I need more mental snapshots.

Someone starts banging on the door and knocks me back into reality.

"Hey, is anyone in there? Can you open up? I really gotta go!" A female voice whines.

"Fuck off! Go use another bathroom!" I look down at Peyton, who is looking up at me, her pupils blown with lust.

I drop her from my hold and back away from her, and she falls back into the door to brace herself from falling.

"What the fuck was that? Of course, you're a fuckin' dyke," I shoot at her.

I didn't think it was possible but her face takes on an even more shocked look as her jaw drops. "Are you fucking serious right now? *You* kissed *me!*"

"You didn't have to get so into it, though, did you?" I sneer.

"You picked me up off the floor and ground into me!"

"You raked your nails down my back!"

"You bit my lip!"

"You moaned into my mouth!"

"Listen, let's just… agree… that that will never happen again." She crosses her arms.

"Thank you, Captain Obvious," I agree with her.

"Okay, I'm gonna go," She points behind her.

"Yeah, wouldn't want to be late meeting Graham. Who, again, is mine. Got it?" I try to muster up some of my earlier bitchiness, but my hands are clammy, and my pulse is racing.

"Yes, yes, yes. You're the future Mrs. Huntington. I'm well aware." She flips up her hood and exits the bathroom.

I move to the sink, clasping the porcelain and staring into the mirror. I take myself in: my cheeks are flushed, I can see the pulse racing at my throat, my lip gloss is smudged, my clothes are askew. The most damning evidence of all: *my* pupils are blown, blotting out the blue in my eyes. I look away from the darkness of my gaze and focus on what I can fix. I grab a paper towel out of the dispenser and remove the rest of the gloss on my lips, then I right my top and skirt.

I have to calm down. I can't go back to cheer practice looking like this. I look like I'm fresh off a hook-up, which is, I guess, what has happened. I try to review:

1. I have cheated on Graham

2. That cheating has been done with Peyton

3. Peyton is the girl I have bullied for years

I groan, cataloging the snowballing information. When had hatred turned to lust? When had I stopped thinking Peyton was below me and started wanting... Peyton *below* me?

CHAPTER 8

GRAHAM

When I'm done with football practice, I find Peyton sitting on the curb by my truck and I lift my eyebrows in surprise. I'm the last one to leave practice, so the parking lot is empty aside from her figure and the truck looming over her. Her face is in a book so I walk up to her and squat down in front of her, waiting for her to lower her book. She doesn't so I finally put a hand on the pages and push it down out of her eyes.

"Oh. Hi," she startles.

"Look at you being such a good girl for me and following instructions," I marvel. I like it when she fights me, and I like it when she is good for me. I'm beginning to think I just like her.

"It was incidental. I had a fight with the Triad." She paused. "That's my-"

"Sam and Adrian. I know."

She looks at me in shock.

"Of course, I know my little sister's friends. I told you I know everything about you. I wasn't blowing smoke up your ass. "

Her wide brown eyes just stare into mine, and for a moment, I'm captivated. I stand and reach a hand down to her, "Come on. We have a stop before we go home."

She takes my hand, and I pull her up, towing her to the car and opening the door for her. She hoists herself up, and I follow her, buckling her in like I did this morning.

"Graham... I can buckle myself in. I'm here of my own volition right now. I'm not going anywhere."

I click her seatbelt and test the give of it, making sure it's secure. "I'm aware." When I lean back, I grab a quick handful of tit and give her thigh a playful smack, hearing the satisfying sound. I jump down from the running board and close the door. When I get into the driver's seat, I look over and see Peyton's nose back in her book. She's reading *Babel* by R.F. Kuang, and that thing looks like a tome. Realistically, she could probably beat the shit out of me with it if she caught me off guard.

She reads while I drive, and I keep the music low so she can read without distraction. When I get to our pit stop, I inform her I won't be any longer than 10 minutes, and she barely replies as I lower the windows and take the keys with me- she has followed one instruction; I don't trust her not to run off with my truck. When I find what I need at the store, I go back out to the truck, throw the bag in the backseat, and then drive us home with more dulcet sounds and the windows rolled up.

When we get home, she's still engrossed in her reading

so I leave her there while I go to work on the project I had just bought supplies for. I'm surprised I'm able to get through it and start my homework by the time I hear her footsteps in the hallway signaling she has finally come inside. I would say that must be some book, but I know that she's often like this: losing herself in plays or novels and not coming up for air until she's done.

Dinner that night is a less pronounced version of the previous night. Regina drops hints about college- University of Tennessee, specifically- while I toy with Peyton beneath the table. She fights me again, but I take it with a grain of salt.

After dinner I finish my homework and then decide I don't want to wait until Peyton is asleep to have her tonight, so I cross the hall and try her door. It's locked, but I smirk, take out my new key, and open it, stepping into the room.

Peyton's back is to me as she sits at her desk on her computer. I can't see her ears, but I assume she has headphones in because she doesn't turn in alarm as I pocket the key and lock the door behind me. I step up behind her and watch her for a minute. I can't tell exactly what she is doing but it looks like she is working on her lines for the upcoming audition. She has a script opened and highlighted, and a browser tab open on her computer with Shakespeare theory.

Peyton has changed into her sleepshirt, and I look down at her ample legs in appreciation, but then I pause. She has bruises on her upper thighs that look a lot like fingers and I certainly don't remember giving those to her. I wrap a hand around her throat from behind, making her jolt in her seat and squeeze. My other hand goes to her ear, and I pluck her air pod out.

"Fucktoy," I growl in her ear, "Who the fuck has been

marking you aside from me?"

She slowly reaches up to her other ear and pulls out her other air pod. Her pulse is racing in fear underneath my hold. "What do you mean?" She asks slowly.

"I mean, those finger marks you have on your thighs. Those aren't from me. I categorize the bruises I give you, and I only left the mark on your neck. So I'll ask you again: who the fuck gave you the bruises on your thighs?" I punctuate my words with another squeeze to her neck but then slacken so she can have the airway to respond to my question.

"You don't own me, Graham," she whispers.

"If you don't want your ass spanked raw, you're going to answer my question," I growl again.

"What the fuck? Punishment? We're not even together, Graham. You have a girlfriend."

She's doing a good job of keeping strong, but I can feel her start to shake underneath my hand.

"I may not belong to you, but you belong to me. Or didn't you understand that when I told you that you're going to be in my bed every night that Heather isn't?"

"How did you even get in my room? I locked the door," she deflects.

"If you had bothered to pay attention on our errand earlier today you would have noticed we stopped at the Home Depot for a new doorknob. Which I installed when you didn't leave the truck, but I would have done it regardless, so don't be too hard on yourself about having been so into your book. I now hold the key and have access to you all the time. Are you going to tell me who gave you those bruises, or do I have to force it out of you?"

"It's not important," she whimpers.

"I say what's important or not, fucktoy. Come here." I pull her out of her chair by her neck and lead her over to the bed, where I sit and pat my lap. "Over my knee." I want to punish her. I want to torture her. I want to hurt her.

Her eyes bulge. "I'm sorry, what now?"

"Over my knee for your punishment." I pat my lap again and then I shrug and let go of her neck to pull her body toward me and force her face down and ass up onto my lap. She struggles the whole way but I muscle through it. Once I get her into position, I put my hand on her upper back and press down into her, holding her down. With my other hand, I lift her shirt above her waist to reveal her ass covered in lacy cheeky panties.

Unable to help myself, I grab a handful of ass and massage her.

"Look at this ripe ass. So fat," I marvel.

"Don't call my ass fat," her muffled voice comes from the bed.

"Oh, little sister. I don't mean it in a bad way. I fucking love this ass. I want to fuck you so I can watch it bounce on my cock. I want to slide my dick inside it. But right now, I can't wait to spank it."

I hear her whine and it's all too much for me. Having her on my lap, ass out, whining at me because I was about to hurt her? My cock is filling.

I rear my hand back, spanking her hard. She screams in reply and my cock reaches full hardness. "God, I fucking love it when you scream for me."

I hit her over and over, alternating cheeks, hearing her screams and watching her skin bloom an angry purple. I can see her capillaries beginning to burst under my hands and it's delicious.

"Are you ready to tell me whose marks you're wearing?" I ask breathily. This is working me up into a frenzy. I want to fuck her, yes, but I'm loving hurting her.

"Yours! I'm wearing your marks!" I can hear tears in her

voice and I can't wait to see them on her face.

I laugh coldly. "And who else's!"

"It… it was a girl! It's not another guy! You're the only guy!"

I pause, considering that sliver of information. I'm somewhat mollified that I'm the only man on her radar, but I'm still jealous of this unknown girl. On the flip side, now I'm thinking about watching Peyton with another woman, and suddenly my brain is conjuring Heather and Peyton in a myriad of positions: fucking, licking, sucking, kissing… I groan.

"That's fucking hot," I finally land on a reply. "Are you into girls?"

"I… I don't… I don't know…" she whimpers, and I pull her up by the hair to gaze into her eyes. Her pupils are blown, her cheeks are covered in tears, her eyes are glassy with them but they also seem hazy and far-off. "I'm dizzy, Graham."

I prop myself up on her headboard and beckon her to me. "Come here, fucktoy. I'll make it better," I told her as I unbutton my jeans and pull out the length of my cock.

She crawls- a little drunkenly I notice with raised eyebrows- and sits on my lap.

"Turn around," I tell her, but she just looks confused. "Face away from me."

"Oh, okay," she said docilely. I'm not sure why she's listening to me right now but I'm not going to question it. She turns in my lap, and as she raises up I slide her panties to the side, notch my dick at her entrance, and push her down into my lap. God, she is fucking dripping. So much for not liking her spanking.

She squeals and then lets out big, breathy sighs. "I'll never get used to you, you're so big."

I groan in reply. "Come on, fucktoy. Bounce on my

dick."

"Can't… So… tired." She leans back into me and suddenly I regret all the clothes I'm still wearing. I push her forward enough so that I can tear both our shirts off, then pull her warm body back into mine, feeling our skin touch. I grab her under her thighs and begin to lift and lower her onto my cock.

"Don't want to fuck you, but you feel so good, " she cries, and I can feel her pussy fluttering around my cock.

I bite down on her shoulder and her pussy clenches me like a vise, making it hard to slide in and out of her.

"Are you going to come for me, little sister?" I ask her.

"Not close yet," she replies, and I realize I'm not doing anything for her clit. I pull her into my chest by her hair and then run my hands down over her shoulders, over her tits stopping to massage them and then pluck her nipples, causing more cunt flutters. Then I caress my hands over her soft belly, and then finally over her thighs. I draw a hand to her entrance to feel how we are joined. Feeling it makes my dick flex inside her hot wet heat, and I draw a finger around her entrance to catch some moisture before I find her clit and start rubbing it. She squirms around on me and then turns her face into my neck and nuzzles me. I feel her mouth open on my neck as her lips open and close softly over me as she lets out tiny mewling sounds. I keep rubbing circles into her clit and she arches her back against me and suddenly she's raising her arms and plunging her fingers into my hair.

"Fucking shit, you feel so good on my dick. What a good girl you're being for me," I tell her and she nods into my neck leaving another open-mouthed kiss on it. "You're such a fucking slut for me, getting dripping wet from your spanking and then taking my cock so well."

"Graham," she whines and I feel her pussy clenching

hard on me.

"Oh, that's it. You like to be told you're a filthy little whore who loves to be used by her brother? God, you're a deviant, fucktoy." I start rubbing her clit faster and finally she seizes up on me and lets out a healthy groan and I can feel her pussy flood with her orgasm.

"Fuck, you're so fucking hot," I tell her then smack her thigh. "On your hands and knees for me."

She wobbles as she does so, but she follows instructions, getting off my dick and getting on her hands and knees. Then her arms give out and she collapses face first into the bed. I get on my knees behind her and pull her panties to the side again so I can plunge my dick inside her. I grab onto her hips and start fucking her roughly. I'm hitting her cervix on every thrust and every time I do she moans loudly. I know from fucking Heather that sometimes I can give her a C-spot orgasm when she's really turned on.

I watch Peyton's ass jiggle and bounce on my dick and I start spanking her ass again as I fuck her. She's still face down in the sheets but now her hands have balled up the linen around her and she's grasping onto it so hard I can see her knuckles have a death grip.

She moans my name and I can't take it anymore. I slide my dick out of her, lean down, and bite into that juicy peach of an ass. Her scream spurs me on to bite harder, then I pull my teeth out and lick over the spot as she whimpers. I get back up and start fucking harder into her while she releases a litany of "Graham… Graham… Graham…"

"You feel so fucking good," I moan out. "Such a good little fucktoy for me. No one else. You got that?"

"No one else," she parrots.

I pump twice more into her and then I let loose, throwing my head back and clutching her hips as I fill her with my cum.

When I'm through, I smack her ass again and flop back onto her pillows. "C'mere, fucktoy."

"Can't move," I hear her muffled voice from the other end of the bed.

I sigh and get up, walking over to her where I had left her and rolling her toward me and into my arms. I hoist her up, then pull the blanket back and lay her on her pillow. I shimmy her panties off of her- just because I fucked her when she was awake doesn't mean I'm not going to take her tonight, and I want easy access. I tuck her in, take off my pants and boxers, then crawl into bed next to her and drape her body over me. She's like a puppet right now, all soft, docile, and fucked out. This isn't just dick-drunk, though. Something else has happened to her while I was spanking her and it has turned her inside out. I remember the look of her eyes, glassy and hazy, and the way her movements were like she was drunk. Honestly, I kind of like whatever had happened. And now I was going to enjoy the feel of our skin shifting together.

CHAPTER 9

HEATHER

I manage to get through the rest of the week without running into Peyton. Not willing to let her think she is off the hook, I did deface her locker with a "Dyke Freak" tagged onto it, but I didn't even stick around to see her face when she found it. I don't like the confusing thoughts tumbling around in my head in regards to her. I'm avoiding Graham, too, because I know he will detect that there is something off with me if he spends too much time with me. But it is Friday afternoon now, and I am due in the boys' locker room for his superstitious pre-game blowjob. The whole team knows we do this, and they know to wait outside the locker room until they are granted entry.

It's not like I don't want to suck Graham's dick- I love

the power I get when I give him head- it's just that I don't know if I could manage to be normal enough that he won't catch on to the tumultuous thoughts stampeding through my brain. One of my- many- favorite things about Graham is how much attention he pays to me. But right now, when I am so fucked up about having my tongue in someone else's mouth, I really can't afford to have him peering too closely inside my mind. I can omit things from conversation, but I'm not suave enough to lie straight to his face and not have him see through me. I might as well be a jellyfish, for as translucent as I am to my boyfriend.

I straighten my cheer uniform and walk past the football team who nod to me in greeting, then I open the door and find Graham lying naked on a bench slowly stroking his already erect cock. His other hand is underneath his head and he has his eyes closed.

"That better be my pretty girl," he warns.

"It's me, baby boy," I reply and sit between his legs on the bench. I lick my palm and take over stroking him, running my hand over his length and then teasing his crown. He bucks into my hand and I watch as a dribble of precum drips over my hand. I squirm. Okay, my boyfriend still gets me hot. So, definitely not a lesbian. In fact, I can't wait to taste him.

"How do you want me?" I ask him, as this is for his benefit in order to play his best.

"Can I lay here on the bench while you give me dome? Because this is so relaxing right now. The only thing that would make it better is me being in your mouth." He sighs in pleasure.

"Of course, baby. Scooch up on the bench a little for me?"

"Whatever you want, gorgeous. Can't wait to feel that tongue tracing my vein like you do." He moves up on the bench and then resettles himself.

I straddle the bench and then lean down to take him into my mouth. I take him all at once, deepthroating him immediately and he groans, flexing his dick into my mouth.

"Fuck, that gets me every time," he moans out.

I hum around his dick, suctioning and hollowing my cheeks, circling my tongue, and sliding up and down his length.

"Oh, God, Heather, yeah. Take that dick. No one gives better head than you do. Fuck, that's so good," he praises me.

I slide up and down his length, fucking my mouth with his cock and listening to him grumble in appreciation. I love it when he is like this: when he is just putty for me, and I can do anything I want to him. I love when he just lays back and lets me touch and taste him and bring him pleasure. I especially love it when he keeps a running narrative for me and tells me what he likes. It makes me wet, and more often than not, I like to slip a hand under my cheer skirt and my bloomers and rub my clit until I come too.

I pull off his cock and replace my mouth with my hand, jacking him as I suck his balls into my mouth roughly and tug at his sack with my mouth. He thrusts into my hand.

"Heather... Heather... pretty girl... I need to come in your mouth," he bites out.

I give him a few more sucks and tugs then I trade hand and mouth to move my mouth back to his cock and my hand to his sac. I plunge him to the back of my throat as I fondle his balls and he yells as he empties into the back of my throat. I suck him through his orgasm until he reaches down and pulls me off of him by my hair.

"Fuuuuuuuuuuck," he groans again and sits up, attacking

my mouth with his. I open for him immediately and his tongue tangles with mine as he wraps his arms around my body and crushes me to him. He pulls back and looks me in the eye. "Fuck, I love you. Do you know that? Do you know how much?" He wipes at the tears under my eyes.

"Enough to get me off?" I laugh wetly at his post-orgasm passion.

"You didn't jill off while you had me in your mouth? Yeah, of course. Come here." He slides a hand down my bottoms and runs two thick fingers through my wetness. "Mmm. Yeah. You love giving me head, don't you, pretty girl?"

I gasp when he briefly runs his hands over my clit. "You know I do. You make me so hot, Graham."

"Fuck, you're so sexy." He smiles openly at me and then molds his mouth to mine again. At the same time as he plunges his tongue into my mouth, he plunges his fingers into my cunt. His fingers are fucking thick, but it still isn't as thick as his dick usually is. But when he crooks his fingers and hooks into my G-spot, I forget why I care about thickness. The heel of his palm is grinding into my clit, and that come hither motion of his fingers is hitting me just right. I moan into his mouth and squirm against him.

"Suck my neck. Leave a mark on me," I beg against his lips.

"My fucking pleasure," he replies, and then bends to suck my skin into his mouth. I'm riding his hand and my hands tangle into the soft curls of his hair, trying to keep him up against my neck. I growl, he bites my neck, and my vision goes white with pleasure as I come all over his hand.

He pulls away from me and grins at me. "I love when you squirt for me, pretty."

"Of course I squirted. You went straight for my G-spot." I playfully bite his shoulder.

"You need that intense orgasm. Don't think I haven't seen how stressed you've been this week." Fuck. There it fucking is. He misses nothing.

"Yeah, well, we'll talk about it later. You have a game to win." I run my hands through his hair, coaxing him into compliance.

"Mmm. I don't like it," he returns.

"Listen, baby boy," I start in a low and seductive register. "This season is important. You have to throw your little heart out so you can keep hold of your spot on UT's team. I want you to be stress free so you can think about passes and not about what's ailing your girlfriend's mind. Okay?" I pull his neck to the back so I can nibble on his Adam's apple. "Let me take care of you."

"You're pulling out all the stops right now, with the hair and the throat and the voice. So I know you're doing some serious avoiding. But you also have a point so I'll listen to you and let it go. For now."

He breaks my hold and pulls me to him, kissing me slow and sweet, with just a small amount of tongue. Then he pulls back to look at me.

"I love you." He searches my gaze.

"I love you, too. That's not even in question," I respond, and he visibly relaxes.

"All, right, pretty girl, let me let these jokers in so we can win a football game. I'll be watching you."

I snort. "No, you won't. You'll be playing. I'll be watching you, though. All my cheers are for you."

"Even when you're cheering for defense?"

"That's an indirect cheer for you. Defense has to be strong so you, the star of the offensive line, can shine."

"I can't fault that logic," he smiles at me and pecks my

lips.

I smile back at him.

As I leave, the boys hold up their hands in a high-five line, and I tell them all to play their hearts out.

I head to the girls' locker room to do my makeup. Obviously I waited until after deepthroating Graham to put on mascara. He loves it when I wear mascara and it runs down my face but before a game is not the time to be making a mess out of myself.

When I'm touching up, the rest of the squad comes in and starts doing last minute adjustments to themselves.

Molly's blonde ponytail bobs up to me. "So, Heather. Remember that cheer we made up Junior year about how awful Peyton is?" Our Junior year I had devised a cheer about Peyton that we performed during a pep rally. The whole rest of the year I had the school cheering it in her ear and torturing her when I wasn't around. Turns out it had been really catchy. I mean, of course it was. I wrote it.

I look down at her warily, not sure where this was going.

"Well, she's here tonight! We should do the cheer!"

"She's what? She's here?" I gasp.

"Yeah, she's with Graham's dad and some black lady who I guess is her mom."

This is not what I want to hear. Friday nights are special. Graham plays, and I cheer on the sidelines and perform the halftime show. I don't need for her to be getting in my head.

I come back to, and the girls are squealing.

"Great! We can perform it-"

"We're not doing the cheer." I make sure my voice is loud enough to carry over the ruckus.

"But she's never been to a game. We should chase her off!" Amber yells.

"Yeah! Show her she's not welcome!" Hannah pipes up.

"Listen, we're just going to ignore her tonight," I say sternly and turn around to go back to my mirror.

"Let's take a vote," Molly announces.

I quickly turn and say, "It seems like you've forgotten your place, Molly. This is not a democracy, this is a cheerocracy."

"Isn't that from *Bring It On?*" someone mumbles in the back.

"Yes, it is. And it's the truth. I'm the cheer captain and this is not up for discussion. Got it?" I make sure to put as much venom into my words as possible and I watch as they visibly back down. Some of the girls go so far as to duck their heads and nod.

So. The little freak has come to a game. Well, all I want is to block her out and focus on my performance. But every time I end a cheer I look over and find her watching me. I can't tell what's going on in her mind as she watches me. Maybe puzzlement? But it's not like she can be confused about the content of the cheers or the gymnastics of the movements. She's confused? I'm confused. My boyfriend is playing behind me, and every time I sit down to watch the game I can see he is doing well. But hearing his voice call plays can't drown out the words I keep hearing in the back of my mind, "*You* kissed *me!*" I can't stop seeing her wrecked face after I tore my face from hers. Like a palimpsest over the top of the images I see Graham telling me he loves me. I remember the way it feels to kiss them both. They are so different. Graham is all muscle and strength. Peyton is all soft and sensuality. If someone asked me to choose which one I want? I wouldn't have an answer. I'm straight. I'm Graham's girlfriend. But it comes to me with sudden clarity that I want to kiss Peyton again, and I'm not sure where that leaves me.

CHAPTER 10

PEYTON

Saturday morning, I blissfully wake to no one but me in my bed. Last night Graham spent the night with Heather, which means I have no man masquerading as an octopus clutching me to him and feeling me up. It means I'm not dripping cum out of my pussy. It means I can leisurely lay in bed and soak in my solitude. I sigh and stretch like a cat, enjoying my morning of freedom. Then someone knocks on my door and I curse whomever is ruining the scant amount of isolation that I have found myself in.

"Baby girl!" I hear Mama yell through the door. "Are you up?"

I pull a pillow over my head and try to ignore the noises.

"I wanna talk to you!"

I angrily fling the pillow to the side of my face and get up, knowing Mama won't stop. Good thing I really am alone this morning, or this could be so much worse. I unlock the door and open it. I glare at her, saying nothing.

"There's my beautiful girl! Good morning!" She is so chirpy in the mornings and it drives me mad.

I continue to glare at her.

"Oh, lovebug. Here's some coffee to soften the blow. Did you stay up reading again? It's already noon. The day is a wastin'!"

I glare harder but take the cup from her outstretched hand. "I don't have work until 4. I deserve some sleeping in."

"I wanted to talk to you about that. Ashton and I were thinking maybe you could work for him as a PA? It would look much better than the diner on a resume." She pushes into the room and sits on my bed, patting the space next to her. "I think he secretly wants to have someone in the family he can talk nerd with, too. Graham is no help on that front and neither am I. Plus, it would be a good bonding experience for the two of you. You aren't a football fan like the rest of the family. It could be your thing with him."

"Mama, I'm not that type of nerd." I sit next to her and take a sip of coffee. She's put in the perfect amount of cream, just the way I like.

"You don't know that. When was the last time you fiddled around with a computer? It could be your thing. And you still don't know what you want to major in at school…" she trails off.

"Ohhhhh that's what this is about. You want me to try on… what? Business? Computer science? What's the angle you're going for here?"

"Listen, I can't pretend to know what Ash does. He's the CEO of a software company he founded, and that means little to me. But Graham sure isn't going to take it over for him, so maybe we can keep this a family company with you in it."

"You've been married to the man less than a month, and now you want his stepdaughter of two weeks to helm his company? Mama. I don't think he's interested in that." I take another sip of coffee and close my eyes in bliss.

"Baby, not every man is your father. Some of them are actually good and loving men." She wraps her arm around me and pulls me into her, kissing my temple.

"I'm glad you found someone you feel like you can trust. But I'm not gonna hitch my wagon to someone who I don't know is reliable," I retort.

"Listen, it's better for your resume, and you might learn something fun. You don't have to commit to anything. You're so smart. Maybe this is your niche. You never know."

"Yeah, okay. I'll give my two weeks at the diner tonight. Does that make you happy?"

She kisses my temple again. "Yep, sure does. I know that manager is a pill anyway. And look, if you don't like it or you feel like Ashton is being too hard on you, just let me know, and you can go back to food service. It's not like before. We don't have to scrimp to get by anymore. The boys will take care of us."

"Jesus, Mama. The boys? Like Graham is doing anything to help out around here." Helping test the limitations of my birth control, maybe.

"He doesn't work, but he's a caretaker just like his daddy. You'll see. I bet whatever you needed help with, Graham would step up."

I can't bear how wrong she is about Graham, but I also don't want to poke a pin through her balloon, so I just grunt in affirmation.

"When does Ashton want me to start?" I question.

"You'll have to get your final schedule from the diner and then talk to him about where to go from there. I don't even know what he wants you to do because he commutes into Nashville every day, and you have school," she answers.

"So you're saying this is a nepotism hire, and my job is basically pointless, got it." I take the final sip of coffee and hide my rolling eyes behind the cup.

"Hush, child. Have him teach you some coding basics and see if you can do some more work for him that way. You'll figure it out," she double-pats my leg.

"Yeah, all right. Now get out of my room so I can catnap before work." I pass her back the empty coffee cup and flop back into my pillows.

She tsks her way out of the room and shuts the door. I get up and lock it, knowing the lock is virtually meaningless, before I crawl back into bed and start going through my socials.

I'm thirty minutes from the end of my shift when I see him. White skin, dark hair that is graying at the temples, thick limbs sitting in my section. I gasp, and my hands get clammy. The coffee pot in my hand starts to slip from my hold, but I quickly place it back on the warmer. I turn away and try to get my breathing under control. I search for my manager and spot him, making a beeline toward him where he's sitting at a booth with spreadsheets around him.

"Hey, Scott, can I head out a little early?"

He pauses above his calculator and looks up at me.

"You're on 'til midnight. If I let you go, everyone would want to be let go, then there would be no one to turn over with. So, no, Peyton, you're not leaving early," he scoffs.

I'm trying to think of a good excuse why I should leave early when Mira comes up to us and interrupts.

"Hey, Peyton. There's a guy who is getting antsy in your section. I tried to help him but he's asking for you," she announces.

I have a feeling I know just what customer is getting antsy in her section. And I have no intention of serving him. I turn back to Scott.

"Listen, I would never ask but this is important. Please." My pulse is firing rapidly and my brain is starting to get foggy.

"You can go after you take care of that customer," he replies and goes back to his figures.

"No. That's what I'm saying. I can't serve that guy. He makes me uncomfortable." My legs start to get shaky.

"What's going to happen? You're in public. You'll be fine. Now, Peyton," Scott demands.

"You're not listening to me. No, I'm not serving that guy. Someone else can do it," I insist.

"Peyton, go over there now or you're fired before those two weeks of yours are up," he narrows his eyes.

"Then I guess I'm fucking fired. No one should have to serve someone who makes them uncomfortable. Fuck your bottom line." I untie my apron and toss it on the table in front of him, then I go back to the employee lounge to grab my purse.

I have just made it out the door and into the parking lot when I feel a hand grab my upper arm and turn me around.

"Sweetheart, where are you going?" The man from the diner asks.

"Get your fucking hands off of me," I growl out.

"Not until you stay put so we can talk. I tried texting and calling but you didn't answer." His grip on my arm increases.

"Yeah, that's because I blocked your number. I don't want anything to do with you." I try to pull my arm from his grip again, but he just pulls me into him and puts his arms around me.

"I'm your father. You can't block your father." He squeezes me to him and I can smell the alcohol on his breath.

"Don't fucking touch me!" I push him away and pull out my keys to brandish at him.

"Oh, for heaven's sakes. What are you gonna do? Stab me? You're such a drama queen. Just like your mother. I don't even know why I bother," he mocks.

"Yeah, you really shouldn't. And when you do bother it's a half-assed attempt anyway," I confirm.

"I was in town and I wanted to see my baby girl." He holds his hands palm up, faking innocence.

"I'm over your hot and cold. I used to try to see you when you floated in on whatever bullshit but half the time you didn't show up and the other half the time you were too trashed to even know what was going on. So fuck you. I'm over it," I sneer.

"You're delusional. None of that ever happened. What happens in that brain of yours to get so twisted around? I thought you were supposed to be a smart cookie, hmm? But you can't even seem to get basic things right. Maybe your mother should have you tested," he drawls and I can hear the beginnings of a slur in his words.

"I used to get upset when you'd say that shit to me, but you're just a drunk who can't be held accountable for his actions. You mean nothing to me." I hold the hand with the keys up higher. "I'm going to go now and you're going to let me go or I'll fucking plunge one of these into your eyeballs. Capice?"

He grumbles but holds his hands up in a retreat.

I don't remember the drive home. I don't remember climbing up the stairs to my room. The first thing that tracks is me holding the toilet with one hand and holding my hair back with the other as I vomit into it. Then in a haze I manage to brush my teeth and shower away the day.

I come out of the bedroom to find Graham scrolling through his phone on my bed.

"Fuck. You," I growl at him.

He looks up from his phone.

"Oh, hey, fucktoy. Bad night at work?" He chirps at me.

"I am not in the mood for your bullshit tonight, Graham. Leave."

"Inconvenient, because Heather decided she'd rather get sloshed tonight with the girls

and leave me high and dry. So guess who gets to take care of me now?" He smirks at me.

"No. Graham. No." I stomp toward him, feeling brave. I stand toe to toe with him, me in my sleepshirt and him in his boxer briefs. I have had a terrible encounter with my father tonight. I am full up on asshole men. I want to go to bed in peace and not worry anymore about stacking up on trauma.

"When has you saying 'no' ever stopped me before, little sister?" He raises an eyebrow at me. "I'm getting hard just from you saying it." He grabs my wrist and places my hand on his dick, which I can feel hardening under my palm.

I tear my wrist out of his grasp and spit in his face.

He slaps me across the face and it's like all my senses light up at it. It makes me dizzy, it makes my ears ring, it makes me giddy to get a reaction like that again. So I spit in his face again, and he slaps me across my other cheek. This time, I can't help but to let out a moan.

Time seems to stop. My eyes are closed from when he hit me and I am afraid to open them. Had I really just moaned when he hit me? Had I wound him up on purpose so that he would? My chin is grabbed and tilted up toward his face but I resolutely hold my breath and keep my eyes closed.

"Look at me, fucktoy," he says softly.

I shut my eyes so hard my eyelids are trembling. I make a squeak of dissent.

"Come on, little sister. Open your eyes for me." His hand on my chin is rough but his voice is the soothing drawl he uses for the public.

I slowly open my eyes and they meet his. His eyes search me and I can see surprise written all over his features.

"Did you just moan when I slapped you, fucktoy?" His voice is still soft, still soothing. My day has been trash on fire and I think about sinking into that voice, about maybe getting a gentle man as a lover. What would he do if I capitulated? What would he do if I was good for him? Then I bring a hand up to feel my hot cheeks and wonder... what if I could do more to piss him off? What if I brought all his rage to the surface and he hit me more, hit me harder? What if I could feel filthy in his degradation? What if I could give myself over to it and let it wash away the sins of the day? What if I could become clean by getting dirty?

"Of course I didn't fucking moan for you, you piece of shit. I fucking hate you. I never want you inside of me again," I goad him.

His eyes get wide for a moment and then he smirks at me. He grabs me by the throat and pushes me onto the bed.

"How do you want to be fucked today, fucktoy?"

"I definitely don't want to see your fucking face, asshole," I snap at him, hoping he will take me face-to-face.

He pushes his boxer briefs down and crawls over me. He slaps my face and tears my shirt open. "Now I can see those gorgeous tits." He then proceeds to tear my panties in two, throwing the leftover fabric over his head. "Jesus, these tits."

Smack!

Smack!

He hits the side of each breast with either hand and my pussy flutters.

He grabs one of my legs and throws it over my shoulder and then enters me in one thrust. We both moan. I'll never tell him but fuck he feels good.

"I hate you," I pant out while he thrusts hard into me.

"Yeah, I can feel how much you hate me. Your hate is so warm and slippery," he snickers.

He pounds roughly into me, holding me by my tits, and I can hear the sloppy sounds my pussy is making around his cock. I clench around him and watch his powerful frame as he masterfully fucks me. It occurs to me how gorgeous he is, and suddenly I want to touch his body. I run my hands over his abs, feeling the dips and ladders. God, he feels blissful inside of me. I feel wild and free as he pumps inside of me. But it isn't enough. In the back of my mind the browser tab is playing the scene with my father and all I want to do is forget him.

"Now that I'm not a virgin I should find another guy to fuck who isn't you. I bet I could find a real good lay," I try to say with resolve but my voice is warbling.

Suddenly my throat is being grabbed and the sides of it are being squeezed until I can't speak. Graham leans down and speaks harshly in my ear.

"Listen up. You are mine for however long I say you're mine. You will not fuck any guy but me. This is the only cock that you'll have filling you," he growls out.

My vision is going white at the edges and I try to breathe his name but nothing comes out. Then everything goes black.

I'm brought back by a hard slap to my face and then I'm coming harder than I ever have, clenching around his dick and pulling him down to bite into his shoulder.

"Fuck. Yes, harder," he moans and as I bite down harder I can feel him pulse and empty into me.

I am so empty and yet so full and... I am overwhelmed. I close my eyes as tears start streaming down my face.

"Oh, fucktoy, shhh." I can feel our cum dribble out as he pulls out of me. Feeling him flip onto the bed next to me, he turns me toward him and pulls me into his chest. "Shh, shh. You're okay. You're okay." He runs his hands up and down my back as I soak his chest in tears. "This isn't from me. What happened today?"

"I don't want to talk about it with you of all people," I sob out.

"All right. All right. Of course not. Okay." His voice is buttery smooth and calming as he pets me.

He starts to move away from me and I squeak and grasp for him.

"Oh, fucktoy, shh. I'm not going anywhere. I'm just going to get a washcloth to clean you up. I promise I'll be right back to hold you," he comforts me.

I sniffle and nod.

"Maybe some Kleenex, too, hmm, beautiful?"

I feel his weight disappear from the bed and then a couple of moments later feel my legs being spread to be wiped down by a rag.

"Sit up for me, fucktoy. Let's get some water in you and

get that nose blown," he gently orders me.

I open my eyes and sit up to face him. I'm shocked to find his eyes full of concern for me. I have never seen that before. Taking the tissues from him, I blow my nose. He grabs the glass of water next to the bed and holds it out to me while opening his other palm for me. "Trade me."

Feeling like I am in the twilight zone where Graham takes care of me, I do as he says. I keep my eyes on him while I drink the glass and hand it back to him to place on the bedside table.

He scoots down under the blankets and lifts a side in invitation for me to crawl up next to him. Warily I do, testing the limits by placing my arms around his waist and curling up on his chest. He makes no move to complain or to stop me. He just starts petting my hair.

I feel... safe... comforted... even loved. Which doesn't make any sense because this is Graham for heaven's sakes. But here we are. He holds me while I cry until I fall asleep.

I'm woken up by the feeling of being filled with cock. I lean back into Graham's chest and can't control the whimper that comes out of my mouth. It is so much easier between us in these sleepy sessions. He rocks in and out of me gently and I want to tell him to play with my nipples but... that would ruin the facade that I am still an unwilling participant in this.

"Shh. It's just me, fucktoy," he breathes into my ear, and I bring my hands up to tangle in his hair, gently pulling at the strands. "Thatta girl. Fuck, you feel so good. Always so wet for your big brother."

I moan and I can feel myself lubricate his cock even more than it already is.

He circles my entrance with a finger, wetting it, and then starts rubbing my clit.

"Graham!" I shudder out.

"What a good girl you are when I take you like this. I'm beginning to think the lady doth protest too much. You want this cock. You want me to fuck you. You want me in this bed every single night," he purrs into my neck.

I moan and shiver against him, pulling tighter on the strands of his hair until he growls. I do want him. I want him all the time. But I don't know how to tell him, and I certainly don't know how to tell him I still want to pretend he is raping me. Isn't that a thing fucked-up girls like? Rape fantasies? But at this point I trust him. I know he won't ever seriously hurt me. He had gone so far as to take care of me last night. Graham Abraham Huntington cares about me. And I have no idea what to do about it.

CHAPTER 11

GRAHAM

On Sunday I wake up to a sleepy Peyton in my arms. Slipping my arms from around her and detangling my legs from hers, I grab my phone from what I'm beginning to think of as my side of the bed and leave her sprawled out to attend to my morning workout routine. Sunday is usually my rest day but damn if I need to empty my mind with a run and some weights right now.

Spoiler alert: it doesn't work. I really can't pinpoint how this had all started, but I'm incredibly confused about where this thing with Peyton is now. I haven't been bullying her at school, now I'm comforting her when she cries… I feel protective of her. And no matter how much I tease her about us being siblings I definitely am not feeling very familial toward her. I want to wreck her, ruin her, make her cry. But then after I want to hold her, pet her, tell her that she is mine to protect. This is confusing enough but meanwhile I have a girlfriend that I am not willing to give up. What am I thinking? That I can just have them both? I mean, Peyton and I have an end date at least. We will be going to two different schools. Can I just keep having her until then?

I run a hand down my face as I step into my shower. I love Heather. I do. And it's not fair to say that something between us is missing, because when we are together I feel complete. It's just that when I can let loose with Peyton something inside me is set free. It's like unlocking the secrets of myself. There had been that aborted attempt to see if Heather could ever be interested in the things that Peyton and I do but that had gone over like a lead balloon. And it is clear now that Peyton actually likes the things I do to her. Which honestly had made it hotter last night. Every time she had moaned, it had gone straight to my dick. Combined with her telling me no?

Maybe I should stop. Something is clearly wrong with me. What man gets off on a woman telling him no? Do I need therapy? A lobotomy? Why can't I feel fulfilled with the hot sex Heather and I have? I have to make sex into something creepy and violent instead?

I step out of the shower and run a towel over my body, securing it at my waist. Running a hand through my hair, I wander out of the bathroom and into my room where I find Peyton sitting rigidly on my bed.

"Oh, great. The cardio didn't do it so maybe a nut will." I toss the towel away and move toward her.

"No, I'm here… to talk about the sex, actually." She stands up nervously and starts backing away but then halts. "Actually I should not run. That'll just stir you up."

"We can talk after we fuck. But not too long. Heather is only at church for so long with her parents." I continue to move toward her, my dick perking up.

"Graham, seriously. I want to talk to you. I…" She brings her hands up to try to stop me, and looks around wildly.

"Let's make it a rule that whenever you're in my room or yours, you wear nothing, yeah?" I slip my hands up her shirt and groan in dismay when I find a bra.

"God, how do I make you stop?" She mutters, then says louder and with firmness, "Graham, I want you. I want you to fuck me."

I pause my movements over her tits and look in her rich brown eyes."I'm sorry, what?"

"That's what I'm trying to tell you. You make me so fucking hot. I want you to take me. But I want to talk to you about it first."

I drop my hands from under her shirt and back away, so confused by her shift. She moves toward me now, and slides her hands up my chest.

"We both like it when I say no, right? When I tell you I hate you and I'll never fuck you. When I fight you and you have to put me in my place either by overpowering me or spanking me or slapping me." My dick is thickening with her words and she notices and looks pointedly toward it. She runs a hand down to my dick and starts lightly stroking it. "Yeah, that's what I thought. It didn't… start out that way… but we both know I like it now. You pointed it out yesterday."

"What's your point?" God, I don't want to stop. I love all of what she has just described.

Her hand pauses on my dick. "I… looked it up. Other people like what we like. It's called consensual non-consent, or CNC."

"Other… people do this." It's a question, but I say it like

a statement.

"Yeah, Graham, they do. We're not alone in thinking this is hot. So I want..." She runs a thumb over the crown of my cock to spread the little droplet of precum that has emerged. "I want to ask... sometimes people who are into CNC still have a safeword that they can call if it gets to be too much. Like maybe you hit me too hard and I can't take anymore. Or maybe I'm not wet enough for you and I tear."

I smirk at her. "Fucktoy, you're always wet for me. Your body knows who it belongs to."

"Graham. Please be serious for a second. I want to keep playing this game, but I really want to do it safely. It's called SSC or RACK: safe, sane, and consensual/risk-aware consensual kink."

"Where in the world did you find all this shit?"

"I... kind of went into a rabbit hole this morning while you worked out." I run a thumb over her lips. "My smart little fucktoy." I can't debate any of what she is saying. This morning I was freaking out over wanting to protect her. And this can protect her from me.

"I really like the stoplight system: red, yellow, and green. Red means everything fucking halts, yellow means tread lightly because I'm getting to red, and green means go. So red would be my safeword."

"But you would still tell me stop and no? You would still fight me?" I clarify.

"Sometimes, Graham." She bites her lip and looks up at me through her lashes. "Sometimes I don't want to fight you anymore. Sometimes I want to tell you to hit me again or to fuck me harder or to pull my hair." She shivers and then leans forward to bite my nipple. "Sometimes I just want you and I don't want to work for it."

"Yeah, okay. I can do that." At least this doesn't have

to stop. I want her crying in release, not because I've seriously hurt her. I think… I think if I really hurt her that would fuck me up.

"There are some other things I'd like to do, but we can start here. I know you're a big burly jock but can you go online and try to read some educational things for me?"

"Why would I do that when I have you to do it for me?" I grin at her.

"Graham, seriously. You should understand this. There's so much. Dom/sub dynamics, all sorts of kink that I couldn't even list them all."

I sigh. "Is this really important to you, little sister?"

"Yes. It really is." She looks up at me with wide and sincere eyes, and I stop in my tracks. I don't think she has ever looked at me that way before. She looks so open and earnest. This girl is giving me carte blanche to do whatever I want with her as long as she doesn't say the word "red." I guess I can find the weird corners of the internet and read some kinky shit to appease her.

"Yeah, all right. But I was serious last night, you know. You can spin me up by telling me you're going to fuck other guys," I grab her chin and lift it to look in my eyes. "But you will absolutely not fuck other guys. You're mine."

She glowers at me. "But you're not mine. That's not fair."

"This part of me is yours. That will have to be enough." I stroke her cheek with my other hand. "Now get out before I fuck your face. I have to go pick up Heather from her date with Jesus." I cup her cheeks with my hands and kiss her forehead. When I pull back from her, the way she's looking at me fills me with panic. I'm in over my head with this girl. Now we are negotiating how I will fuck her? And fuck if that doesn't settle something inside me. But now I am being tender with her, too? I grab her hair and pull her head to the side, sinking my teeth into the side of her neck that's absent a hickey and hopefully giving her some fresh bite marks. This is just sex. It can't be more.

When I pull up to Wickersville First Baptist, it's a clusterfuck of folks in their Sunday best rushing to their cars so they can get to Cracker Barrel first. Don't let anyone tell you differently: the church crowd is vicious about their afters. I unlock my doors, lean my seat back, and close my eyes to wait on Heather to find my car.

Moments later, I hear the passenger door open and a grunt of frustration.

"Graham, I need kisses!" My blonde beauty demands of me as she closes the door.

"Of course, pretty girl. But why don't you just come over here and get them?" I open my eyes and pat my lap.

"Mama is already on a tirade today. They never care that every Sunday you pick me up after church but noooo. Today someone invited us to lunch and it was apparently imperative that I go so we can pretend we're a proper family. Then it turned into a big fight and I just left. She tried to threaten me as I walked away, but you know she'll forget I exist the second her martini passes her lips. I can't stand them! Ugh!"

"All I'm hearing are the best reasons to get your ass on my lap, let me tongue fuck you into a coma, and stir up everyone in this parking lot." I reach toward her and run my hand up her arm.

She throws her head back and screams in frustration.

I move my seat to an upright position and lean in toward her. "Okay, love, shh, it's okay." Then I gently open her mouth with mine, licking inside her mouth and painting her tongue with mine. Her posture deflates as I run my hands up her arms and press her body into mine. She sighs into my mouth as she begins to kiss me back softly at first, then more feverishly. She bites my bottom lip and then pulls back.

I push her hair out of her face and frame her temples with my hands. Her hands cover mine and she threads our fingers together as she leans in, bringing our foreheads together.

"I love you," she murmurs.

"And I love you," I say back.

"If I promise not to be a bitch all day, will you still take me to the farmer's market in Nashville?"

"It was never even in question," I promise.

"Ugh, you're so good to me. We'll never be like my parents, right?"

"No, because we're actually in love, and we hold a conversation more than once a week," I confirm.

"What if we fall out of love?" She breaths against my lips.

"Then we'll go to counseling and fall back in love. Didn't we have a variation of this conversation last week?" I peck her lips.

"Yeah... but..."

"Is that what's going on with you? You've been weird all week long. Are you falling out of love with me?" My heart races. I know I'm fucking Peyton now but my biggest fear is losing Heather. I can stand not to go pro in the NFL. I can deal with not getting to play QB for UT. But I absolutely cannot picture my life without my best friend in it.

I feel a tear slipping down Heather's cheek and my heart lurches. I can't think so close to her right now, so I take my hands off of her and back away slowly.

"Pretty girl…"

"Please don't call me that right now." She closes her eyes and more tears fall, running through her perfectly applied makeup. I love to see her mascara running but not like this.

"All right. Just talk to me," I implore.

"I don't know what to say. I'm so confused right now, and I don't have anyone to talk to about it, and that's not normally a problem because I can talk to you, but I can't talk to you about this."

And then it hits me. There's only one conceivable thing I can think of that she can't talk to me about. Fuck, it's the only thing I can't talk to her about. But I'm not confused. She's still it for me. I know that like I know that water is wet. "Is there… is there someone else?"

She brings her hands up to hide her face from me. My heart fucking shatters. It may sound hypocritical of me, but my fucking Peyton isn't confusing my feelings for Heather at all. But there's some dickwad guy that Heather has feelings for and she doesn't know if she wants to be with me.

I slump back in my seat and bring a thumb and forefinger to the bridge of my nose, closing my eyes. This is a clusterfuck of a day: my fucktoy wants me, my girlfriend doesn't.

Heather, meanwhile, is sobbing in my passenger seat. I'm feeling absolutely wrecked and betrayed but it still hurts me to see her like this. Sighing, I pick her up and pull her over the console into my lap to hold her while she cries.

We sit like that for a while, her nuzzled into my shoulder and crying into my button-down while I pet her. After the parking lot has been emptied of even the pastor and ushers she pulls back and looks at me.

"I'm sorry, baby boy."

I flinch. "If you're no longer 'pretty girl,' I don't want to be 'baby boy' either, thanks."

She flinches too. "Right. That makes sense. You're not mad?"

"I'm livid. I just love you too much to be an asshole to you right now."

"Fuck, that makes me feel worse."

"Do you want me to call you names and slut-shame you?" I try to make the joke.

"I haven't fucked anyone else. I just… want to. And it's confusing me."

Honestly, that makes me feel better. I don't want her to fuck anyone else. Maybe there's still time to turn this around. "Great. I thought you wanted to take a break."

"Oh… I… still think we should take a break. Until I figure out what's going on." She wrings her hands.

"You want to take a break so you can fuck someone else and figure out if you still love me. Right. Okay. I'm tracking." I wonder if I could wheedle out of her who it is so I can kill them before they even touch her. I'd go to prison for murder, but then this prick would never fuck her. Ugh but wait. If I'm in prison then some third guy would get his paws on her. Fuck. There's no good solution. I think I'm stuck.

She climbs over to her side of the car and opens up the console to grab some Kleenex. I throw my head into the steering wheel so hard the horn honks.

"Can we… can we still go to the farmer's market?"

"Heather. You are destroying my life right now and all you can think about are the soy candles you like?"

"But I really like that honeysuckle scent and…" she trails off with a watery and hesitating smile as I loll my head on the steering wheel to glare at her. "You're my best friend. I don't know how to live without you."

"So then may I give you some advice and tell you don't live without me. It's pretty fuckin' simple, Heather."

"It doesn't feel simple."

"I'm not going to argue with you. And I don't want to have to beg you to be with me if you don't want to be with me."

"I never said I didn't want to be with you!" She cries.

"You're asking for a break so you can experience a different dick!" I finally burst out.

She cringes, opens her mouth, closes it, and facepalms.

"I'm taking you home. Then I'm gonna go home and get drunk about it. You can do whatever you need to do."

She turns away and buckles her seatbelt but I see her tear-filled expression in the window reflection all the way to her house.

When I get back to the house I go straight to my dad's liquor cabinet and grab a fifth of whiskey. I don't bother looking at the label because whatever it is, it's expensive. If he wants to get onto me about it later, that's fine. I really could give a rat's ass right now.

I've got a third of it down when Peyton walks into my room and finds me propped up against my headboard.

"Not now, little sister."

"Jeez. Was that bottle full when you started?"

"Peyton. I mean it. Out."

"We could talk about it if you wanted," she offers.

"We don't do shit like that," I sneer at her.

"Oh. I see. I'm just good for realizing your deviant fantasies that you can't share with anyone else. But not good enough to share your troubles with."

"Nailed it," I say as I take another gulp of whiskey.

"Well, do you wanna fuck it out, then?"

"I'm afraid I'll actually hurt you right now. I've had too much to drink."

"Will you come in tonight, then?"

"Fuck, Peyton, I don't fucking know. I guess you'll figure it out if I'm fucking you circa two am, won't you?"

"Jesus, you're an asshole when you're drunk."

"Correct. Bye now."

"Do you want me to stay and drink with you?"

"Wha... what?" I flounder.

"Keep you company in your despair. We don't have to talk. Or fuck. I could just... be here with you."

"Have you ever even had liquor before?" I ask her, but then I scoot over on the bed to make room for her.

"Mmm. No. But... I'll only have a little." She sits down next to me and leans in to kiss my Adam's apple.

I take a drink and grab her chin, pulling her lips open with my thumb. She opens her mouth and I put my lips on hers and push the liquid from my mouth to hers. I pull back and watch her swallow. She sputters and coughs, making me smirk.

"That's fucking disgusting." She wipes her mouth with her arm.

"Then leave me alone," I retort.

"I'll get over it," she says and tucks into my side while I take another drink. I put my arm around her and start petting her hair. She nuzzles into my neck and I sigh. I put the bottle off on my bedside table and tuck her under my chin. I'm done drinking for now. Apparently I'm expected to give my fucktoy a sleepy fuck and I've gotta be sober enough to do it. I've already let one girl down today. I don't need to make it two.

CHAPTER 12

HEATHER

I spent the whole last week trying to figure out what was going on with me while simultaneously trying to stay far away enough from Graham so he couldn't tell there was something on my mind. But it had all come to a head in the car and now I feel even more lost than before. But I had also decided I wanted to kiss Peyton again and it wasn't fair to Graham that I do that while still dating him. Even if it was with a girl. I mean... I am a girl. Kissing a girl. That doesn't count as cheating, right? And I don't know what he would say if I told him I thought I... God, I can't even say it. Not even in my thoughts. He hasn't been raised like I have been raised, but there are a lot of homophobes in this town. The biggest ones are in my house. Wouldn't wanting Peyton be wrong, be unnatural? I have always thought I am so normal. I mean, I'm a cheerleader for heaven's sakes! I'm supposed to be the epitome of a girly girl. And now I am sitting in the hoodie I stole from Peyton's locker just to smell her scent instead of my own Shalimar scent.

I am laying in a ball on my bed while I have the hoodie over my face, just like I have seen her do. I feel so close to her right now. Her scent surrounds me and in the hoodie I can pretend she herself is wrapped around me clinging to my body. If Graham and I are on a break- because of *you* my subconscious shouts at me but fuck her- then I'm going to have Peyton and I know she'll be into it because she kissed me back. Yes, she's right... I initiated that first kiss but she had kept up. She had been happy to be pushed up against that bathroom door and picked up into my arms.

The next day at school I'm jittery all throughout the day. I have thought this through. I am going to corner her after school before cheer practice and I am going to kiss her again. And she's going to be willing. And it will be great. And... I really haven't thought about what will happen after that. That's as far as my mind has been willing to go.

I leave my last class early so I can go primp in the mirror. Hair- sleek. Lips- glossy. Pout- kissable. Body- fuckable. I wait across the hall and when I see her I spring into action.

I grab her by her nape. "You're coming with me."

"Heather, I literally do not have the time for this today." She tries to bat my hand away but I just pick her up and throw her over my shoulder. "What the fuck! Heather! Let me go!"

"Listen, little freak. Just give me a second." I shove her into the nearest custodial closet and go in after her. I grab her by the arms and pull her into me, kissing her roughly. God, this is good. This is what I need. This is-

She pushes me off of her hard. "What in the fucking hell, Heather? What actually is your damage?"

"You liked it the other day. I thought we should do it again." I move toward her mouth again and she slaps me across the face.

"Heather, No! I'm saying no. Jesus Christ what is it with you people?"

"What do you mean, no? Everyone knows you're a lesbian, little freak. You don't have to pretend with me."

"Um, actually, you started that rumor, and it's not true. I'm not a lesbian."

"So, what? Are you with whomever is leaving marks on your neck?"

"You know, Heather, this is pretty misogynist of you. I can say no and not have it be because I'm already with someone else."

"But you're... into girls, right?" My heart starts to flutter. I thought this to be safe because she is already into girls but if she isn't... God, I have gotten this all terribly, terribly wrong.

"Fucking hell, Heather. I don't actually know, all right?"

I curl my hands into fists and feel my nails making divots into my palms.

"Fine. Well. I've got to get to cheer practice, so." I make to leave and she follows behind me.

"Great. I have auditions to get to."

"Oh, my God. Did you think you were leaving? No, you're staying in this closet. Either until someone comes and lets you out or until I'm done with cheer practice."

"Are you kidding me? I won't make out with you so

you're trapping me in here?"

"I guess you're as smart as everyone says. Give me your phone."

"Fuck you. No."

I shrug and quickly grab her backpack from her hand, holding it above her head and out of her reach as I discover her phone in the front pocket and slip it into my purse. "You can have this back after I'm done for the day."

"Please, Heather. I'm begging you. Don't leave me in here. Today is so important to me."

"Oh, well." I open the door and she tries to duck around my arm but I grab her by her hair and pull her by her curls back into the closet. I step around her and push her down before I go through the door and close it behind me. I try to think of a way to keep her in there while I go to get something to bar the door with but luckily the girls are coming down the hall toward me.

"Hey, ladies. I've got the little freak in here. Can one of you go get a chair to put under the knob for me?"

They laugh in unison then Amber pipes up, "Yeah 100%. I'll be right back."

"What did she do today?" Hannah asks me. I can hear Peyton screaming and hitting the door behind us.

"Oh, you know. I just didn't like how comfortable she was looking," I say smugly.

"Oh, fun! I love the 'just because' days," Molly adds. Peyton is trying to open the door behind me if the knob moving or the weight hitting the door is any indication.

Amber comes back with a chair and I nod to the door. She tucks it under the door and we all step back to see our handiwork. It's holding.

"Great. Now, we have to work on that kick routine today for regionals." I start walking toward the gym.

"Some of the girls' high kicks just aren't there, Heather,"

Molly chirps in my ear.

"Yeah, I know. I was thinking of adding some rigorous stretching routines to our warm-ups to get more elevation."

After cheer practice, I go back to the maintenance closet. I fully expect that someone has clocked a chair in front of the door and released Peyton from her makeshift prison. To my surprise it's still right under the doorknob just like I had left it an hour and a half ago.

I untuck the chair and open the door to find Peyton curled in the fetal position. She looks up at me as I enter, tears streaming down her face, and glares at me while she gets to her feet.

"Give me my phone, Heather." She holds out a palm.

Silently, I slip her phone out of my purse and hand it to her. We say nothing else as she shoulder-checks me on her way out but as she crosses the threshold of the door she turns and says, "I fucking hate you. I hope the one thing you love disappears from your life and leaves you feeling as empty as your fucking heart is."

Turns out, the one thing I love has disappeared. Graham. And the kicker is that I had been the one to make him just so I could figure out what the hell is happening with the girl who has just rejected me.

I guess that isn't completely true. I still have dance. Resolved, I leave the closet so I can go to my only safe place left: the dance studio for some ballet.

CHAPTER 13

GRAHAM

Peyton is curled up on her bed reading when I walk in juggling two glasses of water, a chocolate bar, and a bag of beef jerky. She managed to evade me after school today and get a ride home with Adrian instead of me.

"So I was reading about aftercare and I decided I should be feeding you after we fuck. I'm always hungry anyway. We can have a little snack."

"Graham, get the fuck out." She keeps the book in front of her face, not even looking at me.

"Love that energy. Keep that going," I say as I sit everything down on the dresser and start peeling my clothes off.

"No, I fucking mean it. I'm not in the mood for this

right now." She turns on her side away from me.

"God, you get me so hard, fucktoy." I crawl up from the foot of her bed toward her body.

"*Red*, Graham, red."

I sit back on my haunches, confused at her safewording. "But I haven't even done anything to you yet."

"Yeah, that's the point. I don't want you to do anything to me right now."

But then she sniffles and that triggers my worry at what is happening with her. This isn't about me, this is clearly about her. My hand pushes the book down from her face. She looks like shit.

"Little sister, what happened?"

"Nothing."

"You've clearly been crying. Your eyes are puffy and red and I know you're into different makeup styles, but I don't think the mascara is supposed to be that far away from your eyelashes."

"Fuck off. We don't talk about shit like that, remember?"

I run a hand down my face. "Listen... I shouldn't have said that. I'm sorry." I continue climbing up the bed, pushing her to her back when I'm above her. I reach over to her bedside table and grab some tissues, then wipe below her eyes.

"Oh, what? I'm too terrible to look at right now? You've got to make me palatable to have a conversation? Just go, Graham."

"Stop trying to rile me up. I'm already hard and not going to fuck you. Stop fighting with me. You're still beautiful. I'm just trying to clean you up a little to make you feel better. Let me."

She sniffles again. "You think I'm beautiful?"

I smile gently at her. "You're beautiful all the time. You think I just cheat on my girlfriend with any girl? I've never fucked anyone else aside from Heather until you, fucktoy." I finish dabbing at her face and then wipe under her nose. Flinging the Kleenex off onto the table I lean down and pepper her face with soft closed-mouth kisses.

"I... I missed my audition for *A Midsummer Night's Dream.* I was so late that Mr. Stephens said I had missed my window and it wasn't fair to all the people who had been on time to take me in a different time slot." Her tears start afresh. "So, the fall play of my senior year I can't even be in. This is the only thing I look forward to. This is the only thing that's just for me. I'm good at academics because I knew I wouldn't make it in athletics, and I knew that was the only avenue available for me to get a scholarship and go to college. But drama club is just for me. My little slice of paradise. And now it's ruined."

"Little sister. You don't have to get a scholarship now. Dad will pay for wherever you want to go to school."

She growls in frustration. "Now it's a matter of pride, but you're missing the point."

"Okay, sorry. Right. But why did you miss the audition? Is that the point?"

"Your girlfriend cornered me and locked me in a closet. She didn't come back for me until after she was done with cheer practice."

"Heather isn't-"

She cuts me off, "I don't want to hear you defend her right now, Graham. I'm really fucking upset. Nothing either of you have ever done is as bad as this is."

"I wasn't-"

She glares at me.

"Sorry. Of course. No defense. I promise." I lean down to kiss her forehead. "What can I do?"

"Unless you can magically get Mr. Stephens to give me an audition, there's nothing to do."

"I see. And sex won't make it better?" I cock my head at her in question.

"Oh my God. This has all been so you can put your dick in me? Fuck you, Graham." She pushes at my chest.

"What? Jesus, fucktoy, I'm just asking. There are very few things sex can't make better. My mistake for thinking this fell under the category." I flop down next to her, face-to-face, and pull her into my body. "What are you reading? Something too smart for me to understand?"

"Um… no… you'd understand this but it's kind of… I'm reading smut?" She buries her face further into my chest to hide her embarrassment.

"Sexy. Can I read it to you?"

"I don't know if you'd think this is sexy. It's a male/male romance about a monk and his ex-boyfriend."

"Do they fuck?"

"Well… yeah." She hesitates.

"You've already told me sex is off the table right now so better that it doesn't make me hot. Give me the book." I push back from her and grab the book that is still in her grasp between our bodies.

I read to her for the rest of the night, until she's limp against me and breathing deeply in sleep. And when I wake up like clockwork in the middle of the night with an erection I just tuck it between her ass cheeks, nuzzle into her neck, and fall back asleep.

The next day at school I slip into the drama room during lunch to find Mr. Stephens hunched over and making annotations in a script. He doesn't notice me even when I'm standing right in front of his desk.

I clear my throat.

He looks up and looks around, as though bewildered to find me in front of him.

"Mr. Huntington, hello there. You're not in any of my classes and you're certainly not in drama club, so I can't imagine what I could do for you." He straightens his horn-rimmed glasses on the bridge of his nose.

"Well, you may not be aware but my sister is in both your class and your drama club."

"Ah, that's right. I had heard your parents tied the knot over the summer. How fortuitous for your family to have found joy. But I still have no clue why that would bring you to my stoop, as it were." He tries to look down his glasses at me. His hackles are already up, I can see.

I pull out my patented good ole boy drawl and inquire, "You're up for tenure this year, are you not, Reginald?"

"Young man, it's Mr. Stephens to you." He sits up straighter in his chair.

"Of course. Being tenured must come with a lot of benefits, not to mention job

security." I continue.

"I don't see how this is relevant to a conversation between the two of us."

"Ah, but I think you absolutely do. Just as I think you know, my father sits on the Board of Education for this school district."

"I... I wasn't aware of that."

"And now you are. So it seems that it turns out that Peyton should have a second shot at that audition for whatever culture shock you're bringing to our beloved school district."

"But... the fairness. The other students wouldn't have had the same opportunities."

"Then I suggest you give all the other students who

missed their slots a second chance as well, or you can simply use the excuse that Peyton had a family emergency which precluded her from arriving on time. You can choose whichever your heart desires."

"I… suppose…" He's visibly wilting in front of me.

"And, of course, Peyton will get whatever part she decides to go out for."

"How dare you! It's one thing to strong-arm me into letting her have a second audition but you can't force me to give someone a part, too!" He finally must have found his courage because he's standing now, although I stand taller and am much broader than his wispy frame.

"I'm not doing anything but reminding you how important I think you are to this school and how talented we know Peyton is. It would be a shame to have to find a new teacher for the drama department. Stability is so important for funding, especially the arts, don't you think?"

He closes his eyes and slumps back in his chair.

"Good talk. And, Reginald? She never needs to know about this conversation. After all, she looks up to you so much. Wouldn't want to rain on that parade, now would you?"

I stroll out of the classroom with a grin on my face.

CHAPTER 14

PEYTON

I shut my locker and lean my forehead on it in despair. I have two options: find something else to do with my time until Graham is done with football practice, or go find Adrian and beg a ride off of him while still giving him the silent treatment. Yesterday he had been too worried about comforting me to try to get back on my good side, but I know that today he will be back up to his old tricks and trying to cajole me into forgiving him. It's hard to stay mad at him but I am pissed that he always co-signs with Sam and never stands up to her with me when she crosses a line.

A shadow falls over my right side and I close my eyes and sigh in preparation. What fresh hell will this be? Heather, who can't decide on kissing me or torturing me? Adrian, who will be bent on cheering me up and pretending everything is fine between us? Graham, who has a genius idea to fuck before football practice? Honestly kind of hot, so I'm hoping for that option.

"Hey," Sam says next to me. She is never one to back down and we haven't spoken since our fight, so I'm shocked to hear her voice.

"Shouldn't you be in play rehearsals? The cast list should have gone up today." I snap out.

"Actually, there's been a delay. According to Mr. Stephens you had an emergent situation. That's what I'm coming to get you for. He wants to see you. He wants you to audition."

I stand up straight and look at her with wide eyes. "I'm sorry, what now?"

"Yeah. He also said in the name of fairness anyone else who missed their time slot could audition today. Kind of crazy. He's usually such a stickler for these things."

"Right." I turn around but I don't get far before her voice stops me.

"Pey... I was wrong."

It's the last thing I expect to hear and it causes me to halt where I stand. I do an abrupt about-face and narrow my gaze at her. "Go on."

"I was... I was jealous. And I didn't even hear you out before I got on what Adrian called my 'high horse.'" Here she stops to make quotations with her fingers. "He called me out and at first I blew him off, but I thought about it for a while and... I guess missing you was a good form of punishment because it made me really stop and think."

"I appreciate what you're saying, and don't think I'm not impressed with both Adrian and you, but I've yet to hear an apology float through your mouth."

"God damn it, Peyton, I'm taking accountability for my

actions. You need the words 'I'm sorry' verbatim for it to count?"

I cross my arms.

"Fine. I'm sorry. I don't know what you're into. I didn't even ask. Marking is like a kink, right? It doesn't have to be patriarchal bullshit. You could be with a no-shit feminist and still do it. And instead of asking I just made a bunch of assumptions because I was hurt it wasn't me but that's not fucking fair. You should not have to worry about your best friend being an asshat about your sex life."

"This is a lot of growth, Sam. I'm honestly so surprised."

She looks down and scuffs a black boot on the ground. "Yeah, I, uh, took it to therapy on Adrian's suggestion and kind of did a lot of work around it."

"Do you think you can handle hearing or not hearing about my sexual transgressions?" She sighs, "Yes, you hooker. I'm here to be a springboard or just to support you. As long as whatever you're doing is consensual."

I mean… it is now. But she doesn't need to know the details and she certainly doesn't need to know with whom.

I open my arms in a hug and she steps into me.

"Ugh I hate this," she whines as we wrap our arms around each other.

"This is also your punishment," I laugh.

I head to the gym unburdened and feeling anticipation for my audition, Sam following me.

"Mr. Stephens, I heard that you were letting me do a make-up audition?" I greet my teacher when I enter the gym.

"Miss Stratford, there you are. Yes. You'll be reading with Mr. Higgins as he missed his audition as well. I understand you wish to read for Titania, so we will start there."

"Oh, yeah. Great!" It's not great. Theo will be terrible to work off of. He tries out every semester and reliably gets put on lighting.

I hand Sam my backpack, then open up the top flap and pull out my well-worn script.

Looking for the scene I'm hopeful will be the best, I turn to Theo and tell him, "Let's start at Act 4, Scene 1, yeah?"

His big puppy dog eyes look at me and he nods. Ugh, this is going to be a feat. His monotone voice and stumbling over words is going to go over so well.

Climbing up the steps to the stage, I look out over the makeshift audience. Mr. Stephens is sitting in a folding chair with some students scattered on the floor around him.

"Uh, can someone read for the fairies?"

At the same time as the words leave my lips, the gym door opens and Heather comes through the doors.

"I can, just so y'all can hurry up with this. We need the gym for practice, Mr. Stephens." She pops a hip and places a fist on it.

"Miss Lovelace, I cleared our time with the front office. They said you could spare 30 minutes of practice for an addendum to our audition schedule. We won't be long."

"Right. Like I said, I'll help by reading for the fairies or whatever, so you can hurry this along."

I watch in horror as Mr. Stephens sighs and then agrees. "I suppose that'll do. You'll need a script."

Heather walks over to Adrian and plucks his copy out of his hands. "Hey!" He protests but Heather ignores him and makes her way up to the stage.

My jaw is still dropped when she turns toward me.

"Show me who I'm reading," she demands of me.

I tuck my script under my arm and wave toward hers,

silently asking for her to pass it to me. She does, and I open it to the page we are on, pointing toward the first line. "You're going to be the fairies. That's Peaseblossom, Cobweb, Moth, and Mustard-Seed."

"Wow. Those are some interesting names." She takes the book back from me.

"You're literally named after a type of fern," I counter.

"Wow. You know what?" She starts, but Mr. Stephens cuts her off.

"Ladies. If we could start soon. Isn't that why you came in here, Miss Lovelace?"

We grumble.

"'Come, sit thee down upon this flowery bed, While I thy amiable cheeks do coy,

And stick musk-roses in thy sleek, smooth head, And kiss thy fair large ears, my gentle joy.'" I begin.

"'Where's Peaseblossom?'" Theo mumbles out.

"'Ready.'" Heather reads but stares me down as she does so.

"'Scratch my head, Peaseblossom. Where's Monsieur Cobweb?'" Theo makes the question sound like a statement.

"'Ready.'" Heather is still staring at me, and this time I stare back. To my surprise,

she bites her lip while she watches me.

Theo continues the scene badly, while Heather and I keep eye contact. For some reason, I cannot look away from her. We cannot look away from each other.

"'Ready,'" she continues, and it still does not break the spell.

What is happening? Yesterday she had been the reason I cried, and yet today, I am… captivated? By her?

"'What's your will?'" This time after she reads a line her mouth quirks up on the right side. Is Heather smiling at me?

I tune back into the scene and read my line, "'What, wilt thou hear some music, my sweet love?'" My voice has gone melodic, soft, and soothing.

"'I have a reasonable good ear in music. Let us have the tongs and the bones,'" Theo reads. I am barely paying him any attention. I know enough of his presence to know he is stuck in his book, but my lines are for one person on this stage.

"'Or say, sweet love, what thou desirest to eat.'"

This is insane. We don't even like each other, but this sexual tension is so thick. The heat in Heather's eyes is scorching as Theo and I continue trading lines, and when I get to my final line, I can't look away from Heather as I utter, "'O, how I love thee! How I dote on thee!'"

After my audition, I try to read but I keep looking up every time someone comes near in the hopes that it will be Graham. I don't know why it's not enough that Sam and Adrian know I have nailed my audition, but Graham has gotten underneath my skin and now I need to tell him how it went.

"Yeah, we can look over your cardio schedule and see where you're getting it wrong. Or even look at what you're lifting- those muscles transfer to cardio too. People forget that. We'll get you running those suicides faster, kid." I look up and see Graham coming toward me with some guy I don't recognize.

"Thanks, Graham. I just want to be able to play half as well as you do when I take your starting position next year." Ah. So the second string QB, then.

"Sure, Tommy. You will. We'll get you there." Graham

turns away, and I watch his eyes light up when he spots me sitting and waiting for him. "Catch you later, man." He doesn't even stop eye-fucking me as he says it.

He holds a hand out to me and I reach up to take it, letting him pull me up off the curb. He tows me to the passenger side, opens the door for me, and helps me in. I stare at him while he climbs up and belts my seatbelt. When has this become our new norm? As of this week, Heather has even stopped showing up in the mornings, as though she is used to our routine of him driving me to and from school.

I wait for him to get in and turn the car on before I turn to him and put a hand on the arm that's outstretched toward the gear shift. "I have something to tell you."

He slowly lowers his arm and turns to face me fully, looking inquisitive.

"Mr. Stephens changed his mind. He let everyone audition who missed their original times. I just got done!" I take his hand with mine and curl our fingers together.

His smile unfurls into a blindingly bright grin. "Oh, yeah? And how'd you do, little sister? Were you transcendent?" His thumb starts rubbing circles into the back of my hand.

"Graham. I was the best I've ever been. It was so great. I was so great. And just... I wanted to share it with you. And thank you."

"Thank me? For what?"

"You were just... I know last night... we aren't like that. And you took care of me anyway."

His emerald green eyes capture mine, and I freeze. Something is happening. I don't know what, but we are on the precipice of something that I can't understand.

We are still holding hands, but he brings his other hand up to my jaw, cradling it. He runs a thumb across my lower lip as I hold completely still for him.

"Fucktoy… you want me to be yours?"

"Yes," I breathe out, still careful to not move.

"Fuck it… then I'm yours," he breathes back, and then his mouth is on mine. His hands are in my hair, tipping my head back, and I'm halfway across the seat because I have wanted this for so long but I haven't known how to wish for it. His kiss is positively searing, and I swear to God it changes the make-up of my DNA. He licks into my mouth like I am a mere possession of his and he can do anything he wants with me. He kisses like he fucks- like I am there for his enjoyment and nothing more. But as I groan into his mouth he growls back at me and pulls my hair, getting rougher with me, and making my pussy gush. It occurs to me then that Graham and Heather both kiss me like they are trying to devour me. It makes me wonder how they kiss each other.

He pulls back from my lips and we stare at each other, panting, trying to catch our breaths.

"You've never kissed me before," I wonder aloud.

"Things were different before. Now they're… we're… different," he flounders.

"But, Heather?"

"Don't worry about Heather," he responds.

And, okay, that's not really an answer, but I am still trying to collect myself after that revelation of a kiss.

My head is spinning, but I realize Graham is unzipping his pants and taking out his hard cock.

"Have you ever given head before?" He smirks at me, which is slightly less effective when he looks so disheveled.

"No. And I'm definitely not doing it now." I glance around the parking lot furtively.

He groans and strokes himself. "That's it. See how hard you make me? You have to take care of it if you're going to make it hard, fucktoy. That's how this works."

"Graham, seriously. Someone will see." I feel my face heating.

"No one is around. Tommy and I were the last ones in there. What's your color?"

I sigh, "Green."

"Great. Now get on this dick." He palms my head and starts to push me down but then hesitates. "Wait. How do you call red if you're suffocating on my cock?"

"Oh. Yeah. I'll tap you three times."

"Perfect. Now shut the fuck up and start sucking my cock." He continues to push me down onto him.

I put my mouth around his dick and try to take him inside. God, this is fucking hard. How do people do this and not gag?

"It's okay to gag, fucktoy. That makes it hotter. And don't worry about drooling. I like sloppy head. Don't overthink it. Try to use your tongue and hollow your cheeks and suck. If that gets manageable, try to hum a little for vibration. But if you can't, just do your best. I know it's your first time. Breathe through your nose."

God, so many directions. I want to be good at this for him. As I lick around his crown, I feel the car start to move, and now I'm even more panicked. I'm giving roadhead for my first time? God, the learning curve with Graham is so steep.

I'm trying to take it slow but fucking shit my jaw is stretched so wide. Can I get TMJ from this? I'm trying to take more of him in my mouth when suddenly I feel his hand pushing me down onto his cock further. He goes to the back of my throat, and I feel the urge to vomit. Oh, shit. Oh, shit. What if I throw up on his dick?

"That's your gag reflex, fucktoy. It's going to feel like you want to ralph. Stick with it. That rarely, if ever, happens." Rarely? If ever? That means that it does happen! Listen, it's one thing to read about all this shit happening or to watch it in porn, but the reality is way harsher than anyone has prepared me for.

But he said he's mine. So I'm going to do this to the best of my ability. I'm not going to tap out. If I can't breathe- and it's difficult, please believe- I'm going to die of suffocation on Graham Huntington's dick. That will make for an interesting eulogy. I hope wherever the afterlife is that I can read it.

He pushes my head down again, and I sputter, leaking drool all over him. It's just flooding from my mouth, but he said he likes it sloppy, so I'm not trying to keep it in. He likes my pussy wet, so I guess it's the same sort of idea when my mouth is the opening in question.

He grabs my hair and starts pulling me off and then pushing me back down. Oh. This is better. He can be in control. Let me just… I hollow my cheeks and start sucking as he thrusts his dick in and out of my mouth.

"Oh, good girl. That's it. Keep sucking. You're doing so good for me, fucktoy. That's my girl."

His girl? His girl? I'm going to faint from more than oxygen not making it to my brain. I try to remember- oh, right. I start humming while he is pulling me on and off of him.

"Fuck. Yeah. Just like that." He groans out above me.

We keep that rhythm going as I feel the truck making all sorts of turns toward the house. Finally, I feel the truck stop and park.

He keeps using my hair as a handhold, but then his dick is jumping in my mouth, and he is using his hips to thrust up. Suddenly my mouth fills with his salty release, and he keeps pressure on my head to keep me down. I try to swallow around his cock, but it's hard since it's already full of his length. Finally, he pulls me off of him by my hair. I think I have a second to breathe, but his mouth is on me the second I start gasping for breath. I push some of the cum I haven't swallowed into his mouth, and he groans before fucking my mouth with his tongue some more. He pulls my hair again to bring me off his lips and finally, finally, some blessed air. I'm panting, my nose is running, my eyes are watering, and I'm spluttering.

"God, you've never looked more beautiful," he praises me.

"Thank you," I tell him.

He grabs my chin with his other hand and turns my face so I look into his eyes.

"Thank you, Sir," he corrects.

I gasp in surprise, and my pussy clenches. "Thank you, Sir."

"Good girl," he smiles.

And that's the story of how I died: death by kink.

CHAPTER 15

HEATHER

Anyone would think, hey, the girl you wanted to kiss didn't want to kiss you, so maybe you should let that go. But maybe anyone wasn't present yesterday in the gym while Peyton was basically reading her lines to me instead of Theo. Which isn't all that surprising since anyone can tell Theo is shit for acting and should be relegated to the part of tree or whatever doesn't have a talking part. Anyway, that shit yesterday had been hot. Not that I was thinking of a girl…

"Miss Lovelace, you'll be paired with Miss Stratford," My World History teacher's voice suddenly breaks into my thoughts.

I haven't been paying attention, but I heard that sentence loud and clear.

"You want me to work with the dyke?" I blurt. I can't help myself. It's a habit to be a complete cunt to Peyton.

"Fuck you, Heather," Peyton retorts. "You fucking wish I was."

That hits too close to home. I stand up, knocking the items off my desk in the process.

"Ladies! That's enough out of both of you. Sit down, Miss Lovelace. Slurs aside, you two will be working together. I suggest you find a way to be civil if you want a passing grade."

Mrs. Roth claps her hands and moves to the front of the room to address the class at large. "I'll give you some time at the end of this class to coordinate some times to get together outside the classroom. I suggest you make good use of it."

People start moving their desks to get closer to their partners, and I just stare Peyton down, waiting for her to come to me. Our eyes connect, and her brown eyes narrow on mine. I wave to the spot next to me, beckoning her to come over. She growls in displeasure and then starts scooting her desk over, ensuring she is making the most noise and causing a scene while doing so.

My eyes rove over her body while she moves closer to me. She's wearing ratty black jeans, her Docs, and a black hoodie advertising "The Julie Ruin." I peer at it. Maybe a band? I'm not sure. Her curly dark black hair is shielding most of her face, especially while she is moving closer but I can tell her makeup is done in her usual heavy smokey eye. Other than her face, it's not like she puts effort into her appearance. All her clothes are always baggy, but maybe that's why it intrigues me. I want under those baggy outfits. Would she be wearing more lingerie like the other day in the cafeteria? Would all those curves be thick and juicy, spilling over the seams of her clothes and making me ache to remove all her stitches so I could touch every inch of her? It's not that I want her... I'm just curious. I want to explore how different our bodies are. I want to see our skin next to each other, her light brown offsetting my white skin. I want to hold her in my arms and feel my lean muscles against all her plump flesh. I want to cup her breasts and weigh them in my hands, whereas mine are so small they don't fill a palm. I want...

"Heather," Peyton snaps her fingers in front of my face.

"Don't snap at me, I'm not a dog," I bitch at her.

"Well, you were zoned out. Anyway, I can imagine what you're going to say. I can do the project myself, and you'll sign your name on it. So we can just pretend you have any input right now."

"Fuck you very much. I do my share of group projects, thanks. You can come over after school today. Do you want to ride with me?" I flip my hair over my shoulder.

"Oh... really? We're actually going to work on this together?" She hesitates, surprise in her eyes.

"Yeah. I'm actually a good student. Not like your level or anything, but I take pride in my work."

"Well, excuse me for not knowing there's more to you than cheer or terrorizing me," she huffs.

"Right. So. After school, then." My heart starts fluttering at the prospect of her in my house. In my room. In my bed.

"Yeah. Um. Okay."

"Meet me by my car after you get out of drama. I usually get out of cheer earlier than Graham gets out of football, so you won't be waiting as long as you do with him."

I told Peyton to wait for me, but after school, when I find her sitting by my Mercedes's bumper, I'm still surprised to find her there. Walking up to my car, I simply watch her for a moment. She's deep into a book, and I crouch down so I can see the title: *Tomorrow, and Tomorrow, and Tomorrow.* I haven't heard of it, but I guess that I wouldn't have heard of a lot of things she reads because I'm not a reader. Her eyes are flitting across the page while she bites her lip like something exciting is happening. I watch as she brings a hand to her chest and squeaks out a sound that sounds like a cry. Then her eyes fill with tears, and she sobs as she flips a page.

I look around the parking lot. Peyton is just sitting here in broad daylight, crying over a book. I can't imagine not caring that someone would find me like that, but she's in her own little world, not giving a single fuck about anyone seeing her like this.

I click the fob to unlock the car, but even the lights flashing don't break her concentration, so I get into the car and honk the horn at her. She throws the book up into the air and looks at me with a startled expression. "Get in," I mouth through the front windshield, and she nods as she picks up her book and backpack. She opens the passenger door and slides in, closes it and buckles herself in. Smirking to myself, I pop the lever on the roof and press the button to make the top fold into the trunk. I want to see all of Peyton's hair fly all over the place when I drive my car with the convertible top down.

"Ugh. My hair is going to go everywhere," she mutters. "Can I borrow a hair tie?"

"Nope. Fresh out," I say, saccharine sweet.

She glances pointedly at my wrists which have two hair ties on them. I pull my hair up using both of them, staring her in the eye while I do so. She glares at me.

"You're such a bitch," she says boldly.

"Thanks for noticing," I kiss my lips at her, and she glares harder.

We make it to my house and I walk her to the kitchen.

"Do you want a snack or anything while we work?" I leave her by the kitchen island while I saunter to the walk-in pantry.

"What? Because I'm so fat I need food constantly?" She parries.

"When have I ever called you fat?" I turn from the pantry and look at her in shock.

"Seriously? All the fucking time." Her face is getting darker under all that brown skin.

"I call you a dyke, sure, and a loser, and a little freak, but I have never called you fat," I walk toward her and trap her between me and the kitchen island.

She looks up at me, "Seriously? The other day when you stole all my clothes so I would wander through the halls in my underwear, you made cracks about my body."

"No, the girls made cracks about your body. I wouldn't have. There's nothing wrong with your body." I do a lot of shit to Peyton, but I never want her to think there is anything wrong with her body. Society does enough of that shit to women. I know I'm stereotypically beautiful, but there is more than one way to be beautiful.

"You… I… there's not?" She looks so puzzled, I feel like I have to let her in on what I'm thinking.

"You don't think you're beautiful?" I ask her, interested to hear her response.

"Um… I… do *you* think I'm beautiful?" She looks down.

"Fuck, yes." I surprise myself by saying. But this feels too important. She needs to know.

She looks up at me with wide eyes, "I think you're beautiful too." And fuck. Wow. I get told I'm beautiful all the time, but it's somehow different when Peyton says it.

"You don't think I'm too conventional?" I blurt out.

She rears back in shock. "What? In what world? You're like Stereotypical Barbie. You're perfect."

Holy shit. She thinks I'm perfect? I laugh to dissolve the tension. "So… snack? Not because I think you have an unbalanced diet, but because I don't want you to not have one if you want one." I walk back to the pantry.

"Will you judge me if it's something unhealthy?" She walks over and peers around me.

"Well, good luck finding something unhealthy in this house. Would you like some beef jerky? That's what I was going with. It's better than the rice cakes Mama tries to foist on me."

"Sold, then. What do you have to drink?"

"Diet everything and sparkling water," I respond.

"Sparkling water, please."

I grab two of each item and then wave for her to follow me up the stairs.

"I forgot your parents are as rich as Graham's dad," Peyton comments.

"But not around as often," I mutter.

"They aren't home?" She asks.

"The only reliable time I see my parents is on Sundays." You know, when they pretend like we're a loving family. What absolute garbage.

I open my door and wait for her to follow me in, shutting it behind me for good

measure. Setting everything down on the bed, I plop down at the foot of the bed so she can take the headboard.

She follows and then we take our books out.

"So we have to pick a country and give a presentation on it, right? I was thinking we could do Russia for our country. Maybe dress up in some traditional outfits, make a traditional pastry- they have tasty baked goods, don't they- and then tell a folktale." I grab my phone to start researching.

"Ooh. Baba Yaga! She's so fun. She's this witch who turns into a house. Like if you look up illustrations, you'll see witch's legs and a house on top where the body goes. She eats small children. She's actually quite fierce. I'll write that down." Peyton grabs a pen and a notebook.

"Ugh, it's so hot in here. Let me just..."

I look up to see Peyton taking her hoodie off. I gulp as her shirt catches on the hoodie's fabric and rides up, giving me a perfect view of Peyton's tits framed by a gorgeous lacy black bra. I watch open-mouthed as her chest heaves before she pulls her shirt back down. She throws the hoodie down onto the floor and looks at me, blushing. And with that, my control is absolutely shot.

"I... um... oops."

"Mmhm. 'Oops,'" I agree as I start crawling toward her. She sinks into my pillows as though to get away from me, eyes wide, as I crawl over the top of her.

"Heather, I-" she starts but then I cut her off as my mouth closes over the top of hers. Her mouth is already open from speaking when I kiss her, but when my tongue chases hers, she lets me catch her. I plunge a hand into her curly wind-blown hair and pull, tilting her head back as I ravage her mouth with mine. She whimpers into my mouth, and then I feel legs capture my hips and hands grab onto my biceps, nails digging in. I let some of my weight go so that my pelvis drops down to grind against hers, and I feel her arch up to meet me.

I pull away, panting, and look down at her to gauge her reaction. The last time hadn't gone so well, after all, but this feels like the first time I kissed her.

"Why do you keep kissing me?" Peyton asks, pupils blown out.

"Why do you keep kissing me back?" I retort.

She doesn't answer; she just grabs my blouse and fists it in her hands, pulling me toward her.

I continue kissing her but move to ruck her shirt up. "I need this off. I need to have your tits in my hands."

Still wide-eyed, she nods at me, and I take her shirt off of her and reach around with one hand to quickly undo her bra. She gasps, and then I follow with my own when I look down and find bruises covering her tits.

"What in the fuck, Peyton?"

She looks down and bites her lip. "Oh. That. Um…"

"Has someone been hurting you?" I growl out.

She blushes again. "Oh, no. This is very consensual. I… um… it's a kink?" She squeaks out, clearly uncomfortable with this conversation.

"Should I not be kissing you? Are you involved with someone?" I hesitate. I don't want to stop kissing her. I think I want to fuck her. But it looks like someone has beaten me to the punch.

She laughs. "Are you going to tell Graham about this?"

"Oh my fucking God, no. No one is ever going to know about this," I say with surety.

"Then we're good. Keep going. If you… want to," She bites her lip again.

"I've never fucked a girl," I tell her.

"You think I have?" She laughs back. "How many times do I have to remind you that you're the one who makes up the rumors that I like girls?"

"Right. Okay. Continuing then," I say directly to her

breasts, and then I'm lapping and sucking at her nipples like they are my favorite hard candy. She moans beneath me, and it goes straight to my center. Fuck, she is hot. I trace the line of her leggings on her belly, and she squirms under me. I need these pants off of her, and I need them off yesterday. I pull the leggings down and over her feet, throwing them off to the side of the bed.

"Little freak, you really have excellent taste in underwear. No one would ever believe you wear shit like this underneath all your baggy clothes," I tell her, brushing my fingers over her gusseted center.

"Thank you. But now literally everyone knows because of the day you stole my clothes," she complains.

"Yeah, that worked out better than I thought it would. You were a wet dream come to life, stomping into the cafeteria in your lingerie. Jesus wept, little freak." I slide her panties down her legs and toss them, too.

I run a finger through her wetness and moan. I look down at her. Her mouth is curved in a grin, and her eyes are closed, leaving long lashes to fan out on her cheeks. She looks gorgeous, and she's at my whim. This is immensely better than bullying her. I can't wait to make her come. I slide a finger inside her, marveling as I do so. She is so wet, and it is all for me. I make Peyton Stratford wet. I slide another finger alongside the first, and she moans, riding my hand. I slide a third finger in, and she bucks against me.

"Oh, little freak, you love to be full, don't you?" I ask as I begin fucking her with my fingers.

"More, Heather, more," she moans out, and I break out in chills. This is surreal.

I fuck her with four fingers, but she's so wet that I slip my thumb into the mix and try to fit my whole fist into her. She keeps moaning as I work her open, and then I'm watching my whole hand disappear in and out of Peyton as she keens. This is maybe the hottest thing to ever happen to me, and all my clothes are still on. I keep pumping in and out of her while I lean down to leave biting kisses all over her lips.

"God, you're so fucking wet for me, Peyton. You're taking my whole fist right now. Such a good girl for me," I whisper into her ear.

"I feel so full of you," she moans back, "this feels so good."

"You're so hot right now, little freak."

"Heather... God..." she whimpers out.

"That's right. Say my name," I fuck her harder.

The scene is so sexy my brain is liable to break. My hand in Peyton's cunt, her scratching my arms in pleasure, the moans of happiness she is making under me, her wet pussy taking me, the way her throat arches as she digs back into the pillows, her soft pillowy skin sheened in sweat as she ratchets closer to an orgasm.

I pull back so I can watch her unravel as I lick the thumb that isn't inside of her and then start rubbing her clit with it. I feel her clench around my hand, but she also growls, so I know that's the move.

"Say my name when you come for me," I demand of her, wondering if she is in a place to listen and, even if she is, if she will follow my instructions. Two hours ago, we were firm enemies and now I'm giving her an orgasm so I'm not really sure what the rules are here.

But then I feel her clench around me hard, followed by a gush of cum. She moans out, "Heather," and it's better than an orgasm to hear her scream my name when I am making her come.

I pull my hand out of her pussy, and my hand is drenched with her cum. Pulling my top off, I wipe my hand down with my blouse and scoot down her body. She's boneless below me, but I'm not done with her yet. I use both of my hands to open her pussy lips and take a second to admire her pink center. She's come so hard it looks like she has been cream pied, but it's just the creaminess of her cum dripping out of her cunt. I put my face up against her center and smell her and am surprised to find that I like the scent of pussy. Or I just like the scent of Peyton's pussy. I lick a path up her center, and she jolts on the bed.

"No, Heather. I'm too worn out. I can't come again," she moans.

"That sucks. Because you're going to," I tell her and then bend to fuck my tongue in and out of her hole. She honest-to-God tastes like raw honey: earthy but sweet. She tries to push my head away, and I sit up, glaring. "Do I need to tie you up?"

She straightens and looks at me. "No, Ma'am," she breathes. "I'll be good for you."

Whatever it was about what she just said, it makes me light up like a Christmas tree. I like her calling me "Ma'am," and I definitely like the idea of her being good for me.

I bend back down and circle her clit with my tongue. This time, she weaves her fingers through my hair. I can feel the stiffness in her joints as she tries not to force me away. She meant what she said. She really is trying to be good for me. She can't stop herself from wiggling her pelvis away from me, though, so I chase her and pin her down with my hands. I lick circles around her clit until I feel like she is about to fall off the edge, and then I plunge my tongue back inside her warm cunt.

"Heather! Let me come!"

I bite into her thigh and then come up for air. "I thought you didn't want to come again? I thought you had enough?" I laugh at her.

"Yeah, that was until you got me close, and now I want

to come again!"

"I'm going to keep edging you, and you're going to be a good girl for me and take it until I let you come," I tell her.

She whines back at me, and I smother a laugh into her thigh, biting it again until she shrieks.

I delve back into her pussy, eating her and teasing her almost into orgasm until she is shaking, and I finally slide two fingers into her opening and find her G-spot while I suck on her clit. Then she's coming hard and squirting into my mouth. I keep pounding her G-spot and sucking on her clit until her orgasm has abated, and then finally, I slide my fingers out of her and remove my mouth from her.

I move up the bed and flop down next to her. There is so much room on my bed that even with her starfished out, we aren't touching.

"Can I hold your hand?" She asks me, but her fingers are already threading through mine.

I don't reply, I just let her hold my hand, basking in the wonder I'm feeling.

"So I guess that settles that. I'm officially pansexual." She laughs.

I tense. "Good for you, I guess. I'm straight," I tell her.

She sits up and looks down at me. "You literally just fisted me, edged me, and ate my pussy like you were starving."

"What's your point?" I close my eyes so I don't have to look into her eyes.

"We just fucked, and you think you're straight?" Her voice is getting higher.

"That's what I said."

"I can't believe you." She lets go of my hand.

"I'm not like you. I'm not into girls." I keep my eyes closed. I don't want to see the look on her face.

"You still taste like me, and yet you're not into girls? You know what? Fuck this. I'm leaving. I'll see you at school tomorrow. Have fun with all the internalized homophobia." Then I feel the bed lift in the absence of her weight.

"Wait. I drove you. Let me take you home," I finally open my eyes and sit up, moving to get off the bed.

"That is the last thing I want right now. I'll call someone to get me." She turns away from me, but I see her tear-filled eyes before she turns.

"Right. So we can work on our project-"

She cuts me off, "We have time. We'll do it later."

I deflate. Maybe I have ruined everything. I'm stuck.

"Look, I obviously said the wrong thing. But I'd like to do that again."

She turns toward me and lets a tear fall. "You're saying you're straight but you'd still like to fuck me again?"

"Can we just not put labels onto it?"

"Do you even hear yourself?" She opens my bedroom door and walks out.

That isn't a yes… but that isn't a no. And now I have to find out who else she is fucking.

CHAPTER 16

GRAHAM

Peyton and I are laying in bed post fuck, lazily kissing when she pulls away.

"I love that you kiss me now." She looks so earnest while she looks into my eyes.

"I like it too, fucktoy," I tell her and dive back into her mouth.

She whimpers for me, and this time I pull back.

"You like being called fucktoy, don't you?" I ask her.

She hides her face in my neck and laughs. "It started out as so degrading, but then it got hot, and now you say it affectionately. It's like the sweetest of degradations."

"Mmm. So very us, you might say," I grin down at her, though she is still tucked into my body.

She laughs and nips my neck. "Very us. Someone else

wouldn't get it, but they don't need to. I know you care about me."

"Don't tell anyone," I whisper jokingly.

She stiffens, and I know I've fucked up. She moves to sit on the edge of the bed, facing away from me.

"Peyton…" I start, but I don't know what else to say. I told her I was hers, but I still feel like Heather's. We aren't together anymore, but there is still a part of me that isn't willing to let her go. I run a hand down over my face and then move in behind her, putting my legs on either side of her.

"You're mine. I'm yours," I tell her.

"Right. But no one can know." She sniffles.

I turn her head toward mine and kiss her tears off her face. "It wouldn't change anything. We know what we are."

"Kiss me," she pleads.

"Of course," I tell her, then I'm softly running my lips over hers. Her mouth is open, begging for me to give her my tongue, but I just keep teasing her. I breathe into her, and she takes my breaths like they are vital to living. I'm barely touching her, but as I palm her neck, I feel her pulse speed underneath my hand. She starts keening as I move from her lips to her jaw to her neck, leaving sensuous open-mouthed kisses. She is panting for me as I reach her neck, and then I open wide and bite harshly into her. Shrieking, her hands fly up to pull at my hair.

"I need you again," she moans.

I pull back and look into her tear-filled eyes. "No. We're going to do something decidedly unsexual," I tell her, even though I absolutely want to fuck her into this mattress again.

She tilts her head. "Like what?"

"Do you know how to throw a football?" I ask her.

Her face shutters.

"Come on, fucktoy. I'll make it fun. Spend some time with me with clothes on."

"Then we can fuck?" She runs her hands over my torso, petting my abs and making my dick perk up.

"No, then we have to go to dinner and pretend to our parents that I don't spend all my free time filling you with my cum."

"I can't wait until tonight," she whines and bites into my shoulder.

I grab her hard by her chin and force her to look at me. "Stop bratting or you're going to make it worse on yourself," I tell her sternly.

She bites her lip and thinks about it. "What if I want to make it worse?"

"I don't think you know what you're asking for," I tell her right before she grabs my dick which by that point is already hard, and starts stroking me.

I slap her face, and she moans for me. "Graham, please. You're making me so wet. I need you to fill me."

I groan internally. Peyton is seriously testing my limits. I pull her hand off my dick and get off the bed. "Up and get dressed." I slap her thigh.

She flops back on the bed. "Graham," she groans in frustration.

"The punishment for not listening is that you won't get fucked after dinner. Keep it up, and I won't fuck you at all tonight."

"But-" she starts.

"If the next words out of your mouth aren't 'yes, Sir...'" I tell her.

She gulps. "Yes, Sir."

"That's a good fucktoy. Now get dressed." I start putting my clothes on. I usually wear sweats after football practice so I'm already suitable for outside activities.

I sit on the bed and watch as Peyton throws a fit. She's stomping around grumpily and drawing out all her actions as she grabs a sports bra, panties, shirt, and shorts.

I decide I will let her cause a scene as long as she is listening to me. The bratting was kind of fun, too. Just like the CNC, I like to work for it a little. I like it when she tests my boundaries. I like getting creative with her punishments. I like it when she is blindly submissive, too, but it adds to our fun that I never know which Peyton I am going to get. Is she going to be a good girl, all wide eyes and sweet disposition? Or is she going to be a prickly little bitch and fight me every step of the way? Sometimes the latter means anything from her having an attitude problem to her actively telling me she hates me and that I can't fuck her. And all of it is an absolute treat.

She finishes dressing and then stands next to me with her hands on her hips. "Well? I'm ready."

I crook a finger at her and then point to the floor. "Kneel for me," I tell her softly.

She bites her lip and then lowers herself to her knees, head bent down.

"I like it when you look at me," I coach her as I tilt her head up gently. She closes her eyes.

"What did I just say, fucktoy? Open your eyes for me." I keep my voice level.

"Please, Sir."

"Thank you for using my title. Now open your eyes for me," I repeat.

She obeys, and two tears track down either side of her face as she looks at me. Even without the tears, I can see the hurt in her eyes.

"Good girl," I praise as I pet her hair. "Who do you belong to?"

"You," she whispers, still gazing up at me.

"That's right. That means all your tears belong to me, too. You will always give them to me, do you understand?"

"Yes, Sir."

"And who do I belong to?"

"I…" she closes her eyes in hesitation.

"Peyton, open your goddamn eyes. Who the fuck do I belong to?" I tug on her hair.

"Me, you belong to me."

"That's right." I start petting her again. "What just happened was not a rejection. Do not for a second think that I don't want to ravage you. Of course, I want that. But more than that you need to see we are more than sex, more than kink. So, we're going to go outside and get some fresh air and have a couple of laughs and make a memory that's not me painting your cervix with my seed. Tell me you understand what I'm saying."

"I understand, Sir." More tears slip from her eyes.

"Come here and give me a kiss," I point to my cheek.

She raises herself by my thighs and kisses my cheek.

"That's my girl."

I take her out into our backyard and put a football in her hand.

"Okay, first, you want to get your stance. You want to stand with your feet apart, feet wider than your hips." I model it for her.

"Have you seen my hips? I'll be falling over. That's too far apart for me."

I take a moment to admire her hips in her bike shorts and grin.

"Graham! Are you even listening to me?"

"Of course I'm listening to you. You asked me if I'd seen your hips, so I had to take a moment to admire said hips."

"I don't think a lot of athletics take into account a woman's proportions and center of gravity. It's like when the PE teacher tries to teach me how to do push-ups and says the center of gravity should be in the shoulders, but that just doesn't work when you're pear or apple-shaped."

"All right. Point made. Your stance should be hip-width apart, considering a comfortable position."

She moves into position.

"Great. Now your dominant foot should be leading, and it should point toward wherever you're throwing. In this case, that would be me."

She nods.

"Okay, now the actual football." I take her hand in mine and tuck the football around her fingers, arranging them around the laces of the ball. "See where your fingers are? This is where they should be all the time."

"It's not very comfortable," she complains.

"Your hands are small, gorgeous. That's why. I'm not training you to go out for the team. This is just something for us to do to spend time together."

"Can't we just read another book together? I liked that. You do good voices for the characters." She looks up at me beseechingly.

"We need other things to do besides that. We'll do that again, though. Even though you tend to fall asleep on me." I hide a smile.

"Your voice is soothing, I can't help it," she smiles at me.

"Mhm. Anyway. When you throw, the ball should be between your chest and your belly button, with the nose of the ball facing down."

"Okay, move back so I can try," she uses her non-football holding hand to shoo me back.

"Last thing, fucktoy. Don't shift all your weight to your front foot when you're throwing. Keep your weight on your back foot."

"Graham. This is getting complicated."

"Okay, that's all I'll say. This is what I want to do for a living, fucktoy. I geek out a little. I'm trying to simplify it for you."

"I feel like baseball could be easier for me. Sure, you don't want to take a sudden interest in that?"

"We don't even have a team in Tennessee. This is not a baseball state," I retort.

"Isn't there a minor league team here?"

"Do you hear yourself? This is the south. We do sweet tea, barbecue, and football."

"We have a hockey team. Although I don't want to learn how to ice skate. That seems hard," she continues to ponder.

"Pey!"

"All right. Let me try to throw this."

I step back so she can feel like she's getting distance and watch as the ball limply soars all of ten feet.

"That was..." I start, trying to muster up something supportive to tell her.

"My fingers slipped," she excuses.

"Okay. No problem. Let me get it and throw it back to you. Maybe catching is more your speed."

I jog forward, pick up the ball, and then jog a little away from her. I don't want to hurt her with a throw, so I pick a nice easy distance and do an easy spiral toward her. It hits her in the chest, and falls to the ground. She throws her head back in frustration.

"Graham, I'm just not athletic!" She yells with her face still tilted toward the clouds.

I look up at them and then have an idea. Making my way over to her, I take her hand and tug her down onto the grass with me.

"How about guessing cloud shapes? You tell me what you see, and I'll tell you what I see."

She rolls toward me and says into my shoulder, "We could be having sex right now, you know."

"Peyton. For fuck's sake."

She sighs and rolls onto her back. I tighten my hand on hers, pulsing and then letting my hand relax but keeping my fingers threaded into hers. We lie there for a couple of minutes until I hear her voice.

"That one looks like a pig wearing a hat," she points with her hand that isn't holding mine.

"Counterpoint: it looks like a house with a steaming chimney."

"Wow. Okay. I'm better at this than you."

"You're better than me at a lot of things." I bring her hand up to my lips to kiss her knuckles.

"Does that bother you? Is that why..." she trails off.

"Jesus, Peyton. No, that does not bother me. I know where my strengths lie. I'm okay at school, but I'm great at sex and football. You don't emasculate me whatsoever."

She doesn't respond, but I can hear her wheels turning. I don't know how to make her feel better about us without broadcasting that we are a couple. And I don't know how to be a public couple without letting go of what I thought my future had been for as long as I can remember. I still want Heather to be my wife, but now I have the added confusion of wanting Peyton in my bed every night. Do I feel forever about her? I still am not sure. But I also am not willing to let her go. Even if I was, how long before the forced proximity led us back together? We are stepsiblings now, trapped in this house, doomed to be stuck together.

CHAPTER 17

Between trying to keep up with being valedictorian, learning my lines and blocking for the play, working with Ashton and learning how to code, and fucking Graham, I am exhausted. Content and fulfilled, but exhausted. I would say I'm looking forward to the weekend, but I have work and Graham, and somehow in all that mess, I am supposed to be hanging out with my two best friends now that I have forgiven them.

Friday night sees Graham at an away game, so I capitalize on his absence by having Sam and Adrian over.

We're all lounging on my bed, and Sam has been making us listen to a new song by one of her favorite bands, Varials, but all I hear is angry screaming. Adrian and I had looked at each other in companionable misery when she excitedly put it on, but now we look toward her with what we both hope are supportive expressions.

She pauses it and looks toward us. "What do you think?"

I dip the brush back in my nail polish bottle, then slick the excess off on the lip of it.

"I think we should just put on some Sleater-Kinney and call it a day." I brush the black polish onto my fingernails, careful not to get any on my nail beds.

"I love the Riot Grrrl movement as much as you do, but we can't listen to oldies all the time." Sam throws her arms out wide.

"We have to because we don't agree on modern music. You think I listen to pop, and I think you listen to angry shit." I put the brush back in the bottle and screw it closed.

"Adrian, what do you think?" Sam inquires.

"I don't know why we can't just put on Dixon Dallas and call it a day." He flashes a grin.

"Oh, God. I know it's gay, but it's still country. It makes me feel like I should be barefoot and pregnant in the back of some redneck's pickup truck." I blow on my nails.

"You're halfway there already. Do you even remember how to drive, or does Graham take you everywhere now?" Sam teases.

"Stop. I know how to drive. He's just protective of me," I move my hair toward my face in an effort to cover up the massive bruises on my neck.

"He made your life hell for two years, but all of a sudden, his daddy marries your mama, and he treats you like his precious baby sister? Oh, because you're in the family you're an extension of him now? Why are men? Adrian? Help us out." Sam pulls one of Adrian's purple-tipped fingers toward her and examines them.

"Why are men what, sugar?" Adrian asks.

"No, that's the whole question. Why are men?" Sam flings a hand over her eyes.

"Oh, I see. No, that's a legitimate question. I presume present company, being myself, is excluded?" Adrian posits.

"Of course, love. You would never," I jump in.

"Speaking of men," Adrian begins and looks at me like an excited puppy begging for a treat. "Someone is still marking you, and I know we've been tiptoeing around it because last time we fucked up the questioning, but we're dying to know who you're hooking up with, Pey."

"I, uh. Well. That's the thing. I think… actually, I know… please don't be upset with me, Sam," I stumble over my words.

Sam sits up and gazes at me. "Okay. I am here to listen and not get upset with you based on who you're hooking up with." She crosses her heart.

"Um, so actually. It's not about who I'm hooking up with. I mean. I guess it kind of is. Or. Maybe it will just happen the one time. Or. Ugh." I'm having a rough time getting this out. It had seemed so much easier to say after Heather had fucked me.

Sam and Adrian exchange a look. Sam waves toward me as though telling Adrian to go ahead.

Adrian clears his throat. "Look. We're your best friends. You should feel like you can tell us or not tell us anything. It won't make us love you any less."

"That's not what happened last time. Sam got jealous and lashed out, and you didn't even stand up for me. You just let it happen."

Sam sighs. "I fucked up. I can't guarantee I won't get jealous, but I have fully processed the situation now. Yes, I'm attracted to you. Yes, I would love to date you. But we're friends first. That's always going to be the most important thing. And I'll make sure my actions show that I mean that."

"Okay. Well. I'm pansexual." I shut my eyes so I don't have to see a reaction.

I feel arms wrap around me and start squeezing me. "Yay! Now we're all queer!" Adrian pulls back and clasps my biceps. "Oh my God, maybe the bigots are right. Is it catching? Do you think you caught the gay from us? Tell the Christian alt-right!"

I laugh and open my eyes. "*Stop.* I'm serious."

"That's what you were nervous about? Telling your two queer friends that you're also queer? Did you think we'd disown you? Because bisexual erasure is so early '00s, Pey."

"Well, I don't know. I was nervous."

"Do you think you want a girlfriend? Are you biromantic as well? Is this just an idea, or do you like someone? Because I want to validate that you don't have to fuck the same gender or date them in order to be a full pansexual. You can be with men for the rest of your life and still be pansexual, although I don't know why you'd do that because… men." She shivers.

"I appreciate the validation, and I do think I'm biromantic as well because I'm pretty sure I have a crush on a girl, and we might have… already fucked?" I squeak out.

Sam and Adrian's jaws drop. I cover my face with my hands and try to disappear.

"Does this girl also go to another school so we conveniently wouldn't know her?" Adrian says derisively.

I hear what I imagine is the sound of Sam smacking him. Then I hear whispers.

"I meant what I said. We're friends first. So while I would have been thrilled to be your initiator into the sapphic world of sex, all I'll ask is: it's better than it was with the guy, right?"

Adrian snorts. "Men are perfectly good at sex."

"We're talking about het sex, not gay sex," Sam retorts.

"Like you know anything about being a heterosexual. We're both gold star gays!"

I remove my hands from my face to watch them argue. "So… no one cares?"

"Fuck no!" Sam says.

Adrian huffs. "What she means to say is that we are glad you told us, and we are proud of you for realizing, but the important part is whomst, woman!"

"I'm sorry, but this has to be a secret too." I bite my lip.

"So, who are you going to continue hooking up with? The girl? The guy? Are you going to add a nonbinary person next? Because this is getting spicy." Adrian leans back on the bed and kicks his feet in the air.

"Okay, well. The guy and I are kind of… a thing. But he doesn't want anyone to know that we're together. And the girl also doesn't want anyone to know we're together, and meanwhile, she's insisting she's straight. So… I was just going to keep hooking up with both of them. Neither of them has really made me any promises, and there's some other complicating information that I cannot disclose at this time, and… do I sound like a greedy whore?"

"Greedy is a passé stereotype regarding bisexuals. If you don't think I would be in a TINK situation, you are positively mad," Adrian quirks an eyebrow.

"TINK?" I ask.

"You know. A polyamorous situation. Three incomes, no kids. A throuple," Adrian explains.

"Wow. I think that's pushing the envelope. I mean. Do I want that to be a thing? Yes. Could I see that being reality? No."

But Adrian has named my darkest hope. Graham and Heather are already together. And now Graham is with me, too, and Heather is fucking me. Is it too much to hope that we could all be together? But then Graham would have to admit he is fucking the freak, and Heather would have to admit she likes girls. Probably an unfulfilled wish. Still. How is this supposed to end?

"Let's back up and unpack all the batshit things you just said," Sam folds her hands in her lap. "First order of business: you're giving it up to a guy who doesn't even want to go public with you?" She raises a bisected eyebrow.

"It's-"

"We've established that it's complicated. Can you give us a different adjective?" Sam coaxes.

"Look. I'm not going to say that it doesn't matter to me because I wish I could tell people who I'm with. It's very upsetting to me, in fact. But I don't want to make an issue out of it because I feel like I'll lose him. And... look, the things we do... are not what I could imagine literally any other guy our age doing." I rush to explain.

"Oh my God, you're totally dick drunk!" Adrian bursts out. "Sam, she can't be reasoned with in this state. She's past all logic and reason. All we can do is wait for this to end in tears and clean up the mess."

"Hey! Who's to say it's going to end up in tears?" I counter.

"Sugar. The guy never leaves his wife. The asshole never comes around to commitment. You can't make a guy emotionally available if he doesn't want to be."

"Who's not emotionally available?"

We all turn to see Graham in the doorway, casually leaning on the frame, throwing a chip into his mouth. He's shirtless, and my eyes rake over his body, taking in the ladders of his six-pack and his Adonis belt. I feel my cheeks get hot.

"Since when do you care about Peyton's goings-on?" Sam inquires.

"Since she became my little sister, of course," Graham drawls out in his golden boy voice.

"Oh, really? Then how come your girlfriend is still bullying her?" Sam demands.

Graham straightens and frowns. "Heather's not-"

"Don't put him on the defensive, Sam," Adrian cuts Graham off. "The eye candy is fabulous. We don't want him to leave." Adrian bats his eyes at Graham.

"Oh, really? You don't mind if I stay?"

I feel Graham come up behind me and brush my hair off my neck, revealing the bruises I had tried to hide. As he traces his knuckles up my neck, Sam and Adrian watch on in stunned fascination.

He leans down to my ear and whispers, "Only them, fucktoy." Then he kisses my cheek sweetly and saunters out of the room, closing the door after him.

I look between Sam and Adrian and smile awkwardly.

"What the fuck was that?!" Sam bursts out.

"You sneaky little bitch!" Adrian yells at the same time.

"Okay, so that's one secret down. Oopies." I shrug.

"How kinky is this? You're fucking your brother?" Adrian trills.

"I think it gets kinkier, Adrian. Look at the state of her body. She's like a Pollock painting IRL." Sam smirks.

"So you see? Complicated!" I flop down on the bed.

"God, too bad Heather's a bitch. What a throuple that would be. I'd totally hate-fuck her," Sam sighs.

"Heather's straight. And I'm already fucking someone, remember?" I remind her, leaving out that Heather is the girl I'm fucking. What a fucking mess.

"No wonder she's dick drunk. That man is a god,"

Adrian muses.

"Don't let him hear you say that, I'm sure the man's ego is big enough. Especially now that he's dating the cheerleading captain and fucking the valedictorian on the side." Sam turns to me. "Are you sure this is what you want? We can't talk you out of it? Because this is worse than I thought. What happens when it doesn't work out and you have to spend the rest of your life sitting across from him at family dinners because your parents are married? Did you even think about that?"

"Fuck, Sam, I didn't think at all. But it's so Goddamn good. We push each other's limits in the most delicious way. I didn't think sex could be like this."

"Respectfully, you don't know how sex could be. You've fucked two people. Branch out. To someone who isn't your stepbrother. Oh, my God. He calls you little sister! This is an incest kink thing, too?" Sam explodes.

Adrian puts a hand on her arm. "We said we wouldn't kink-shame her, Sam."

"I'm too vanilla for this shit. Give me a strap and a girl, and I'm set to go." Sam pushes her straight black hair behind an ear. "Listen, we won't tell anyone. But I still think you should give him up. And probably the girl. She can't even come out, Peyton. That's a red flag."

"There's never too late a time to come out, Sam, that's just not fair. And we live in an incredibly homophobic state. Do you know the rate of queer kid homelessness in the state of Tennessee? I can't ask her to ruin her future for a hookup." I sit up and look into her eyes.

"Okay, point. But counterpoint: she could come out to you, the girl who is diving into her muff. But she can't even say she's queer to you? That is for real for real a red flag." Sam tries to soften her words by laying a hand on mine.

Adrian pipes up, "I have to co-sign on this one, Pey. She should at least be able to say what she is behind closed doors. With the person she's sleeping with. Otherwise, that's invalidating to you. I've been with guys like that. They treat you like there's something wrong with you but still expect you to get on your knees or your back. I wish I could say I've never done it, but I have."

"Maybe she just needs time…" I trail off.

"Okay. It's clear you're not going to listen to us about either Graham or this mystery girl. So just… keep us in the loop? Promise you won't hide it from us when it goes wrong and try to muddle through on your own? We won't say I told you so.' We'll just go to the store for some chocolate-covered potato chips and eat our feelings." Sam taps Adrian.

Adrian looks at her. "What?"

"She needs a hug, and that's your department," Sam explains.

"Oh, right. Come here, sugar," Adrian croons and opens his arms for me to snuggle into.

And I go. Because I'm exhausted with everything. Because I'm relieved that my two best friends know part of it, even if not the whole thing. I feel like my life has become a Telenovela and while that's pretty exciting, now I just feel unsure about how long this can be sustainable. I want Graham. I want Heather. Is there a world where I can have them both? I'm just a senior in high school. Even if this doesn't work out long-term, I will survive. Who seriously marries the first people to fuck them? It's just a passing fancy. That's all this is. Just sexual experimentation before college. I know most people did this shit then, but maybe I'll have a leg up when I actually go. I'm sure whatever happens, Graham and I can still be civil at future holiday family dinners. If not, then I guess my future career can take me far away, and I will just use that as an excuse to stay away. This is getting out of hand. These are tomorrow problems. Graham and I are together. Heather and I are probably going to fuck again- she keeps trying to stay away from me, and it isn't working, and I am clearly shit at saying no to her. The rest will, as they say, come out in the wash.

CHAPTER 18

HEATHER

I'm with the girls Halloween costume shopping, but I'm only halfheartedly going through the racks. Not even wispy fabric masquerading as a costume can cheer me up. I'm pining over two people, and I don't know how to move forward with either of them. I've pissed Peyton off by telling her I'm straight, and I don't know if she wants me to like… come out? To be with her? That seems like a little much for a fuck. And will Graham even want me if I've fucked someone else? Will he be disgusted that I've fucked a girl? Why am I not disgusted that I have fucked a girl?

I think back to the other night. Peyton's wild curly hair sprawled on my pillow, head thrown back in rapturous pleasure, her amber skin sheened with sweat as I brought her to orgasm, her dark brown nipples peaked as she was turned on by me, her sumptuous body laid out for me like a feast.

Fingers snap in front of my face, and I turn to see Hannah's brown ponytail smack me in the face.

"She's daydreaming again," Hannah is saying to Amber and Molly.

"Like none of you zone out from time to time," I snap at them.

"I was asking if you think we should do a group costume," Amber catches me up.

"Ugh, no. Pass. We already match like half the time with our cheerleading uniforms. Can I not have one individualistic thing?" I start perusing the racks again.

"Like conformity is too good for you now?" Molly turns to Amber. "Next thing you know, she'll have dyed her hair blue and gotten an eyebrow piercing."

"Calm your tits, Mol. All I said was that I didn't want to wear a matching Halloween costume. I'm not going to join band or start doing interpretive dance. Chill." I hold up a sexy firewoman costume. "How about this one?"

"Great! I'll be a sexy cop!" Amber trills.

"No, never mind. I'll keep looking." I turn away.

I hear whispers behind me, and I turn back toward my girls and raise an eyebrow.

My friends shut up immediately, but Amber nudges Hannah with her elbow so hard that Hannah stumbles and mumbles out a "bitch."

"What the fuck is on with you three?"

"Okay, don't get mad... we heard from some of the football guys that Graham has been showing up to practice with bites and scratches." Molly bites her lip.

I look at them blankly.

"But like... aren't you two broken up? So, he, uh. He

must have moved on." Amber adds.

I feel wetness on my palms, and I look down, noticing that I have made fists and dug my nails so deep into my skin that I have started bleeding. With a calm that I do not feel, I open my purse and dig out tissues to wipe the blood away.

"Well. He's free to do whatever he wants. I broke up with him." I feel like I am not in control of my mouth.

"Yeah… but like… you two have been together since the womb. I can't believe he just moved on that way. I mean. No grief period or whatever? Like, what the fuck. How disrespectful to you, Heather." Hannah flips her hair out of her face with her hand.

"Did the guys say who Graham is fucking now?" I casually ask.

"He told them not to worry about it. Said it's no one that's on their radar, so they didn't need to know," Molly replies.

"What the fuck does that even mean?" Amber complains.

"I guess it means it's not a cheerleader," Hannah tells her.

My mind is whirling. Graham is fucking someone new? And she isn't a cheerleader? I have always thought that if we weren't together, it would be someone else in the squad. He's the quarterback. It makes sense that he would date a cheerleader. But what if I'm not his type? What if we had just been together so long that I've assumed I'm his ideal, but in reality I actually am not? Had he just been waiting for me to give up on him? Had he not been as invested in us as I thought?

What the fuck is going on? Everything I think I know is flying out the window. I'm sleeping with a girl I have bullied for two years. Graham is fucking someone who isn't me. Am I in an alternate reality?

"Surely he just means she's another type of athlete. Maybe a volleyball girl? That seems his speed. They're like the girliest sport aside from cheerleading," Molly is saying.

"Ew. Don't gender sports. That's so early 00's of you. What are you- a millennial?" Hannah retorts.

"Okay, whatever. But you know what I mean," Molly protests.

"So, are you going to fuck someone to get back at him?" Amber cuts off their argument.

"How do you know I haven't fucked someone already?" I raise an eyebrow.

They all snap to attention.

"Oh my God, Heather. Who?"

"I'm dying."

"You've gotta spill the tea."

"I'm not telling you anything more. Just know he's not the only one who has moved on." I turn away.

And while it is true that I have fucked someone new, I certainly haven't moved on. I love Graham with everything that I am. I wish we hadn't broken up. I wish we hadn't had this rupture. I wish that I could go to him and explain all the crazy things I am thinking so he could be my sounding board and talk me down. But none of that is going to happen. For the first time in forever, I'm alone. It's not like I can talk through my issues with the girls. It sucks to admit, but Peyton is right. My friendships with Hannah, Amber, and Molly are superficial. I don't trust any of them, so I certainly can't lean on them for support. Which really sucks. What am I supposed to do?

Later that night, I'm lying in bed watching Bridgerton after begging off going out with the girls. They're used to me being absent from Saturday night hangs because I'm usually with Graham, but even though I don't have that excuse they seem to not have put two and two together. It makes it easier to keep them at arm's length when they give the impression that they have no desire to be let inside my inner walls.

I pick up my phone and open my messages with Graham. I start typing out "I miss you," but then I backspace and delete the message.

I start over. "You're my best friend," I type out, but I delete that too.

"I don't know how to live without you," I write, but that seems desperate.

Me: I heard you moved on already. Should I say congratulations? Pretty fast.

Baby Boy: Heather, don't start. YOU broke up with ME so you could fuck someone new. And you're mad because I did the same?

Me: Who is she?

Baby Boy: Okay, I'll bite. I'll tell you who it is if you tell me who your guy is

Me: I can't do that

Baby Boy: I figured you'd say that

Me: Did you even ever love me?

Baby Boy: JFC Heather OFC I loved you. I would have been happy to be with you for the rest of my life

Me: How can that be true if you moved on so quickly?

Baby Boy: You hate me so much that you wanted to move on while I stayed fixated on you forever?

Me: It would have proved that you loved me

Baby Boy: So then by that logic you never loved me. Is that it?

Me: What??? No!

Baby Boy: You were the one dissatisfied with us so much that you had to go be with someone else. Fucking remember that.

Me: What if I made a mistake?

Baby Boy: I don't know what to tell you. It's done now. We've both dragged different people into this now. The circumstances have changed.

Me: You already heard that I fucked someone? I knew the girls were gossips but that was fast even for them. I just told them this afternoon

Baby Boy: I didn't have to hear it. I know you, remember? You wouldn't have broken up with me and not pursued what you wanted. It's not like you. You would have had to go shoot your shot

Me: Okay, but how would you have known that they would go for me?

Baby Boy: Heather. You're a wet dream. I can't conceive of someone turning you down unless they were already with someone else

Me: So you… still think I'm pretty?

Baby Boy: You will always be my pretty girl, Heather. Always.

Tears drip down onto my pillow before I can wipe them away. I want to keep this conversation going, but I have already made myself massively vulnerable by asking him if I have made a mistake. I do not like his answer to that. I know it had been officially over before, but now it feels really, truly real. Graham and I are over, and there is no hope of us getting back together. That means I have to make a real go of this with Peyton for this not to have been a massive fuck-up on my part.

Me: You should come over and work on our project ;)

Little Freak: Are you fucking kidding me right now?

This is your move? A booty call?

Me: You know I took care of you last time. It could be just as good

Little Freak: Seriously, Heather, fuck off

Me: Okay, but seriously. We need to finish this project

Little Freak: I could literally do it alone so we never have to be alone together ever again

Me: And the fun in that would be…? Also, you shouldn't have to do all the work alone just because I was an asshole

Little Freak: Was or is?

Me: Both

Little Freak: …That was almost an apology, but not quite

Me: You can't just force me to come out

Little Freak: So you're saying you do indeed need to come out

Me: No, that's absolutely not what I'm saying

Little Freak: Can you at least admit you're not straight? That you're… questioning? Because saying you're straight and then fucking me is pretty fucking invalidating

Me: I really liked what we did. I want you to come on my tongue while I lick you like an ice cream cone

Little Freak: You ignored what I asked

Me: You do know I'm going against years of religious programming and a house of conservatism right now, yeah? I don't know. All I know is that I want to kiss that smartass mouth again

Little Freak: And that makes you a lil bit gay, just so you're aware

Me: How can you be a little bit gay?

Little Freak: You know what? Look up the Kinsey scale. That's your homework for tonight

Me: The what?

Little Freak: Just look it up. And keep an open mind.

There's nothing wrong with being queer, Heather

Me: It's unnatural

Little Freak: No, it's not. Plenty of animal species have homosexuality and some animal species even are trans and intersex

Me: You're breaking my brain

Little Freak: Okay, we'll walk before we can run

Me: So we can work on the project sometime this week?

Little Freak: Sigh. Yeah. All right.

Me: Can I get a sexy picture?

Little Freak: Isn't there one somewhere of me in the cafeteria when you stole my clothes? You can track that down if you want one. Otherwise, I'm going to bed.

Me: Sweet dreams, little freak

Little Freak: Night, psychopath

And then, as instructed, I hunt down the picture of Peyton in her lingerie.

CHAPTER 19

GRAHAM

We've just ended practice and are sloughing off our gear for the shower when I feel a hand grab my shoulder.

"I think I could take DNA evidence off your body, man. That is a full set of teeth that's sunk into your shoulder," Bo, my fullback, comments.

"I like it rough; what can I say?" I shrug and continue taking off my thigh pads.

"When are you gonna tell us who's marking you up like this? You never looked this rough when you were fucking Heather," Luke, my wide receiver, presses.

"Not to say that the sex with Heather wasn't amazeballs, but this girl and I... rough isn't even the right adjective to describe it, man," I laugh.

"Right. So who is she?" Bo asks and then turns to Andy. "You're his best friend. Who is this chick?"

Andy laughs and throws his helmet in his locker. "He won't tell me either. I'm as in the dark as y'all. The most I know is it's not Heather."

"Do you think we should start inspecting girls for tell-tale bruises? Who looks wrecked lately?" Luke chortles.

"I can't imagine any of the girls in our circle getting freaky like that. They're all so uptight. They wouldn't want to ruin their nails or hair," Bo surmises.

"That's not true. Heather didn't like it this rough, but she got nasty," I defend her.

"Mmm, go on. Tell us more," Luke eggs me on while he unlaces his cleats.

"Fuck off. I'm not going to disrespect Heather that way. I'm just saying not all the girls we know are afraid to have a little fun if the incentive is right. And also, I know none of you would break bro code and go after Heather now that we've broken up, so you're asking simply out of curiosity," I casually offer.

"Dude, no."

"She's off limits."

"No disrespect."

They all talk at the same time, and I smirk to myself. Good. Although, if Heather approached them, I couldn't exactly blame them for giving in to her. Wasn't I just telling her last night that no one could say no to her? I wasn't blowing smoke up her ass. I fucking meant that. She's a prize, and I wouldn't hold it against any of the guys unless they made the first move.

"The girls said Heather is already fucking someone new, too," Andy pipes in.

"Yeah, we've talked about it. What am I gonna do though?" I sigh.

"You're not upset about it?" Bo looks shocked.

"Oh, dude. I want to fucking murder his ass. I'm pissed. But I'm fucking someone else, so of course I expect her to fuck someone else too," I shrug.

"Way more mature than what I would do," Luke laughs.

"Well, that's why I'm also the captain of this ragtag bunch. I'm the most mature out of all of you dumb fucks," I preen.

"Oh, here he goes. Ego activated," Andy jibes me.

"Okay, enough talking about who is fucking whom. Time to shower," I say as I wrap a towel around my waist, slide my feet into a pair of shower shoes, and walk away.

"Hey, do you think she'll bring the dude to Andy's Halloween party?" Bo inquires.

"For that matter, are you bringing your girl to the Halloween party?" Luke asks.

"If she brings him, I'm doing shots the whole night, I won't be able to stand watching some guy be possessive over her. But also, I'm not bringing my new girl. We're very low-key," I respond.

"You mean you're very secretive," Andy mumbles.

I ignore him and keep walking.

As I soap up in the shower I mull things over. One of my main reasons for hiding Peyton's and my relationship is that I'm convinced Heather and I aren't over. But it really does feel like that now. The other night when we were texting, I basically told her things couldn't go back to the way they were before. I'm sure that hurt her as much as it hurt me. I certainly hated saying it. But the other thing that's holding me back with Peyton is that we're stepsiblings. Would that piss people off? Would it piss our parents off? Maybe it's better to hide the whole thing until it runs its course.

That night at dinner, Peyton keeps sneaking me longing looks and I am crawling out of my skin. I can tell she's going to be a brat tonight, and I can't fucking wait for it. Finally, I can't take it anymore.

"I think you need more wine, Regina. I'll go to the cellar to find some more," I announce.

"Oh, that's nice of you, son. I'm sure Willow will appreciate not having to go down there," Dad beams at me.

I push my chair back and stand, then hold a hand out to Peyton. "Peyton, you've never been down there. I can show you where things are."

"Oh, I don't need to know where things are in the wine cellar, Graham. I'm hardly a drinker." She turns back to her food.

I consider my next move carefully and then decide to snap my fingers. We've been working on her submission cues. She straightens.

"You know what? For Mama, I'll go. I don't know if I'll ever need to grab wine for her." She stands and takes my hand and I lead her away from the table and out of the room.

"Graham. You can't snap at me in front of our parents," she protests.

"Fucktoy. They won't have a clue what I'm doing," I assure her as I guide her down the stairs to the cellar.

"That seems risky," she bites down on her bottom lip.

"Shh. You were such a good girl, though. You listened right away," I praise her.

"Thank you, Sir." Her cheeks darken for me, and I ache to touch her, but not yet.

We reach the bottom of the stairs, and I back her into a shelf.

"Sir? Is there a problem?" She asks sweetly.

"Oh, you're being good for me now, but you weren't at dinner. If you don't stop looking at me the way you're looking at me…" I trail off as she palms my cock through my pants.

"You'll do what to me? Spank me? Hit me? Tell me what a slut I am?" Her voice has gone low, and she's stroking me to hardness through the fabric.

"You're playing with fire, little sister," I growl.

She moves closer and pushes her tits into my chest. Then she stands on her tiptoes and licks my neck.

"Graham, please. I need it. I need you. I'm so hot for you right now. Nothing's even happened, and I'm so wet for you." She's squirming against me, and I'm fully hard now. This is the hardest time to Dom her: when she's so hot for it. My brain starts to blank out, and the only thing that goes through my mind is a need to claim her and fill her with my cum. But I can't.

I step back and bring a hand up to her neck, squeezing until she lets go of my cock and gasps for air. "We are in the middle of dinner, fucktoy. You can wait thirty minutes. You need to eat, anyway."

Her eyes fill with tears, and her lower lip wobbles. I let go of her neck and pull her into me.

"Oh, fuck. You're hormonal. It's okay, little sister. I'm not saying I don't want you. I'm just saying I'd like to finish my snapper first." I pet her hair and try to soothe her.

"You still want me?" Her voice is wobbly.

"I do. How about I fuck you any way you want tonight. Does that work?" I ask, trying to mollify her.

"Thank you, Sir." She nuzzles into my chest.

I pet her hair for a moment and then disentangle myself from her, grabbing the wine that Regina is drinking. I turn toward the stairs to go back up to the dining room and hold out a hand for Peyton to take. She slips her hand in mine and yanks on it to get my attention.

"Sir? May I have a kiss before we go back upstairs?" She asks.

"Of course, fucktoy. Come here."

Then she's in my arms as I hold the bottle of wine with one hand and tip her chin up to me with my other. I brush my lips over hers, and she immediately opens for me. I give her soft kisses with the smallest amount of tongue, just giving her enough. I want these to be sweet. She needs sweet from me right now. She melts into my body, and I feel her hands run up my back underneath my shirt. The skin-to-skin contact feels so good. I break the kiss and move my hand from her chin to her mouth, running my thumb over her bottom lip.

"You're going to be a good girl during the rest of dinner," I instruct.

"Yes, Sir," she responds.

"Then I'm going to take you upstairs and do whatever I want with you."

Her breath hitches, but she nods her head.

"Now, Sir needs your help. Reach into my pants and tuck my cock into the waistband of my boxers so our parents don't think I've been ravishing my little sister in the wine cellar."

Peyton unbuttons my jeans and reaches for my cock. I know it's coming, but I still twitch when her hand wraps around my length. She doesn't get bratty, she just tucks it into my waistband like I told her to and rebuttons my jeans. I reward her with a forehead kiss. I gaze at her for a second. It's a good thing that she always wears a hoodie because I'm pretty sure the darkening of her cheeks has spread down to her chest. It makes me smirk at her, and in return, she gives me a soft smile. I'm so glad that we're comfortable with each other now. She lets herself go with me, and that's not a privilege I take lightly.

I take her hand and lead her upstairs, kissing her on her knuckles before we enter the dining room. I let go of her and open the door for her, gesturing for her to go ahead of me. I double back to the kitchen for the wine opener and open it with a small pop of the cork releasing, then I head into the dining room. I set the wine in front of Regina, but when she moves to pour it into her glass for a top-up, I stay her hand.

"You'll want to let that bottle breathe for fifteen or so minutes, Regina. Finish the rest of what's in your glass and then pour a new one," I tell her.

"Oh, thank you, Graham," Regina beams at me. "Ashton, your son is so cultured." It'll come in handy that Regina thinks the sun shines out of my ass if she ever finds out about her daughter and me.

"Yeah, the benefits of raising a son with money, I suppose. I didn't know this shit when I was his age. And I'm pretty sure he knows more about wine than I do," Dad sighs.

"Speaking of culture. Ashton and I have discussed it, and Peyton, you're going to debut, and Graham will be your escort," Regina informs us.

"Um, excuse me?" Peyton shrieks.

"A debutante ball. You're the perfect age," Regina continues.

"You want me to prance around like a crème puff with all those white girls?" Peyton deadpans.

"It's a once-in-a-lifetime event, baby girl. You'll be glad you did it when you're older," Regina coaxes her.

I can see Peyton is getting legitimately upset, so I take her wrist under the table and start rubbing her pulse point where no one can see. I feel her soften a little under my ministrations, but her pulse is still fluttering.

"Mama. Since when are you even interested in stuff like that?" Peyton tries another tack.

"I've been making new friends. I got invited to join Junior League!" Regina looks off into the distance. "I always wanted to be in it, but we were so poor and classless, and now so many doors are opening because I'm with Ashton." She turns to him, "Not that that's why I'm with you, dear." She pats his arm lovingly, and he covers her hand with his.

"Of course not. I'm just glad there are benefits to loving me. More than the obvious. You know what I mean, right, son?" Dad winks at me.

"Please stop," I say just as Peyton says, "Fucking gross."

"Well, there's a problem with this scenario anyway, Mama. Graham certainly doesn't want to escort me. He's got a girlfriend who is also debuting." Peyton removes her wrist from my hand and flings her hand out to gesture at me.

"Nonsense. He's your brother. He should be escorting his sister," Regina counters.

"Actually, that's true. I would be honored to be your escort, fu-," I cough, "Peyton."

Peyton turns and glares daggers at me. "Oh, you would, would you?"

"Around here in our circles, it's like prom. You wouldn't miss prom, would you?"

She glares harder. "I actually hadn't planned on going to prom. So, yes."

I can see that this is not the battle with her I want to have, so I shut up.

"See? Even Graham sees how important this is. What do I have to do to get you to do this?" Regina begs.

"I want you to stop pressuring me about school choices," Peyton tells her.

"Okay, great. Done. Now that's settled. You start

rehearsals after Halloween, but we should go dress shopping this weekend to get it altered in time," Regina pulls out her phone and starts putting things in her calendar.

"I'm not done. Once I've picked out a school, you will not pressure me to join a sorority," Peyton sinks back in her chair, and I feel her slip her hand into mine on my lap.

"But-" Regina's face falls.

"Mama. I know you like to try to relive your life through me, but this has got to stop," Peyton tells her.

"That's not what I'm doing." Regina holds her hands up in a stop motion.

"I think that's exactly what you're doing. And it needs to end. I think my choices are pretty good ones, and if they're not, I need to make my own mistakes." Peyton squeezes my hand for comfort, and I squeeze back.

Regina sighs. "I... I guess I didn't realize I was doing that. But okay. I can agree to both of those things if you agree to rush just to see if you like any of them. You don't have to bid!"

"Are you even listening to me right now?" Peyton clutches my hand.

"Graham is going to join a fraternity, aren't you?" Regina turns to me.

I hold up a hand. "No, thank you. I've done enough damage in this conversation already."

"Mother, fucking seriously! I am putting up a goddamn boundary! If you want to accept my terms, then do it. If not, please believe you will have the hardest time getting me to that ball." Peyton stands up, throws her napkin on her plate, and storms out of the room.

"If I may, Regina-" I start.

"No, you may not," Regina cuts me off.

I continue anyway. "She wants to make you happy. But

she's never going to even give you a chance if she puts up a boundary and you steamroll her." What I don't say is that I'll help get her to the debutante ball. I want to claim her in this small way in front of the world, and as her escort and brother, I can do exactly that.

Regina picks up her glass and downs the rest of her wine.

CHAPTER 20

PEYTON

I'm walking out of theatre rehearsal after school when I feel my hand being grabbed, and I am roughly slammed into the janitor's closet. A leanly muscled body follows me, and I know even in the dark that it's Heather.

"What the fuck is your deal with closets, you psycho? You are literally and metaphorically stuck on them," I complain.

"Very funny, little freak," she returns.

I hear her bumbling around until the light flickers on, and there she is in her black and gold cheerleading uniform, glossy blonde hair pulled into a ponytail, makeup done in a natural style, leaning over me and gazing at me hungrily. That is new. It's like all the anger has been transposed into lust. I guess since I am thinking about how good she looks, mine has too.

She puts her elbow on a shelf above my head and leans into me.

"Text Graham and tell him you won't be needing a ride home," she demands.

"Oh, you're just bossing me around now?" I ask but only half angrily.

"100%. I've made you come, so I basically own you now," she informs me.

"What if I don't want it to happen anymore?" I cross my arms in front of me and look away from her.

She grabs my chin roughly and pulls my focus to her. Her sapphire gaze bores into me, and I feel trapped like a fly in a spider's web.

"I think you do. I think you're going to take your phone out of your bag, text him, then follow me to my car. We're going to drive to my house, and then I'm going to make you beg for me. And you're going to do it because you're desperate for my pussy. You're a fucking whore who lets her bully fist her until she comes. And today, I'm going to prove that you're such a slut for me that you'll squirt for me."

And then her mouth is on mine, her hand sliding down to my neck to punctuate her words with a light squeeze. It's just enough that it makes me gasp and open my mouth for her tongue's entry. She dominates my mouth with hers, punishing me with bites and making me moan into her mouth. I'm present in the moment, and I'm not. Half of me is electric with want, while the other half is watching from a distance as I give credence to her words. The part of me that isn't in control reaches toward her face, one hand cupping her neck and the other delving into those silky locks. Feeling her hair slip between my fingers emboldens me, and I sling a leg over her hip to get closer to her. I don't know if I jump into her arms or if she picks me up, but then I'm being held up, both legs around her waist, legging-covered pussy grinding against her like if I try hard enough, I can get enough friction on my clit to come. I can't decide what I want more: her cunt in my mouth or mine in hers. I had gotten so drunk off her last time that I couldn't reciprocate, but if I'm going to hers, I hope I can hold it together so that I can learn the sounds of her orgasm. What will it feel like to see this girl who has tortured me for years buckle under the power of my body?

She pulls away from me, her arms bolstering my body under my thighs, and scoffs.

"You're such a whore," she provokes me.

"And you're such a bitch," I offer back.

She lowers me down, and I delicately detangle myself from her and straighten my clothes. I can feel how wet my pussy is from how much has soaked through to my leggings.

I pull my phone out of my bag and give a quick text to Graham.

Me: Hey, doing a thing after rehearsal. Don't need a ride home

Graham: And what's my little sister up to after school?

Me: Heather and I have a project to work on for history

Graham: I know it was okay last time but are you okay being alone with her?

Me: I appreciate your worry, but I'll be fine

Graham: Let me know if you need me to pick you up from hers

Me: xoxo

I watched the ellipses for his typing pop up, drop off, pop up, and finally, they drop off for good.

I tuck my phone away and look back up at Heather who is looking at me bored.

"Jesus, it needed to be a whole thing? Is he worried I'll flog and torture you?" she scoffs.

I feel myself heat, and she narrows her eyes.

"Oh, for fuck's sake. You'd just like that, wouldn't you? You're such a fucking freak. Come on. Let's go." She turns and opens the door.

"At least you have no problem leaving this closet," I prod her.

"Keep it up, little freak," she cautions.

Molly is passing us as we close the maintenance closet door.

"What the fuck is going on in there?" She looks at Heather with intensity.

"The usual," Heather says nonchalantly. "Just some low-key threatening so she knows she has to get me a passing grade on a project."

Jesus. This woman can lie without remorse at the drop of a hat.

"Oh, right. You coming to afters?" Molly flips her blonde hair.

"No, we have to work on said project," Heather offers with a shrug.

"Ew. Can't she just do it alone and put your name on it like how all the nerds do for us?" Molly wrinkles her nose.

"Yeah, but I'm not stupid," Heather says pointedly and crooks a finger at me. "Anyway, we're off. Ciao." She brings her hand up and kisses her fingers twice in Molly's direction.

I have barely gotten into Heather's room when she turns to dwarf me, closes the door behind me, and then presses me up against it.

"Here's what's going to happen. You're going to strip for me, and then you're going to be a good girl and eat my cunt." Her mouth is at my ear, her body is pressed against mine, and I can smell the soft bergamot and floral notes of her perfume. I have never taken the time to catalog it before, but now that I have become somewhat comfortable in her presence, I am taking the time to notice such things.

"You smell so good," I blurt out.

She leans back and down, eye level, to me, and her gaze heats.

"Imagine how good I'll taste," she growls out.

I feel my pussy clench, and I let out a little whimper. Just like Graham, all the intensity of her previous bullying has now become acting out lusty scenes. Has this always been there? Have the three of us always wanted each other, but instead of passion, it had been pain? Now it is both pleasure and pain in the most delicious of ways, and I can't wait to plum the depths of Heather to find out how good it can be between the two of us.

She backs up to her bed in the middle of the room and takes off her panties. My mouth waters as she lets her hair down out of her ponytail. Her bed linens are hot pink, and the contrast to her blonde hair is striking. I want to touch her hair more. I want to sink my hands into those tresses. I want to braid it. I want to dote on her.

She sits down and spreads her legs, pointing between them. "Crawl to me," she commands, and my basement floods.

Are both Graham and she natural Doms? How lucky can I be? Also, how does that work between the two of them? Either one or both of them have to be a little switchy. And oh, heavens, thinking of watching one of them Dom the other has me feeling a heartbeat in my pussy.

She snaps at me, and I immediately get onto my

hands and knees. I look up and she seems pleased but also surprised by my submission.

"Clothes off first, little freak." She twirls a finger in the air.

I stand and tear off my Docs, leggings, panties, hoodie, shirt, and bra. My face heats as I think of crawling to her.

I get back on my hands and knees and start crawling to her. I can feel my thighs, ass, breasts, and belly jiggling as I move toward her. The mix of humiliation and pleasure at it winds me up deep inside my stomach. On the one hand, I feel like this cannot possibly be attractive. On the other hand, I am deeply pleased that she is demanding this of me. I make it to her legs and sit back in the nadu pose: head bowed, sitting on my ankles with my knees apart, hands palm up on my thighs. My eyes are closed in deep embarrassment.

She leans down and raises my chin to look at her. I open my eyes hesitantly, and I am gloriously rewarded when I do. Her eyes are blown black, and she is trying to hide a smile by biting her lip. I still feel the humiliation of my submission, but now I am not embarrassed by my body. This gorgeous creature is staring at me like I'm an ice cream sundae, and she's the spoon that gets to dip into my scoops. It gives me the courage to lean forward and nip at her inner thigh, but she delves a hand into my hair and presses me to her core.

She smells musky yet sweet, and it stirs something within me. I have never even thought of eating kitty until Heather, but in true nerd fashion, I looked it up on the internet. I bring my hands up to spread her folds open and run a finger through her wetness. She looks so different from me. She is pink in the center, just like me, but white skin surrounds the pink. It's a softer look than my own. Her clit is bigger than mine, and I want to find out if it is more sensitive than mine. I lick a circle over it and am rewarded with a gasp from above me and hands clenching my scalp. I start making the shapes of the alphabet with my tongue over her clit, and she responds by bucking into my mouth.

"God, you're doing so good, little freak. Fuck, the mouth on you. You're wasted on men," she compliments me and presses my face further into her center.

I want to tell her how good she tastes, how she is my new favorite flavor, but I just keep exploring her. I press harder on her clit until she is moaning and starting to shake, then I ease off and move down to her opening, where I plunge my tongue in and out of her until I feel her clench around me.

"Be a good girl and make me come, little freak," she demands.

Moving back up to her clit I flick quickly over it as fast as I can until she is screaming, pulling my hair, and coming all over my face. I lick her through it and then move down to her hole to lick up her cum. Before I can do much, she's pulling me away by my hair.

"Enough!"

Panting, I look up at her. She is the most disheveled I have ever seen her, and at that moment, I know I am addicted to her. Fuck. Getting orgasms from her is a head-fuck, but giving them to her is transcendent. She's still fully dressed, but she looks wrecked: her eyes are still blacked out and now glossy, her hair looks like she has run her fingers through it and pulled it, her lips are red and bitten from her trying to stanch her cries, and she has a flush that covers her body. Our eyes meet, and she growls.

She pushes me down on my back and follows me down to the floor. Her body covers mine as she ravages my mouth. Our soaked pussies grind sensuously together as she grips my legs and throws them around her waist. Her short nails dig into my thighs, and she presses into the bruises I have from her boyfriend.

"I fucking love your curves. You feel so luscious against me. So fucking soft," she purrs between kisses. The words, the feel of her pussy slipping against mine, her tongue in my mouth…everything has me dizzy with wanting her. But I don't want to ask her to reciprocate. First of all, because even though we haven't talked about the dynamics, I feel submissive with her. Second of all, she hadn't gotten off last time, so maybe this was just to even things out.

But then I feel her move her pussy to grind on my leg, her wetness soaking my skin, and I feel her slide two fingers into me. She crooks her fingers to find my G-spot and uses her palm to grind against my clit.

"Right fucking there!" I yell out because she feels so fucking good.

I can feel myself clenching around her fingers, already half gone, and I feel her pussy get wetter on my leg. God, it turns both of us on to please the other. I have that with Graham, too, but I've been thinking that is unusual. I never would have thought Heather would care about my pleasure enough that she would want to bring me to orgasm over and over, but here we fucking are.

With her other unoccupied hand, she grabs one of my tits and then pinches my nipple, and I'm gone, coming so hard my vision whites out.

I feel a splash on my face and open my eyes to see Heather flicking liquid from my pussy onto my face.

"You squirted for me, little freak," she smirks.

"Sorry, I've been killed. Please leave all messages with the receptionist to be given to me at a later date." I close my eyes again and smile to myself.

"I'll be right back," she tells me, and I feel her leave the room and then feel a washcloth wiping my pussy down.

"Mmm. Thank you. You know, this floor isn't so bad when you have no bones," I comment.

"You get so seriously drunk. I don't know what to call it when it isn't a dick. Clam-drunk? Pussy-wasted?" She snaps her fingers. "Clam-baked! You get clam-baked, little freak."

"It's called subspace. It can happen with pleasure or pain for me. It's really easy for me to go there," I explain.

"What now?" she asks.

"Subspace. It's when you get so into a scene as a submissive that you start to lose track of reality. You get dizzy. Everything feels euphoric. A lot of people think that it has to be brought on by intense pain, but sometimes it's just intense pleasure for me. Plus, being in a scene. Not every submissive experiences it, but it's really easy for me to go into."

"But I'm not your- what do you call it? I'm not your Dominant," Heather protests.

"You were acting like it, so I fell into a submissive headspace. But we should probably talk about it if we're going to continue doing this," I drunkenly explain. I raise my head so I can look at her. "Can I braid your hair?"

"Oh. Um. Yeah?" She walks over to her dresser and grabs a brush. Then she sits on the floor at the foot of her bed and pats the bed in welcome.

I go over and sit behind her with my legs caging her in on either side of her. Taking the brush from her, I part her hair in sections and start brushing her hair out. As I untangle her silky locks, I explain D/s dynamics and how they fit into BDSM. I also explain the stoplight safewording system and aftercare.

"This is what you do with your other partner. Why you're so covered in bruises," she guesses.

"Yes. His and my sex is very physical. But ours doesn't have to be if you aren't into that," I tell her.

"Hmm… but you liked crawling to me. And I can tell you like it when I'm… mean to you," she parses out.

"I like humiliation and degradation, yes," I explain.

"Oh my God. All those years I thought I was torturing you, I was just making you wet?" She laughs.

"Shut the fuck up, no. I didn't know I liked it until recently," I correct.

"Until you started fucking this guy, you won't tell me the identity of," she presses.

"Right," I agree.

"So I guess you're okay with keeping this a secret if you're with someone else," she goes on.

"You're also with someone else," I complain.

She interrupts my brushing by turning her head. "God, little freak, you are out of the loop. Graham and I broke up."

"Um… what?" The brush in my hand hovers in the air.

"Yeah. He's fucking someone new, too," Heather grabs my brush hand and puts it back on her head.

I continue brushing mechanically. "How do you know he's fucking someone new?"

"Well, the football team has been ragging on him for showing up at practice looking like he's met his personal Wolverina, and also, he told me. I want to feel your fingers in my hair," she demands.

"Yes, Ma'am," I put the brush down and let myself feel her strands.

"Oh, yes. I like that," she moans, and I don't know if she is talking about me calling her an honorific, me touching her, or a combination of the two.

"But you don't know who she is?" I dizzily ask.

"Nope, he told me I could know if I told him who I was

fucking," she breathes out in pleasure.

My head is positively spinning. This web of deceit has gotten out of control. So before, when I had thought I was fucking a boyfriend and a girlfriend, now I'm fucking an ex-couple. I don't know which one is worse. But I have a feeling that I have to keep my cards close to my chest so I don't bring this house of cards down. I'm in way over my head. Luckily it seems like Heather wants to keep us a secret because "she is straight," but what possible reason did Graham have to keep us a secret? Because we are stepsiblings? Speaking of not keeping things straight…

"Okay, so. Right now. You're kind of giving me aftercare instead of the other way around?" She hazards.

"Well, technically. But this is really relaxing for me. I love touching you. Also, Doms need aftercare, too. There's such a thing as Dom drop; it's just not as common as sub drop," I tell her.

"Drop?" She inquires.

"Yeah, it's like when you've used so much dopamine, it shocks your body when it leaves your system, and you end up depressed," I explain.

"Like when you take molly, and the day after, you're a steaming sack of shit?" She questions.

"I mean, I wouldn't know. But it sounds like it," I affirm.

"Hmm. What are you doing for dinner?" she inquires.

"I don't know. I've probably missed it, so I'll find something in the kitchen when I get home," I posited.

"Okay, letting you eat girl dinner is definitely not indicative of good aftercare. Let me order us something. Do you have a craving for anything?" She pulls out her phone and starts scrolling through restaurants.

"Sushi sounds good. A nice spicy tuna roll and edamame, maybe?"

And that's how I end up with two Dominants.

CHAPTER 21

PEYTON

Saturday rolls around, and my alarm goes off. Surprisingly, I still have the parasite named Graham attached to me. He's usually up on the weekends to go for a run. I stretch in his arms and wiggle my ass against his erection.

"Ugh, you fucking cocktease. I know you don't have time for me this morning, and you're getting me all wound up," he sleepily growls.

"I thought you were such a hardened Dom that you would never have such a weakness. Aren't you supposed to pretend you're impervious to my advances and that you're so in control?" I tease him.

"At the end of the day, or shall we say the beginning of the day? I am just a man with a cock that points straight in your direction, fucktoy." He punctuates his words by grinding against me again and pinching one of my nipples.

"Ugh… baby," I mewl, and I feel him stiffen behind me. "Sorry. I didn't mean…" Fuck. Shit. That's too reminiscent of Heather.

"No. It's okay. If we're not in a scene, you can call me baby," he softly says.

"Just not baby boy?" I try to keep my voice level without the laughter I want to inject.

"No," he responds, and I turn in his arms to look him in the eye.

"Is that because you've broken up with Heather and have neglected to inform me?" Again I try modulating my voice to something akin to normalcy.

He runs a hand down his face. "Fucktoy…"

"I've done the adult thing and assumed it was for other reasons than that you're embarrassed by dating the nerdy theatre kid," I bite my lip. I don't want to push him too hard because, hello, I am fucking Heather. But I also need the reassurance that he isn't a toolbag.

He grips my hips and pulls me close. "I happen to like every single thing about you, so I appreciate that you aren't buying into that piece of your brain." He gives me a peck on the lips. "I like that you always have your nose in a book." Kiss. "I like that you are a performer." Kiss. "I like that you're too good for me." Kiss.

I pull back, shocked. "You think I'm too good for you?" "You're going to be Valedictorian, little sister. No one is good enough for you. And when I have to meet your future husband as your big brother, I'll tell him he's not good enough for you either." He kisses me again, but I'm wooden.

My future husband? What the fuck is that? I guess I have been deluding myself that even with all the web of secrets and the fucked up circumstances, he could see me as something as permanent as I'm beginning to see him as.

I push him away from me. "We should get ready for the day." I hurriedly get up and put my back to him so he can't see the tears that are starting to arise in my eyes.

"What? What did I say? Are you upset about the future husband comment?"

I feel him come up behind me and wrap his arms around my neck in a hug. I sniffle.

"Little sister… I'm just being realistic. You're going to go to college and see what a great big world is out there, and you're going to forget about me. And that's okay. I'll have been your first. And I'll be your big brother forever."

But I don't want to hear his bullshit. I lean down and bite him on his arm.

"Agh! Peyton, what the fuck?" His arms slip away from my body, and I turn to him.

"You know what? I'm glad this has a deadline. We can keep this going until we leave for college, and then I can go meet someone a little more my speed. Perfect. Now get out," I yell at him.

He narrows his eyes and raises his fingers as though to snap but stops himself. "A good Dom never Doms in anger! Fuck!" Then he turns and leaves, slamming the door behind him.

I crumple where I stand and let the tears start flowing when a knock sounds at my door. I know it must be Mama because Graham's ass would never; he would just walk in. I wipe my face on my arms and hurry for a sleepshirt.

Once I'm clothed- relatively- I call out, "Come in!"

Mama enters but then blanches at the sight of my face. "Why are you crying?"

"If I say the prospect of having to dress up and pretend I'm a lady is what's causing me so much turmoil, will you call the whole thing off?" I parry.

"Very funny. But I'm serious. We don't have to do this today. What's going on?" She sits on the bed without an invitation, and I walk over to her and take a seat.

"It's boy problems. Honestly, I think the torture of trying on clothes to be paraded around like chattel will make my problems feel small. So let's do it." I pat her thigh twice.

"You continue to work on your stand-up routine. Hey! Have you considered-" she begins, but I cut her off.

"Mother, I am not becoming a stand-up comedian. When I try to be funny, I am so dour. I'm only funny off the cuff without intending to be. That's not my future career," I explain.

"Yeah, all right. It was just an idea. I'll let you get dressed, and I'll make some coffee. Meet me downstairs." She gets up from the bed and leaves, the door standing open in her wake.

I go to shut it and look straight into the eyes of Graham, who is leaning against his doorframe in low-hanging sweatpants that would make me ogle his dick if I weren't so pissed at him.

"You were crying?" His face betrays how concerned he is, but I don't want to deal with him right now.

"Fuck off, Graham. Like you give a shit. I'm not your future wife, I'm not even your girlfriend!" I explode.

"Who the fuck said you aren't my girlfriend?" He blusters.

"A girlfriend is someone you see a future with, or at least someone you can publicly acknowledge!" At this point, I don't even want him to acknowledge me because of the repercussions it would have with Heather, but I'm too worked up to be thinking straight right now.

He stalks toward me and grabs me by the throat,

squeezing hard.

"You are mine. You are my girlfriend. Regardless of who knows it," he growls at me.

I slap his face and then grab his hair and pull him down to kiss me. He groans into my mouth and plunges his tongue inside me. Our tongues fight for dominance. We're both so angry and so worked up right now that I'm dying to have a scene with him, but there's no time. Mama is downstairs waiting for me. I push him off of me and slap him again for good measure. We're both panting.

"You're an asshole," I announce.

"And you're a bitch," he smirks back.

I rear back to slap him again, and he catches my wrist.

"I know you're pissed, but I already let you have two. If you don't want to explain to your mother why you missed your dress appointment, keep at it. I'll tie you up and scare you so bad you'll wonder if I remember what red means," he threatens.

"You wouldn't ignore my safeword," I huff.

"I wouldn't. But you'll start doubting yourself mid-scene, won't you?" He steps further into me and looks down from his massive height. "You'll be screaming and crying and wondering if this is the time I'll hurt you for real. If I'll take it further than you want."

I'm gasping for air. I haven't felt this terrified of him in a long time. It's delicious. Electric. I want more.

Then he steps back from me and I take the opportunity to shut my door and get dressed for the day.

Later I'm mainlining my sparkling cider like it has alcohol in it, as though I actually know how to drink. But

I'm wishing I do right about now because I've tried on 10 dresses, and all that's happening is I feel like an imposter in this nice shit. Luckily Mama waved away all the dresses that weren't suitable for my body type, so I didn't have to go through the indignity of trying on gowns that weren't made with plus-size bodies in mind.

I step out of the changing room in something that Cinderella would get a lady boner for and stand in front of Mama.

"Ta-da. This is probably the worst out of all of them. So it's definitely the one you want me to wear," I deadpan, twirling.

When I come to a stop I see Mama's eyes are filled with tears. Oh, for fuck's sake.

"That's the one," she sobs.

"Great. Can't wait to try to waltz in this thing. Love this journey for me," I huff.

I go sit on the couch next to her and grab the bottle of sparkling cider, taking a drink from the lip.

"Oh, what the fuck? That's not cider. Is this what you're drinking? God, that's vile," I splutter.

Mama laughs and puts her arm around me, cuddling me closer to her. "I'm so glad I don't have to worry about drugs or alcohol with you. My sheltered little sweetheart."

"I'm not such a good girl. I do things you don't know about," I pout.

"Actually, I wanted to talk to you about that. I think you were too sleepy to realize this morning, but you were barely covered, and I saw a lot of bruises on your body. It's pretty worrisome. Is someone hurting you?" She leans back and looks me in the eye. Her concern is apparent.

Fuck. How do I go about explaining to my mother that I'm into BDSM? That's not really a conversation I ever expected to have.

"I mean… someone *is* hurting me? But it's consensual?" I try to hedge.

"Fucking shit, Peyton. Are you trying to tell me you're into BDSM at your age?" She breathes out.

"You know what BDSM is?" I stare at her.

"I'll have you know I know about a lot of things. I never really went in for it, but I had a couple of boyfriends that tried to change my mind," she explains.

"Wow. Okay. This conversation is too bizarre. It's breaking my brain," I try to wiggle out of her hold.

"Wait a second." She pulls me back. "Are you sure this is something you want and not something a boy is telling you that you should want?"

"Ew, Mother. I have agency in this. BDSM is so stigmatized, but both of us want this equally. There are rules for safety, and my partners know my safeword," I tell her.

"Partners? Plural?" She lifts an eyebrow.

"So… I guess now is a good time to tell you I'm pansexual," I hesitate.

"Oh. Okay. So your partners are…?" She fades out.

"One is a guy, and one is a girl," I say.

"Do they… know about each other? Is this a poly situation? Is this a ménage?" She questions.

I blank out. "Um… what? Is that a thing?"

"Well, I don't think it's common, but I have friends from high school who are polyamorous. So I'm not unfamiliar with it." She pats in the direction of my tulle-covered thigh.

"People… do that for real for real?" This is blowing up my brain.

"Sure! So. Are you?" She cocks her head.

"Oh. Um. Being that I didn't know that was an option, no. I'm kind of… seeing them behind the other's backs?" I grimace.

"Peyton DeVal Stratford! You cannot two-time people! I taught you better than that!" She brings a hand up to her collarbone in disgust.

"Okay. But like. He wants to keep me a secret. She wants to keep me a secret. I don't know…" I trail off.

"Neither of them wants to go public with you?" She says, aghast. "Who isn't proud to be with my baby girl!?"

"Calm down, Mama. I only suspect his reason, but she's afraid to come out. She's still convinced she's straight. It's kind of ridiculous." I hug my arms to my chest.

"Well, they're both crazy for not being sure of their place with you. But it doesn't give you the right to cheat on people, Pey," she admonishes me.

"Okay, right. But like… there's more to it that I can't go into," I shrug.

"There's more? This is better than a CW show. Should I get popcorn?" She playfully pushes me.

"Mama! I know this isn't great long-term but I think it's working for right now. I know for a fact neither of these people sees this going past the summer. So I feel like it's okay for now," I fold my arms together.

"Okay. You're going to do what you want. But know that I have lodged my complaint. You know now I don't approve," She picks up her glass and takes a sip of bubbly.

"Oh, now I can do what I want? But when I didn't want to participate in this antiquated affair it was your way or the highway?" I throw my voluminous skirt up as punctuation.

"You'll be happy I made you do this when you're my age. The networking alone is worth it. You want to get in with these women, baby girl. They're the people who are going places, and if you play your cards right, you'll go places, too." She pushes my curls over my shoulder.

"Ugh. It's such elitist bullshit, Mama," I protest.

"I'm not arguing that with you. But the elite run this country. You might as well get in the race," she parries.

I look down at the yards of fabric encircling my body. "Great. Can I take this thing off so we can charge an ungodly and unnecessary amount to Ashton's credit card?"

"Absolutely!" She claps her hands together, and her locs sway with the movement. "You would tell me if things start to spiral out of control and you're being abused, right? Well. If you even realized it?"

"Yes, Mother. Please stop," I hide my face behind my hands.

I may not have my shit together, but at least I have Mama, Sam, and Adrian behind me. Thank God for good support systems.

CHAPTER 22

HEATHER

The bass line of a Bad Bunny song filters out through the front door of Andy's house as I walk up the stairs in my thigh-high black boots. The PVC makes a crunchy sound as the material crinkles, the fabric coming together and tearing apart as my legs bend. I straighten my mini-skirt and don't bother to knock at the door, just walking in.

I'm greeted over and over by my peers as I walk through the house to the kitchen, litanies of "Hey, Heather, looking good!" from the guys and jealous "Oh my God, so hot, girl" from the girls. It's always the same, and somehow I've never clocked how superficial this all is. None of these people are my friends. They either want to fuck me or be me, and none of them bother to know a fucking thing about me. I guess not having Graham on my arm to share my true self with is a shocking revelation. For a second, I wish I could have brought Peyton with me, picturing her dressing in a sexy nun costume to match my own, but that's a different shitstorm I don't want to deal with. What a laugh: I'm a closeted ball of religious trauma.

I clock my girls pouring shots, and I swoop a hand between Molly and Amber to grab one, knocking it back before anyone can get a word in.

"Ugh! What the fuck? Why are we shooting gin?" I roll my lips together to get the excess wetness off of them and preserve my cherry red lipstick.

Hannah answers, "Andy said he was trying to get rid of the gin, so we thought we would help."

My eyes search the counter and alight on a bottle of vodka. "How nice for you," I reply sarcastically as I pour a shot of Goose and down it, followed by another. I push the bottle into Molly's hands. "Find a mixer and make me a drink with this."

She scowls but moves to the refrigerator to do as I demand.

"You're in a mood tonight," Amber observes.

"Yeah. I guess I am," I shoot back with some force.

"Is this about the possibility of seeing Graham with a date?" Hannah asks.

"Oh my God, Hannah. Why would you bring that up? You want her to drink even more?" Molly joins us again and pushes a Solo cup into my hand.

"This has nothing to do with Graham," I mutter, despite it definitely having to do with Graham. I take a sip of Molly's concoction and make a face. "Not so sweet next time, hmm?"

I turn from them, ignoring what I imagine will be a hurt expression on Molly's face, and move into the living room. I'm sure it won't be too hard to find someone to grind on. It's not my main motivation, but if Graham happens to notice, all the better for me.

The night passes as such: the girls feed me approved drinks, I tease half a dozen guys into half-chubs but manage to avoid anyone putting their mouth on mine- ugh, as if- and I get so drunk as to not even notice if or when Graham shows up to the party.

I weave toward the bathroom, where there is a sizeable line, and as soon as the current occupant departs, I block the first girl from entering. She's in chemistry with me. Amanda? Amy? Alecia? Who cares, really?

"Hey! I was next," she sputters at me.

"And now you're not," I inform her.

I feel someone come up behind me, and I'm about to turn and lay into whoever thinks they are entitled to be in my fucking space, but then I hear a molasses sweet and slow drawl.

"Sorry, Ashley. She overdid it a little. Thanks for waiting, darling."

He's still at my back so I can't see his charming smile, but she's in front of me and suddenly all smiles and stars in her eyes.

"Of course, Graham," the girl who is apparently Ashley demures.

"Come on, pretty girl," his voice is butter in my ear. "Let me take care of you." He takes my elbow gently and prods me into the bathroom, shutting it behind us.

"I don't need you to take care of me." I push him away and cross my arms.

His eyebrow flicks up. "Really? Heather, you're three sheets to the wind. I'm getting drunk secondhand from the alcohol seeping from your pores."

"You know, I don't know how I didn't get fed up with

this good guy, savior, martyr, hero, whatever complex when we were together. You're just soooo good. Sooooo sweet. Soooo charming. How do you not get exhausted?" I move to lean back on the sink counter and misjudge the distance, tripping backward, and then managing to trip- again- over my heels.

Graham, being as predictable as he is handsome, takes me by my waist and hoists me up onto the counter. I sit against the mirror and look up into his green eyes, our gazes locking together. I feel the weight of his hands on my waist as he soothingly runs his thumbs over the exposed skin between my skirt and the bralette that is my top.

"What's going on with you? You lash out when you're upset over something, so something is the matter."

I break eye contact and look down, closing my eyes. Maybe I did overdo it. The room is kind of spinny.

He pushes my headdress back and lifts my chin. I feel his lips against the tears I hadn't realized I was crying.

"You're a priest for Halloween," I murmur.

"And you're a nun," he says softly.

"We're not even together anymore and..." I cut off, my voice breaking with a sob.

"Hey. It's gonna be okay, pretty girl," he coaxes, continuing to kiss my tears. Suddenly his lips are on mine, giving me the most chaste of kisses. He pulls back. "Fuck. Heather. I'm so sorry. I shouldn't have-"

I cut him off, "I need you." I whimper, and I grab him by his priest costume back down to my mouth, opening for him. He immediately plunges his tongue into my mouth.

Our kiss is so familiar and comforting, the push and pull of Graham and Heather, always trying to out- dominate the other. I push my hand into his hair and grip the strands, so much shorter and silkier than Peyton's. Peyton. Fuck. I shouldn't-

But Graham is pushing my veil off, grasping my hair in a fist and pulling, giving me a bite of pain that has me moaning into his mouth. I'm hiking his robe up his body, the fabric bunching in my hands as I finally get to his boxer briefs. I push them down, and his erect cock springs free. Which… of course, he's already hard. This is so delicious, so forbidden. We're in priest and nun costumes, and we're cheating on our partners. There's not one sliver of this that is not forbidden.

"Be a good boy for me and put that thick cock where it belongs," I pant out.

He pauses and looks at me wide-eyed. "Shit, Heather." Then he pulls my panties to the side and forces his cock inside of me in one thrust. "Oh, fuck, pretty girl."

"Worship me like you worship your God," I demand of him, and he moans, pumping harshly into me as he grasps my chin and cants my head so that he can bite into my neck.

My pussy clenches around him as he pounds into me, my oversized crucifix thrashing against my chest with the athleticism of our bodies.

"You are my true religion. You are my goddess, my queen. Fuck, Heather," he bends down to lick up the center of my cleavage while his hands go to my hips and start massaging into me, heightening my pleasure.

I bring my hands up to his neck and squeeze. "Are you gonna come for me like a good boy? Are you gonna fill me up, baby?"

He's putty in my hands as his eyes widen, and he tries to nod with my hands around his neck. "Fuck, fuck, fuck. Yes, Ma'am. All of my cum is for you. Thank you."

I'm probably as surprised at his usage of "Ma'am" as he is at my calling him a "good boy," but I'm too close to an orgasm to care that we both picked up honorifics since breaking up and the shocking revelation that Graham makes the sweetest submissive for my latent Dominant side.

My fingernails dig into his neck as my orgasm crests over me, and I shriek out a "Yes!" which is echoed by Graham growling as he unloads into me.

His head is resting in the crook of my neck as we stay frozen, clutching each other. My hands have relaxed on his neck, and I'm cupping his cheeks and running my thumbs over the apples of them.

"Heather…" he starts hesitatingly.

"Shh. You were so good for me. It's okay. We're so used to being together. It was just an accident. It's all right, baby boy. We're okay." I keep one hand cupping his face while the other goes to his hair, and I start petting him.

He melts against me and nuzzles more into my neck.

"I feel so bad, but that was so good," he punctuates his words with a soft kiss on my neck.

"I know. Are you submissive with your new girl?" I continue petting him, letting myself be distracted by how he feels in my hands. I don't know if I can deal with his answer, but I'm asking anyway.

"No… I didn't know I would like that until just now. I'm her Dominant," he laughs out onto my skin.

My whole body feels electrified. He's only submissive with me. He's still mine. A little. For now.

"Are you… Dominant with your new guy? No, don't answer that. Of course, you are. Fuck, I'm so jealous."

"You're jealous of someone else when you're the one with your cock still inside of me?" I taunt him.

"I don't want to pull out because then this moment will have to be over. I want to be selfish and greedy for just one second longer."

"Come here," I beseech him and pull his mouth toward

mine.

Our kiss is soft yet achingly passionate, the slow press of lips and tongues that have memorized each other over the years. His arms have come fully around my back, and we are as close as possible, even with the layers of his costume keeping us from skin to skin. He hardens inside my channel again and starts to move slowly in and out of my pussy.

He breaks away and gazes at me. "One more time. Just… one more time." His voice breaks on the last "time."

"Give it to me slow, baby boy," I agree.

"Yes, Ma'am," he whispers and moves his mouth back to mine.

This time we are all sweetness and softness, and we fuck achingly slowly. Actually, what we do is make love: our bodies say what we don't dare offer to one another. But there's no other way to decipher what is happening on Graham's best friend's bathroom sink. Our moans coalesce into one melodious sound that seems miles away from the thumping beat of the party's riotous noises. And when I come, it's the slow creeping euphoria of an orgasm that always reminds me of stepping into a hot bath and being flooded with pleasure.

Graham kisses me on my temple and steps back, pulling out of me and tucking himself back into his robes. His cum slides down my thigh, and it occurs to me that I miss the messiness of male ejaculate. Peyton comes, but she can never leave a piece of herself inside of me. I have to take it from her, lick it from her body. It's different.

"You need aftercare," I tell him, lolling my head against the mirror.

"That was the aftercare. I didn't deserve that," he looks above me and fixes his hair in the mirror.

"You did deserve that. You were always the best

boyfriend, Graham. I'm sure you're as wonderful to her as you were to me. Consider this the breakup sex we never had."

He nods at me and then turns on the sink and wets some tissue, starting to scrub at the red lipstick prints all over his mouth.

"Do you want me to take you home? I'm okay to drive, and the reason I came in here was to check on you... not to fuck you."

"I'll take an Uber. I think we should separate now while we are experiencing post-coitus clarity." I hop down from the sink and move to the toilet.

"And here I thought I had gotten out of watching you pee after we had broken up," he chides me.

I give him the middle finger with one hand and wipe with the other. "Just clearing out all the cum you deposited into me. Anyway, you don't have to stay. There's the door. Thanks for the fuck."

He grins at me and opens the door. On his way out he turns to me and says, "Yes, Ma'am." Then he gives a little wink, and he's gone.

CHAPTER 23

GRAHAM

"**W**hat if I just don't get out of the car?" Peyton petulantly asks, placing a protective hand over her seat belt buckle and glaring at me.

It's a week after the Halloween party, and I'm escorting a grumpy Peyton to her coming-out rehearsal. Do I want to be spending my Saturday afternoon trying to avoid Heather, not betraying to Peyton that I cheated on her a week ago while also not looking too comfortable with my little sister in my arms? Hell no. But we're here, and I'll be damned if I don't get this girl into that ballroom to practice a waltz.

I take her chin roughly in my fingertips. "Fucktoy, I swear to Christ, if you don't stop being a brat and get your delicious ass out of this truck, I'm going to punish you."

I watch her wiggle around on the seat in anticipation. Her eyes are lit up. She's gearing up for a fight, and she's hoping to win one way or another. But I know now how to shut her shit down.

"I'll sleep in my bed for a week if you don't get in there and behave." I stare into her eyes.

Her face falls and she looks at me, panicked. "You… but… that's no sleepy sex or cuddles."

"I know what it is."

"You wouldn't miss me?" She cants her head, and my fingers follow, still grasping her chin.

"Of course, I would miss you. That's not the point. It's a punishment." I stroke my thumb over her chin and pull my hand back. "Now come on." I boop her on the nose and turn to open the driver's side door.

"I'll get out if you give me a kiss." She crosses her arms and nods her head.

I look around the very full parking lot warily. "Quickly," I agree.

She unbuckles her seat belt and half climbs over the console to get closer to me. Then her eye catches on something, and I follow her gaze. Heather is walking past the truck, adjusting her purse on her shoulder. My eyes climb up her body, clocking her hot pink leggings and a black sports bra, the whole look accentuating her muscular frame. I mentally shake myself, hoping that Peyton hasn't noticed me eye-fucking my ex-girlfriend when my mouth is supposed to be on hers, but when I look back to her side of the truck, she's halfway out the door.

"Come on, Graham. We're going to be late," she chides me.

I'm baffled at the flip of the script but eager to go inside before she changes her mind as quickly in the wrong direction. I follow behind her, clicking the fob to lock the doors behind us. Opening the door for her to go in before me, I give in to the temptation to grasp the nape of her neck and guide her inside. I feel her breath hitch, and I know she likes that possessive gesture. I know we're in public, and it's my decision to keep this hush-hush, but sometimes I can't help myself. This woman is mine.

I walk us into the ballroom, and the first thing that grabs my attention is that Heather has decided to be escorted by one of my defensemen. Caleb is an excessively large linebacker, and I would feel some type of way about her choice, but as I eye them speculatively, I don't think this is the guy that she dropped me for. They're standing too far apart to be comfortable with each other's bodies, and she's not even paying him attention as he tries to talk to her. She looks over at Peyton and me, and Peyton wiggles out of my hold, putting distance between us.

Caleb rambles up to me and holds out a hand. "Hey, man. I just want you to know that Heather and I aren't, you know, a thing. Our moms concocted this plot to have me escort her since you two aren't together."

I take his hand and give my patented good ole boy smile. "No sweat, man. Someone was going to have to escort her since I'm taking care of little sis."

"Yeah, cool. No disrespect," he nods at me and releases my hand, turning to Peyton. "So this is the sister. Hi, I'm Caleb." He eyes her up and down appreciatively, and I growl. "Yeah, no. Okay. Not this one, either. Got it." His eyes widen and he backs up toward Heather again.

I close my eyes and breathe deeply, trying to let go of the need to show this entire room that Peyton belongs to me. Jesus fucking Christ, am I feral for this woman. My eyes are still closed but I feel Peyton move close to me, still keeping distance due to all the eyes that could be drawn to us.

"Sir," she breathes quietly enough for only me to hear her. "I'm yours."

Just hearing the honorific calms my blood, but the added reassurance allows me to breathe fully. I open my eyes and look down at her, locking our gazes. She's looking at me so earnestly, so openly, so… do I dare to hope? Lovingly.

Fuck.

I've been keeping her at a distance to try and avoid this, but suddenly it hits me like a freight train. I'm in love with this girl. I'm in love with this girl, and she still thinks of me as a fling. I'm in love with this girl, and I'm going to have to let her go. I'm in love with this girl, and I'm going to have to watch her go to a different school, fall in love with some asshole, marry him, and talk to him about their children across the dinner table at Christmas.

"Do you want children?" I burst out.

She rears back and blinks her eyes at me for a couple of beats. "Um. I don't think so."

"Okay, good," I reply without pause, thinking that this imagined scenario of her future is infinitely more palatable sans children with the man who is my arch-enemy- you know, the one I haven't met yet but hate more than anyone else in the world.

"Good?" She arches an eyebrow at me.

I panic and stare at her. For being known as a smooth talker, I am absolutely fucking this up right now. Luckily I'm saved by the dance instructor interrupting my flailing.

"Please find your partner. The gentleman's right arm will be around the lady's waist, the lady's left arm will be around the gentleman's neck if you are comfortable being that close, or for a less intimate placement, the left hand will rest on his shoulder. Both parties' other hands will be clasped together at neck height. We will be focusing on the waltz, which was invented in the 13th century in Germany and Austria, has been in style in greater Europe since the 17th century, and has never gone out of style, perhaps because of how easily accessible this dance is."

The tall and thick brunette's voluminous skirts swish as she goes over to a speaker system and picks up her phone, and turns on music.

"The basic steps of a waltz are called the box step, and I want you to think of the pacing as 'slow, quick, quick.' It's going to be in ¾ time. Some popular songs are waltzes, so you may recognize the tempo." She gestures to her partner. "Philip, please."

I stifle a laugh as Philip appears to be a head shorter and perhaps 30 years her junior. I imagine this is her son, who has been bullied into helping her teach a class. Bless his heart.

I take Peyton's waist and hand as guided, and we mirror the instructor and her son. As soon as we start to find our rhythm- I'm repeating slow, quick, quick in my head like a metronome- my phone dings a very discernable sound.

"Do you want to put that on silent?" Peyton asks as we continue our steps, managing not to step on each other's toes.

"Of course not. Then I wouldn't hear my ESPN alerts for the game," I tell her.

"You can't go one Saturday without your precious Vols?" She makes a face at me.

"Listen. You carry a book everywhere you go. Of course, I'm going to have my game alerts on if I'm required to be here. We all have our passions, little sister," I explain without a shred of shame.

"What are you gonna do, check it every time it goes off?" She asks with scorn.

"Again, yes. You're lucky I'm not propping my phone

up on your shoulder for the gamecast. That alert was for the start of the game. Next time it goes off, it will be when someone scores. So obviously, I'm going to check who scored," I tell her.

"Can't you just DVR it and watch it later?"

"And have the whole thing spoiled by the entire internet? I think not. This is my only option." I lean down and near her ear, whispering my next words. "Don't think that I can't pay attention to both the game and you, fucktoy. And you're obviously my priority since I'm here with you instead of watching the game at home. Okay?"

I lean back to catch her eyes, noticing a darkening under that light brown skin. The thing about Peyton is that you wouldn't notice the blush unless you look for it... but I'm always looking for it. I live to make my girl blush for me. Sometimes I think Heather is missing the part of her brain that gets embarrassed. She never blushed for me, even though it would have shown up great under her skin. But Peyton? I can just growl "fucktoy" in her ear, and she will be biting her lip and turning rosy for me. And it's addicting as hell.

I look over at Heather and meet her gaze for a moment before she rapidly turns back to Caleb, who is filling a D-man stereotype to the letter and bumbling over his feet whilst apologizing to Heather constantly. Heather, to her credit, is not verbally beating him to a pulp, but she is rolling her eyes to the ceiling, and I can see her nails digging into his shoulder.

We learn a natural spin turn, a whisk, and a chassé before we end for the day. Tennessee has managed four touchdowns and the four accompanying field goals, while Arkansas is struggling to keep up. But the most interesting thing about the afternoon is that I catch Peyton and Heather sneaking looks at each other the whole dance rehearsal. I want to ask Heather about it, but honestly, I'm afraid I'll kiss her as soon as look at her if we're in a hidden alcove together, so I wait until Peyton and I are back in the car and driving home.

"Is Heather still giving you a hard time?"

Peyton looks up from her book, which is *King of Scars* today. "Hmm?"

"You two were exchanging looks the entire rehearsal. Something seems like it's up." I shift my eyes to my passenger seat to try and catch her look before my eyes shift back to the road. She refuses to look up from her book, going so far as to bury her face in it even more.

"Up? Nothing's up. She hasn't done anything to me in a while," Peyton assures me.

"Then what was the predator/prey thing you two had going on today?" I push.

Peyton giggles abruptly and then indiscreetly covers it with a cough. "I don't know what you mean."

"I mean that it looked like Heather wanted to corner you, and it looked like you were afraid of her doing it," I explain.

"I think you read it wrong. Maybe she was watching you. I don't know if you know this, but she's your ex-girlfriend. So she's probably way more into watching what you're doing. And just a thought, but she's probably upset she has to be escorted by Caleb, who seems sweet but like he doesn't know what to do with that big frame of his. So." She flips a page in her book.

"Mmm. All right. So I don't need to have a talk with her about her bullying you?" I query her.

"Graham, that's very sweet of you, but no. It's not an issue anymore," Peyton responds.

"Well, that's weird in and of itself, isn't it? Why did she just stop torturing you? I mean I know why I did and-"

"Graham!" She cuts me off. "I am trying to read! Why don't you turn the radio to the game?"

"Oh, yeah, sure. That's a great idea, little sister," I thank her and scroll to the AM radio station broadcasting the Volunteers vs. Razorbacks game. There's obviously something going on with her that she doesn't want me to notice. For now, I allow my attention to meander to the game as it's the Vols' 4th down.

CHAPTER 24

PEYTON

It's been weeks since Mama came to me and proposed I work for Ashton. I really thought it would be some bullshit job because it's not like my stepfather doesn't already have a dedicated assistant. But instead of me "working" per se, it's more like I'm enrolled in Ashton's Computer Science for dummies course. I would be mad at both of them for trying to steer me in a direction of their choosing, but I've taken well to it. Ashton has taught me binary and basic coding. He doesn't do any of the coding or programming for his company anymore, but when I started "working" for him he would grab some of the code for outgoing software for me to "proofread" and for me to learn off of. My favorite is when he writes a basic code for me to troubleshoot. I love finding the errors in a program and correcting them. I love that Ashton encourages me but never pressures me. If Mama knew how into this I was getting, we would have already had several conversations about making this my major when I go to school. But instead of it being yet another thing I have to perfect, I can just have fun with it.

I'm working on troubleshooting something he wrote for me right now, but I'm having a hell of a time with it. The numbers are beginning to swim on the screen, and I'm getting really frustrated with it.

"Okay, that's the third big sigh I've heard from you," Ashton interrupts me. "Why don't you take a break and come back to it?"

"No, no. I can do this," I tell him as I squeeze the bridge of my nose.

"Peyton. There is no deadline for this. I'm the only one who is going to see this. Please stop being so hard on yourself," he gently chides me.

"I know you're right, but... I can't help the negative self-talk if it's incomplete."

Ashton sighs and places his hands on his thighs to stand up at his desk. Sometimes I forget how tall he is because he's skinnier than Graham, and his personality is not nearly as imposing, but he's at his full height right now. As a person of authority to me and with me feeling like I'm fucking up it's a little disconcerting right now, but then he comes around the desk and opens his arms. I just stare at him.

"I know you and I aren't that close, but I feel like you could do with a hug right now," he tells me, still with his arms out toward me in welcome.

I stand slowly, as though he's going to change his mind, and press my body into his. He folds his arms gently around me and pats my back.

"Kiddo, it's okay not to be perfect all the time. I don't know that you know that, but it's true. I certainly don't expect that from you," he begins.

I start to cry because this is such great dad energy and I've never had that in my life. I feel him tense for a second, and I think I've fucked it up until he relaxes again and starts rubbing soothing circles into my back.

"Just let it out. It's okay. It's definitely time for a break. I think we're done here today. But you just stay right here until you want to let go." He gives me a little squeeze and then loosens, but as promised, he just stays where he's at, letting me sob on his dress shirt until I pull away.

"Sorry about your shirt," I mumble, and gesture to the wet tear and snot stain on him. I wipe under my eyes and nose.

"Don't worry about it, Peyton. You're free to use me as a handkerchief anytime. I know I'm not your real dad, but I'd like to be as close to that role as you'd let me. So hugs are always included." He adjusts his glasses.

"Okay. Well. I'm gonna," I gesture with my thumb toward the door. "Take that break now."

"Like I said, I think you're done for the day. Why don't you go relax and read a good book." He smiles down at me.

I nod and walk out toward the kitchen, where I find Graham staring listlessly at an open jar of peanut butter. He's got a spoon turned down in his mouth, and I want to make a joke about silver spoons here, but I've got the presence of mind, even in my post-cry haze, to notice he does not look okay. He doesn't even seem to clock me walking in and standing across the kitchen island from him. He's still staring at that peanut butter like it's going to do tricks.

"Graham?" I ask hesitantly.

He responds with an "Mm."

"Baby?" I try, but his eyes close at that. "Can you talk to me?"

"I just… I saw you and Dad hugging," he turns out in a lower register than normal after he removes the spoon from his mouth.

"Jesus, Graham, are you jealous of your father? Because, first of all, fucking gross. Second of all, that was the most paternal thing that's ever happened to me, and you don't get to change that into something wrong," I immediately defend.

At that, he bolts upright and looks me dead in the eyes. "Christ, Pey, no. I am not jealous of you hugging Dad. That's not- ew is right. No, that's just the first time that I know of that you two connected like that and…"

"So, what? You're jealous of me as a sister?" I fill in.

"Peyton. I am not jealous at all. I just… I call you little sister as a joke, but what are we doing? We're supposed to be family. My dad sees you as a daughter. And I," he laughs darkly. "I do not see you as a sister at fucking all."

"Okay. Is that supposed to be news? Because this just in: I definitely don't see you as a brother. I'd like to think you're my boyfriend," my voice gets small and quiet on the last sentence.

He runs a hand over his face and turns his head to look away from me.

"Oh. Right. You don't see me that way. I'm still just a fuck to you," I say in a monotone voice, absolutely shocked to realize that after all this time, he still doesn't see me seriously.

"Fucking hell, Peyton-" he starts, but I don't want to hear anything else come out of his mouth, even if I know things are serious, because he only uses my real name when he is.

"You know what?" I turn around and start walking

away. "Fuck this and fuck you," I tell him with my back turned, thankful to not see his expression as I say it to him.

I walk for approximately an hour until I look up and see Heather's house looming in front of me. Did I mean to walk here? Absolutely not. But I stormed out of the house without my phone, so I'd really like her to take me home instead of walking the hour back.

I ring the doorbell to the massive McMansion- heaven knows no one would hear a knock- and think of what I'm going to say when Heather opens the door. Obviously, I walked here without a plan. I didn't even think of where I was going- I just went. And now I'm here, standing in front of the door of the girl who I have a sometimes thing with who sometimes still insults me in class. Am I thinking clearly? 100% no, I am not. I should just walk home. Heather and I fuck- we don't talk about our feelings, and we most certainly don't lean on each other for comfort.

I turn around and walk down the steps. I hear the door open behind me, but I hope it's one of Heather's parents, so I just continue to walk down the steps.

"Little freak? Why are you at my house?" Heather calls after me.

I turn and look up the steps at her. Fuck, she's hot. She's already changed for bed and she's got a two-piece satin cami and short set on. I can see her peaked nipples through the top, peaking between strands of that golden blonde hair that she's set loose from her ponytail.

I realize I'm staring, and I look up into her sapphire eyes. "I'm sorry. I was upset, so I started walking and..." I trail off.

She raises an eyebrow. "You started walking, and you ended up here?" Her mouth twists into a smirk. "Well, look at that. What an absolute upset."

I shrug my shoulders.

She opens the door wider and beckons me in. "You gonna come in? You're already here."

I feel my eyes widen. "Are- are you sure? What about your parents? Aren't they home?"

"My mother is definitely doing some sort of post-charity work chemical peel in her bedroom, and my father is assuredly drinking in his study. And neither of them will even fucking notice that the occupancy in the house has been increased by one," Heather flips her hair over her shoulder, giving me a glimpse at the fabric molding to her round breast. "Come inside, and you can touch them instead of looking at them," she purrs.

"I wasn't- I'm- ugh. I'm not here for that," I stammer out.

"Fine. But seriously. Come inside. I don't want to be eaten by the skeeters. I'm allergic," she waves a hand toward the door again.

This time I follow her, and when I'm inside, all I want to do is touch her, but I know I'll be rebuffed when her parents could walk around a corner at any time, so I keep my hands to myself.

She leads me to her room and locks the door behind us. I take my Docs off and lie down on her bed.

"Listen. I'm not really great at comforting people. I never know what they need. So you'll have to tell me what you want from me. Do you want to be held? Do you want to cuddle? Do you want me to tell you to toughen up and rub a little dirt on it? Help me out here," she bites her lip and shifts from foot to foot.

"Honestly, this is helping out tremendously. Heather

Lovelace, uncertain of herself and before my very eyes. I should charge admission: this is gold," I tease her.

"I'm trying very hard to remember you're upset, and I'm supposed to let you have this," she teases back.

"To answer your question, I absolutely do not want to talk about it, but I would like snuggles," I tell her and bat my eyes to punctuate my words.

"Mmm," she answers and slides into the bed next to me. She lays flat on her back and opens an arm for me to nuzzle into her, and I do, laying my head in the crook of her arm. Her tits are right in front of my face, and I press my face into the one closest.

Heather acts like she doesn't know how to comfort someone, but here she is, absolutely nailing it, petting my curls with her hand and twining her long legs into mine.

"If you don't want to talk about what happened, how about you tell me about the book you're reading," she prods me.

I lean up and kiss her shoulder. "Yeah, okay. So there's this handsome king named Nikolai, and his general is named Zoya, who is magical and such a Blanche," I begin.

"Hold up. What the fuck is a Blanche?" she asks.

"Oh. You know. Blanche DuBois from 'Streetcar Named Desire,'" I explain.

"I remember that play. We had to read it in English class. What about her?" she prompts.

"Okay. Well, like. You know how she's villainized, but really she's just completely misunderstood and a flawed woman? And society hates a flawed woman. We are expected to be perfect and polite and kind, and she is none of those things. She is unique and refuses to be anything but herself, and so everyone just writes her off as a bitch. Sam, Adrian, and I call any character like that a Blanche," I tell her.

"Hm. I don't know. I liked her. We were supposed to hate her?" Heather queries.

"Of course you liked her. You're a Blanche," I say, and stroke the strip of skin between her cami top and her short shorts.

She laughs sharply and loudly. "I'm a Blanche?"

"100% you are." I trail my fingers up under her top to her breasts, delicately circling a still-peaked nipple with the tips of my fingers.

She twitches underneath me but makes no move to stop me.

"So you think I'm a bitch?" she breathes as I continue playing with her body.

"You know you're a bitch," I parry and mouth at the breast I'm not stroking with my hand.

"But am I to understand that you don't think that's a bad thing?" she moans out.

"I like it when you're a bitch. It makes me wet," I tell her and grind my fabric-coated pussy against her leg as though she can feel my hot, wet heat.

"Do I, now?" she asks as she brings the arm I'm not laying on to the top of my leggings and slips a hand under them and my panties. Two of her fingers slip through my slick, and I throw my head back as she brings her wet fingers to my clit, rubbing with the perfect amount of pressure.

I remove my hand from underneath her cami and use it to push it down beneath her breasts so they are exposed, immediately taking a breast in my mouth and suckling at her. I'm rewarded by her gasp, and then I feel her fingers sink inside of me slowly. It spurs me on to suck harder as I grab her other breast and flick her other nipple.

She removes her hand from my pussy and pulls her nipple out of my mouth. "Taste how wet your cunt gets for a bitch," she demands, and I open wide for her to plunge her fingers inside my mouth.

We both moan as I lap my tongue around her fingers, chasing my essence. Then she pulls her fingers out of my mouth and replaces them with her mouth, immediately pushing her tongue into me and taking command of my mouth.

"Play with my tits, little freak," she orders me as she pushes me to my back and stretches her body out on top of mine.

While she's dominating my mouth, I bring my hands up to either breast and brush my fingers over her nipples. I love how small and perky her tits are. We're both grinding our cores into one another and tasting each other's sighs, and I need more. I pull away.

"Ma'am, please. I need to fuck it out," I say as I press up into her.

She grins. "Do you now?"

"I'll beg. Of course, I'll beg. I need you to fuck me and fuck me hard. I need you to degrade me and turn me into a well-fucked puddle. You're so hot, Ma'am. I don't deserve it, but I need it. Please give me your attention," I whine at her.

"Good fucking girl," she growls and then climbs off of me.

I raise onto my elbows. "No- wait- did I not do a good enough job of begging? I'll try again. Please don't leave me like this. I'm so wet for you. I want you so bad. I-"

She starts going through her closet. "Shhh. It's okay. You did well. I'm just getting a treat for you, that's all."

I swallow in relief. And then I swallow again when I see her holding a harness with a dildo on either side.

"Oh, fuck," I breathe out harshly.

My pulse rises as I watch her take off her sleep set and

slip the harness over her hips, then rises again as she slips one of the dildos into her pussy. She watches me as she does it, biting her lip as the flesh-colored silicone slides into her easily because of how wet she is. She adjusts the straps on the harness, and as she stands next to the bed, she points down at her cock.

"Suck my dick, little freak," she demands, and I get markedly wetter.

I take off my hoodie and shirt, then wiggle out of my leggings and panties, finally removing my socks. I throw all of them off the side of the bed, a problem for later me, and crawl on my hands and knees to the side of the bed.

"On your back," she orders, and I acquiesce, putting my head under her body and almost hanging off the edge of the bed. "Open," she demands, and I do. This is new. I don't know what I'm doing.

She slowly pushes her cock into my mouth, and I close my lips around the silicone. I just lay there, letting her fuck in and out of my mouth, getting a feel for sucking dick at this position, when I feel a sharp smack to my breast, and I moan, letting the cock slip deeper. Now I get this position. She has access to my body this way, and my pussy tingles in anticipation. I feel another smack, this time to the other breast, and I moan around her cock again.

"You're doing so well for me, little freak," she praises me, and I go molten. "Let's see if you get off on being treated like a slut." She plunges two fingers into my pussy, and I clench around her fingers. "Mmm. Definitely a fucking whore for me, aren't you?"

I'm getting wetter around her fingers with the degradation, but then she pulls out of my pussy and my mouth at the same time.

"Lay back on the bed, slut," she tells me, and now I rush to obey.

She crawls on top of me, pushes my legs open, and pauses at my slit.

"Tell me how much you want my dick, little freak," she orders.

"Yes, Ma'am, I want it so bad. I want your cock inside of me, please," I beg.

She laughs. "You're so obedient it's pathetic, do you know that?"

She pushes inside of me, and it doesn't feel as good as Graham's actual flesh and blood cock, but it feels good. Then she reaches between us and turns it on, and suddenly it's vibrating inside of me, and I can't help but to loudly moan.

"That's right. Tell me who makes you feel so good," she asks of me.

"You do, Ma'am. Oh, fuck. I love your cock. You feel so good inside of me. Fuck, harder, please." I'm a needy little mess, and I can feel my juices seeping out over the toy inside of me.

She reaches down to my thighs and throws my legs over her shoulders. "Hold on to something. I'm gonna fuck you so hard that your pussy will clench with the memory of it for days."

I reach back to her headboard to hold on while she grabs either side of my hips and starts powerfully thrusting in and out of me. I'm moaning a litany of "fuck fuck fuck," and my orgasm is coming on so quickly.

"Be a good little whore and open your mouth for me," Heather says. Like the obedient little fucktoy I am, I open my mouth and wait.

Heather spits in my mouth. "Now swallow for me."

And I do.

"Such a worthless little slut, aren't you? Everyone thinks you're such a perfect little good girl, and here you are under me, being degraded within an inch of your life and being fucked rough like a doll," she sneers.

And that's it. I'm done. My orgasm rises like a wave, and I come all over Heather's strap-on. I'm exhausted by my orgasm, and I lay there limply as Heather continues to fuck me. She's so into degrading me that she keeps going even though I'm not even clocking the rest of it, too fucked out to even let any of it penetrate my thoughts. I just watch her, so beautiful above me, watching her abdomen muscles clench as she rocks her body into mine, watching her biceps flex as she holds on to my body, watching the sweat sheen her limbs. She's absolutely stunning. I know I'm in a daze, but I'm with it enough to realize that there's a reason she's the queen bee at school, and it's because Heather Lovelace has it all. As I watch her throw her head back as she comes, I think that if she wanted me, I'd be hers too.

CHAPTER 25

PEYTON

eeks pass, and suddenly it's the weekend after Thanksgiving, which means the turkey is not the only thing being dressed against its will. I'm in the worst gown I've ever seen in my life, and the shade of it is so white even Anish Kapoor couldn't create a purer color. The hair and makeup artist Mama hired is gazing at me like I'm her finest creation, but I can't stop myself from scowling. I can't believe I'm having to go through with this. I'm mad at Mama for making me become a debutante, I'm mad at Ashton for being the one to drag Mama into his elite fucking circle, and I'm mad at Graham for not helping to talk Mama out of this. I'm just mad at everyone.

I'm trying not to be mad at the woman who is getting

paid to make me up for the evening, but she is complicit in my torture.

"You had better smile when you walk across that stage, young lady," Mama points her finger at me.

I scowl harder, cross my arms, and look away.

"Peyton DeVal, I swear to everything under the sun if you don't paste it on when the time comes, there will be a reckoning you have never seen before," she threatens.

"Okay, well, we aren't even at the event, so this is what you're getting until then. Deal with it," I retort and pout my lips.

"Fix your face. Andrea isn't going to be with us after this, so you can't be fucking up your face," Mama chides.

"I'm not gonna do anything to it, Mama! Ugghhhhhhh. Can we just get this over with?" I stand up and immediately teeter on the heels I'm not used to wearing. Mama told me to practice walking in them, but I thought that would give into the idea of the ball, so I refused. Now I'm going to have to cling to Graham the whole night and hope he doesn't let me take a tumble. We'll be taking the "escort" position very seriously.

"Thank you very much, Andrea. Your work is lovely," I compliment because, despite Mama's complaints, I was raised right.

Andrea nods as she closes up her makeup kit. "Of course, hon. I'm leaving the lipstick here so you can do touch-ups. Don't forget to put it in your clutch."

Ah, the clutch. The dumbest purse I've ever seen in my life. It's just large enough for that one lipstick and my phone. Good thing I don't need a wallet or a tampon because it most assuredly wouldn't fit. Who is in charge of women's fashion? I can't get a pocket because they want me to have a bag. But then I can't get a bag big enough for anything to go into? Please explain the logic here. It's atrocious.

Mama flits around me and fluffs out my skirt, which doesn't need to be fluffed. I look like one of those cakes that strippers jump out of; the hoop on this thing is so big. I hope I don't need to go to the bathroom because I won't be able to find my cunt under all the tulle.

I wobble out of the room, managing to make it down the hall and to the sweeping staircase. I grip the banister and pray my arm can hold me up as I walk down. I go slowly, and I'm about halfway down the staircase when I look down and see Graham staring up at me.

I don't know what to look at first. First, he is fuckhot in his black tuxedo with his little bow tie. I've never seen him so dressed up, and as soon as I see him, I'm thankful for the lipstick in my clutch because as soon as I can get him alone, I'm going to positively maul this man. His hair is slicked back, but a little curl has escaped in the front and is hanging down over his forehead. But second... dear God, the way he's looking at me. Like I'm every fantasy he's ever had come to life. Like I'm everything he's ever wanted. He looks at me the way I'd want someone to look at me for the rest of my life. And with that thought, I look back down at the banister. Because Graham is my right now. He's made that abundantly clear. I can't want him forever because he can barely see past tomorrow.

I clear the rest of the stairs and look up triumphantly. Graham steps forward, but Ashton waves him off and steps forward instead, taking my hand in both of his.

He lays a gentle kiss on my knuckles and then keeps hold of me. "I know I'm not your real father, Peyton, but I'm so proud of you. And I know you would rather be anywhere else but here tonight, but I appreciate you representing our family with such grace, poise, and beauty. You do it every day by working hard at school, with me, and on your play, but tonight you show everyone how you have beauty as well as brains. You're the total package, and I'm sorry you didn't have the opportunity for a real gentleman prospect to escort you instead of your brother. But young men are going to start taking notice of you- maybe even tonight- and I want you to remember that you're worth everything. I want you to make them remember how you're more than just a pretty face because you could outsmart all these fools."

I am tearing up in the middle of Ashton's speech, but at the end, I start to panic. "Wait. Do I have to dance with random guys?"

Mama steps in and starts, "Well, baby, it would be good if-"

But Graham cuts her off with, "Absolutely not, little sister. You'll be dancing with me all night." He takes my elbow, and Ashton's hands slip away.

He steers me away, and I can hear the murmurs of an argument that we leave in our wake.

Our parents follow us to Ashton's car and we slip into the back seat. My skirt is so voluminous that we can hide our clasped hands under the folds. Graham strokes his thumb over the back of my hand the entire drive to the event.

I'm vibrating in my seat the entire drive. The second we get there, I'm pulling an excuse and getting Graham alone. He's so hot right now I think I'm getting pregnant just sitting next to him.

As we walk to our table, Graham's hand is on my lower back, and I wish it was my nape, but there's a room full of people, not to mention our fucking parents, so I can forgive him for his discretion.

I set my clutch down at the table and turn to Graham. "I think we need to check in. Come with me?"

"Baby, don't bother Graham. You go and leave him here," Mama cuts in.

"You know how Pey's anxiety gets, Regina. I'll go with her," Graham covers.

And it's true. I usually would need him to get through something like this, but right now, the only thing I can think of is unbuttoning that dress shirt and digging my hands under that cumberbund to touch his taut abs, maybe licking a line up his body and tasting his sweat.

Graham takes my hand in his and begins leading me toward what I hope is a secluded space, then turns and gives me a "one moment, please" signal, going back to the table for my clutch. He comes back to me and takes my hand in his.

"I assume this has lipstick in it for when I absolutely wreck your mouth," he leans in and whispers to me.

"That would be correct," I smile shakily at him.

"And I would also be correct in thinking that the check-in was just an excuse?" he asks.

"Graham," I start and then think better. "Sir. Please."

"Okay, okay, come with me," he soothes.

We leave the ballroom with its catwalk, its dancing area, its spread of tables and chairs, and the tasteful black and white decorations that are layered over it all. I follow him blindly until we reach a maintenance closet, and I briefly think I'm starting to have a problem where these are concerned before Graham opens the door and yanks me inside.

"Can we find a light? You're fucking melting my panties off right now, and I need to see how hot you are before I climb you like a tree," I practically demand of him.

"I'm working on it, fucktoy. Be a good girl and be patient for me. You also look incredible. Stunning. Fan-fucking-tastic. Ah, there it is."

The small space finally fills with light, and I look up into his eyes to see him grinning down at me.

"You look fucking bridal. Which is the point, but good goddamn, woman. I've been hard since the second I saw you descend those stairs. I can't wait to fuck you in this," he praises me and cups my cheek.

"Yes, Sir, please," I breathe. "If I don't have your mouth on me in the next five seconds, I'm going to perish. Take me to bed or lose me forever."

He looks toward the ceiling. "And now she's quoting *Top Gun* at me? Bless it."

His mouth comes down hard on mine, and I open for him, loving the taste of him as our tongues twine together. At this point, he tastes like home, so warm and familiar. Falling into his body is still as exciting as the first time, but now not so thrilling. I'm way past the point of being afraid of Graham. Afraid of him leaving me? 100%. But not afraid of him hurting me.

He backs me up into the wall, and I wish I could feel his hardness, but through the yards of fabric, there's no way I can feel his length even when he grinds into my body.

Suddenly the door opens, and we break apart. Everything grinds to a halt as I take in Heather, standing tall in a strapless white wiggle dress with a tutu at her ankles. You know the Solo in the Spotlight Barbie dress? This is that, but all in white. I feel my jaw drop as I stare at her. Her makeup is smoky, her blonde hair is artful waves, and the whole look is topped off with white opera gloves. She's never been so beautiful, and she's stunning every day of the week. I definitely have to steal a copy of a picture she takes tonight so I can look at it every night for the rest of my life.

"Are you fucking shitting me right now?" she screeches, and I stop eye-fucking her and tune back into the situation at hand.

Right. My stepbrother and I were just making out. The evidence is smeared across his lips. And the girl I'm fucking discovered us. The girl who happens to be his ex.

"Um. I can explain," I say. But I don't think I actually can explain. I'm just buying time.

She crosses her arms. "I'm really interested in hearing how the girl I broke up with my boyfriend for found herself making out with said boyfriend."

"This is who you broke up with me for?" Graham asks incredulously.

At the same time, I burst out, "You broke up with Graham for me?"

We all hear someone come down the hallway toward us at the same moment, and Graham pulls Heather in by her wrist. "Come in, pretty girl. Let's have this conversation out of hearing of Wickersville's country club elite."

She shuffles in and closes the door behind her. The move puts all of us in very close proximity. Which come to think of it, I don't actually mind except for the part where both the people I'm fucking just found out about the other. I don't think my luck is good enough to walk away with both of them at the end of this conversation, which is what I realize with clarity is what I actually want.

"Don't 'pretty girl' me. I can't believe you're fucking Peyton," Heather turns to him.

"Let's not gloss over the fact that you're fucking Peyton, too. You're into girls?" Graham asks.

"I'm pansexual. It's not a thing. Let's move on," Heather huffs.

"Aww, Heather! You said it. I'm so proud of you!" I beam at her.

"Don't start, little freak. You're in enough trouble as it is. How could you not tell me you were fucking my ex-boyfriend? Don't you think that was pertinent information?" Heather narrows her eyes at me.

"I'm interested in this answer, too, little sister," Graham prompts.

"Ew. Do you seriously call her little sister?" Heather scoffs.

"In bed, too. We like it, don't we fucktoy?" Graham grins at me.

"Fucktoy, too? Pick a lane! You know what, never mind. Peyton! Explain yourself," Heather orders.

"Um. Well. Graham and I have been fucking since I moved into his house. And he told me to keep it a secret." At this, I shrug. "So when you two broke up, and Heather and I started fucking I thought it would rock the boat to tell either of you that I was fucking the other. I didn't know the circumstances of the breakup, and I wanted you both, so… you know, this is y'all's fault! Neither of you publicly wanted to be with me." I pout.

Graham turns toward Heather. "So, you broke up with me to fuck the girl you didn't know I was fucking?"

Heather nods. "Wait. You were cheating on me?"

Graham grimaces at her and then turns to me. "But apparently fucktoy was cheating on both of us."

"Oops," I feel my face burn with shame. "Sir, Ma'am, I'm so sorry, I-"

"Well, this situation has a really easy fix," Graham continues as though I hadn't spoken. "Let's all be together."

Heather rears back, "You would want to be with me after knowing I like a girl?"

Graham laughs, "First of all, Peyton came out to me weeks ago, and I didn't care. I can't believe you didn't think you could trust me with sharing that. Second of all, pretty girl… I'm gonna let you in on a little secret. There are very few men who would say no to having two girlfriends.

Especially if he gets to watch the two girlfriends fuck." He runs a hand down his face. "Fucking Christ, I don't think I'm prepared for that. I'm going to implode. I'm going to come untouched, just watching the two of you. I'm going to-"

"Okay, Graham. We get it. You're into it. Well, I do miss your dick," Heather admits.

Graham grins at her and cups her cheek. She turns her head and kisses his palm.

"You just had my dick at the Halloween party, or were you too drunk to remember?" he teases her.

"Wait one fucking second. You two cheated on me?" I accuse.

"Little freak, stop while you're ahead," Heather admonishes me without looking at me. To Graham, she says, "Of course I remember."

"I miss your pussy, but I miss you more, pretty girl. I never stopped loving you. I don't think I can ever stop loving you." He strokes her cheek and leans in to kiss her forehead.

"I love you so much. I was so adrift thinking that I'd lost you forever," she murmurs.

I watch as he kisses her achingly slowly. They have a dance that I'm not sure of the steps of. It's clear both of them are fighting for dominance, but they both give and take in equal measure. I once had wondered how they kiss each other and now I have my answer: like a song. Not an angry screamy one or a love ballad, but intense and strong, like something that would accompany one of Heather's solo performances in a ballet.

Heather pulls back and runs her fingers over his throat. "Mmm. Missed that, baby boy." Then she turns to me. "You are in so much trouble, little freak."

"Fucking hell, it's going to be so much fun to punish

her with you, pretty girl," Graham drawls.

"Wait. But. Everything worked out, didn't it?" I hedge.

"It did, but you're not out of the woods. Let me make one thing crystal fucking clear, Peyton," Heather begins, and I straighten my spin at her use of my real name. "There will be absolutely no more cheating. Not from any of us. If we want to bring someone else in, we fucking discuss it like adults."

"Yes, Ma'am," I mumble.

"That goes for you, too, Graham," Heather turns and glares at him.

"Yes, Ma'am," he says but with a shit-eating grin.

I feel my mouth make an "o" of shock. Graham calling Heather "Ma'am" kind of does it for me. Can't wait to see where that goes. Did she Dom him when they fucked on Halloween? How positively delicious.

"Now let's seal it with a kiss," Heather declares, and I tip my mouth up greedily for a kiss from my girlfriend.

CHAPTER 26

HEATHER

After wiping Graham's mouth of the remnants of not one but two different shades of lipstick and a quick reapplication, Graham shuffles us back out to the dining room. All I want to do is grab Graham's bow tie and pull him into me or crawl underneath Peyton's skirts, but unfortunately, I have to go sit with Caleb and listen to him try to talk to me while I make it clear I could not give a shit about him. I keep getting bitchier, but all I'm doing is making him try harder, and that is the opposite effect of what I want. Especially since I finally feel settled for the first time in a long time. Graham and I were happy, but I had felt like something was missing for a while. Peyton was that puzzle piece.

Post debut, I smooth my dress down my ass as I sit

sandwiched between my parents and Caleb, Caleb's parents on the other side of him. I try not to grimace. What a cozy little group. At least I can tell my mother I'm back with Graham. She'd rather me be with him than Caleb. Well. Can I? I look over at Peyton and Graham and watch them. Maybe we should have that conversation.

I start sipping on my wine- no one pays attention to who is drinking what at these things, thank heavens- and settle in to watch the two most beautiful creatures in the room.

Peyton is looking up at Graham like he hung the moon, and Graham is looking at Peyton like she's commissioner of the NFL and he's just been awarded MVP after winning the Superbowl. I'm not jealous of their obvious feelings, but I am jealous that they get to sit next to each other while I'm trapped with the white-bread motherfuckers at my table.

I look around the room and find that no one is paying them any attention, which is good... I think? But how did I miss this intersection of the two most important people in my life? I guess I've been so focused on *not being gay*TM that I hadn't clued into the fact that these two are quite obviously fucking.

I feel a tug at my elbow and turn to face Caleb.

"Is there a reason you think you can touch me?" I ask with an arched eyebrow.

"Oh. Fuck. Sorry. It's just... you weren't paying me any attention," he says stupidly.

"Yeah. There's a reason for that. I don't want to," I inform him.

"But... we're here together," he attempts to explain.

"Good deduction skills," I reply.

He scowls. "Are you going to at least dance with me?"

"It would be appropriate, so yes," I agree.

He brightens. "Maybe we can go somewhere after this?"

"Didn't you just explain to Graham a few weeks ago that you were decidedly not trying to cut in on me?" I narrow my eyes.

"I mean… yeah. But my mama said that your mama said you were looking for someone new and that-"

I cut him off, "Let me stop you right fucking there. You and I?" I gesture between the two of us. "Never gonna happen. We will dance an appropriate amount, at least three dances. We will part ways at the end of the night. I will not hug you, I will not kiss you, and I'm certainly not going to fuck you. If you should happen to tell anyone that we did more than dance, I will find you, cut the testes out of your ball sack, and preserve them in a jar. And then all you'll have between your legs is that micropenis you call a dick and bloody flaps where your balls used to be. Capiche?"

"So you've thought about my dick, huh?" He grins, and I've had enough.

I subtly slip a fork from the table and make a fist around the handle. We're at the country club, which means these rich fuckers have spent good money on the silverware. This is actually silver. Which is going to come in handy for what I'm about to do next.

"If you know what's good for you, you're not going to make a scene," I warn him.

"Huh?" He cocks his head in confusion.

I raise the fork high enough to gain momentum but low enough so that it's not above the table, and then I bring the fork down over Caleb's thigh with force.

Caleb squeals in pain, and the whole table pauses to look over at us.

"Bad salmon," I shrug and explain, and because no one actually cares about anyone else's welfare at this table, they all turn back toward each other and continue eating and chatting.

"I thought I told you not to make a scene," I chide him.

"That was before you stabbed me with a fork!" He whines.

"Are you going to take me seriously?" I ask of him.

He nods.

"Are you going to stop hitting on me and behave?" I ask again.

He nods.

"Excellent. Now I'm going to take this fork out. Shut your mouth. It's going to hurt again; just another reminder not to fuck with me," I tell him.

He quickly nods again, and I brace his thigh with my other hand, getting the leverage I need to pull out the fork with my hand. I watch Caleb grit his teeth as the tines come free from his thigh, leaving trickles of blood on the four jagged holes in his suit pants. Casually dropping the fork on the floor, I flag down a waiter.

"It seems I've lost my fork. Get me another, won't you?" I smile serenely at the waiter.

"Of course, ma'am. I'll be right back with that," the waiter responds, and I nod, turning back to check on Caleb.

He's gone pale and is using his napkin to blot up some of the blood on his pants.

The orchestra begins an instrumental "Moon River," and I hold my hand out to him.

He looks at my hand dumbly.

"Ask me to dance, you dunce," I spell out for him.

"My leg hurts," he whines again.

"You play football for God's sake. You take harder hits than that. Stop being a pussy," I tell him and thrust my hand out toward him again.

He blanches but does as I've demanded, standing and taking my hand. I let him lead me out to the dance floor but he pauses when we get there.

I put one hand on his shoulder and raise the other to the side to clasp his hand, but he's just frozen solid.

"Oh, for fuck's sake. You can touch me to dance with me. Just keep your hand on my waist and go no lower," I coach him.

He grasps my hand in his and delicately holds my waist. I let him lead us in a swaying slow dance and turn my attention to where Graham and Peyton are dancing next to us and looking positively gorgeous together as he gives her a twirl. She giggles at him, and it makes me smile.

Caleb follows my look. "I've never seen a black girl debut," he begins, and my happy expression quickly turns dark.

"Watch your fucking mouth," I warn him.

"I'm not saying nothing. I've just never seen it, that's all," he hedges.

"That's because this backward ass town has done a bang-up job ensuring its people of color stay in poverty," I mutter.

"What do you know about it?" he mumbles out.

"TikTok has more than thirst traps and trendy dances, you know," I grit out.

"Oh shit, really?" he asks. And I'm about to go off on his sarcastic response until I realize this himbo is serious right now.

I sigh. "Really, Caleb."

The song ends, and I look over to see if Graham and Peyton are leaving or staying. They look like they're settling in for whatever's next.

"Caleb. You're going to go cut in on Peyton and Graham. You're going to dance with Peyton. You're going to be the most upstanding gentleman. That means you're not going to hit on her. You're not going to feel her up. You're not going to say anything that's a fucking microaggression," I insist.

"A micro what now?" He asks confusedly.

"Don't say anything about the color of her skin, you big brute," I say with frustration.

"Oh. Well. Okay. What if-" he starts.

"I said no," I sternly say.

He nods and drops my hand and my waist. I follow him over to Graham and Peyton and watch him ask to cut in. Peyton and Graham both look at me in question, and I nod my head in approval. They both visually soften and break apart, Caleb taking Peyton's hand and waist, and then I'm sliding into Graham's arms.

"Oh, fuck, this is so much better. I belong here," I sigh at him. He's at eye level since I'm wearing heels.

"Yes, you do, my love," he agrees and kisses my cheek.

"We can only do one dance, though. I'm not leaving Pey with that idiot," I tell him.

"I agree," he says.

"I did want to ask you, though. This would be better if we had hashed it out with Pey, but we got so caught up in the excitement. Are we publicly a throuple now? Because I don't know that I'm ready to be out," I blush.

"I'm not ready to tell Regina I'm fucking her daughter, so maybe we should just say that you and I are back together. It's not like this is going to work out long-term, anyway," he explains.

"Wait. What?" I look at him wide-eyed.

"I don't mean you and me. I mean the three of us. She's made it clear she's going to Vanderbilt. She's made it clear this is just a fling. This has an expiration date," he tells me.

"Wow. Okay. Wow. Are you sure? I just..." I trail off.

"You really like her, huh?" he brings me in close to his body so that we're hugging more than dancing. I fit myself into his body and sigh into his neck.

"Don't," I tell him. "How about instead of thinking about that, we think about tonight? I can come over, we can peel her out of that dress, I can Dom you, you can Dom her." I lean back so I can look him in the eye, and I do it just in time to see his eyes flash with heat.

"Fuuuuuuck, Heather. I can't wait to have you both," he growls out, and his hands move from my waist to my ass. He grabs a handful of each cheek, and I grind up against him, feeling his hard cock through my dress. His eyes arrow down to my lips, and I smirk.

"Are you going to kiss me or what?" I purr out.

"I can't do what I want to do with you in front of all these people," he laughs.

"It would let everyone know we're back together. So it serves a point as well as quenches a thirst." I feel my lips twist in a smirk. "Actually, you know what? I forgot we had decided I'm in charge in this chapter of our relationship," I laugh but then I grasp his bow tie and pull him to my lips.

We both open up to each other immediately, and it's like coming home. I moan into his mouth as our tongues dance together, licking into each other. Our kiss is fevered and electric after being denied each other for longer than either of us would like. We have been each other's forever, and we will be each other's until we no longer exist.

Breaking the kiss, I move away, and we pant into each other's mouths.

"Forever," I tell him as I stare deep into those beautiful green eyes I know better than my own.

"Forever," he agrees and pecks my lips again.

"I don't want to stop kissing you," I smile. I love being in his orbit again. I've missed the familiar home smell of

Dior Sauvage.

"I know. But we made enough of a scene, and neither one of us wants to leave Pey longer than we have to," he smiles back.

"Accurate AF," I say. "I'm going to go fix my lipstick. You can go tell her what we decided."

"Oh, good. I love being the bad guy," he groans.

"You can make it up to her with orgasms," I laugh and pat his cheek.

"That's a Band-Aid, not a solution," he says seriously.

"I know. I know," I say soberly.

Then I walk over to my girlfriend and the idiot who escorted me and drag him away from her by the ear. I deposit him at our table, grab my lipstick, and head to the bathroom. On the way, I see Peyton vibrating with anger as she storms out of the ballroom. Guess Graham told her we aren't going to be a public throuple. I cringe as I step into the bathroom.

CHAPTER 27

GRAHAM

The tension on the way home from the ball is palpable. Peyton threw a fit about sitting in the back of the car with me, but it's not like she can tell Dad and Regina what I did to piss her off, so we ended up sitting together despite her appeals otherwise. Regina keeps turning around to look back at us, Peyton keeps glancing over at me but glaring when I look at her, and Dad is blissfully ignorant and humming along to the radio as he drives. What a perfectly dysfunctional family we make.

I can't even use the miles of fabric around Pey's waist as cover because she's sitting demurely with her hands in her lap. Frustrated to the nth degree, I finally man up and reach for her hand, but as soon as my fingers start to slip into hers, she pulls her hand back and then slaps me across the face.

"Peyton DeVal!" Regina screeches.

"Little sister," I growl warningly.

"Fucking asshole!" Peyton yells.

"Listen, I don't know what happened between the two of you tonight, but you need to figure it out. It's bad enough that you made a scene at one of the biggest nights of your life," Regina intones.

"Mother. It's not even a footnote in my life. You made me go to that dog and pony show. I went and performed like all the other lemmings. It's not my fault that your stepson is the world's biggest twatwaffle," Peyton grumbles.

"It's not even a footnote? Seems like some things happened that are worthy of more than a footnote," I question her.

She turns and glares at me again. "I fulfilled my end of the bargain. If you didn't tell Graham that he needed to behave too, then that's not my problem," Peyton insists.

"Little sister," I say, and this time it's pleading, not a warning.

She crosses her arms and huffs.

"You two looked so sweet dancing with each other. Let's go back to that energy," Regina coaxes.

"Not a fucking chance," Peyton says and looks away from me toward the window.

That's fine. I'll bide my time. She can't be mad at me forever.

When we get to the house, she starts to leave the car but I snap my fingers. She freezes, then uncrosses her arms and slowly turns toward me. She narrows her eyes but awaits further instruction as our parents exit the car after I tell them we will be a moment.

"You're going to leave that dress on, fucktoy. I told you I'd fuck you in it, and that's still happening tonight," I say with warning.

"You're not coming anywhere near me. Fuck you," she hisses, and my lips curl into a grin.

I slap her face, and she loudly moans before I take her chin in my hand and tilt her face up to mine.

"You filthy fucking whore. Here's what's going to happen. We're going to wait for Heather to show up, then you can try and run into the woods but Heather and I are going to catch you. And you can cry all you want, but we're going to fuck that sopping wet cunt of yours. Because I know you're angry at us, but I also know how drenched that slap just got you." I move my hand from her chin to the curls that are framing her face and twirl a lock around my finger. The rest of her hair is in an elaborate updo that I can't wait to positively wreck.

She rears her head back and spits at me. I laugh at her and grab her throat, squeezing the sides and making her gasp for air.

"Tsk tsk tsk. What a bad girl," I chide her.

"I don't want to be a good girl for you," she gasps out.

I take her mouth with mine, but she resists. She's clenching her lips together so my tongue can't gain entry, and I'm frustrated but also so hot for her right now.

"You know when you fight me it makes me harder," I purr against her mouth as I take one of her hands to run across the length straining in my pants.

She's really fighting me, but when she runs a hand over my cock she opens her mouth with a moan, and I take the opportunity to push my tongue into her. She resists at first, but then her tongue is stroking mine, and she's melting into me. Forgetting that she's supposed to be upset with me and that we're in a CNC scene, her hand starts rubbing me in earnest through my suit pants.

I run my hands down her body, stopping at her tits to grab them roughly, over her waist and ass, then to her thighs as I pick her up and deposit her on my lap. Leaning back against the seat, I let her follow my mouth as she tries to grind into me with all that tulle between us. I yank the bodice down under her tits, and it props them up, making them look even more delicious than usual. Bending down to worship them, I take one nipple in my mouth and bite down. She bucks against me, then threads her fingers through my hair and holds me close to her chest. I lap at her eagerly, tasting the saltiness of her skin.

The car door opens next to me, and we both spring apart, Peyton hiding her breasts from whomever just popped their head in.

"Seriously? This is how careful y'all are being? What if I were Regina or Ashton?" Heather shakes her head. "Good to know little freak isn't still mad, though."

"What gives you the impression I'm not still angry?" Peyton bites out.

"Um. Maybe because your lipstick is smeared all over Graham's face and your tits are out," Heather appraises her and then reaches out a hand. "Mmm, look at these. I'd kill to taste those dark brown nipples." She traces a hand over one nipple, then two. Peyton arches her back, pushing her tits into Heather's hand, and Heather notices. "That's it. Such a good girl for us," Heather praises.

That breaks Peyton's sex haze. She slaps Heather's hand away. "I'm not your good girl."

"No?" Heather raises an eyebrow.

"Are you in the mood for a little CNC, pretty girl?" I ask Heather.

"That could be new and exciting," Heather smirks.

I look up at Peyton sitting on my lap, and I know that

when I grin, it's mischievous.

"Run, fucktoy," I growl out.

"In this dress?" Peyton pouts.

"I'm giving you a ten count, and then I'm coming after you," I tell her and lean back so she can get off of my lap.

Heather moves to the side so Peyton can exit, and she does, pulling up the top of her dress to cover her tits and kicking her heels off so they don't sink into the soft ground. I watch her run toward the backyard as Heather sits in the place where Peyton just left.

"What's the plan, baby boy?" She watches her fingers as they run through my hair.

I close my eyes and enjoy the sensation of her playing with the strands. "The plan is to give her a moment to get ahead but then chase her down and take her rough. Even when she fights us and says she doesn't want it. Do you know her safeword?"

"We use the stoplight system," she responds and gives my hair a little tug.

"Great; same. Now let's go get our girl," I say, leaning up to kiss her. Now that I can kiss her again. Fuck, that's nice.

CHAPTER 28

PEYTON

I make it to the forest's edge, and I'm already panting. Your girl does not do cardio, and I'm already exhausted. I know I have to keep running to make it fun, but I can take a second to breathe because I haven't even heard Heather or Graham running behind me.

I notice that the bottom of my dress is coated in a sheen of dirt as I pick up my skirt to inspect it. Mama is gonna have my ass for getting this dress fucked up, and I'm not sure how I'm going to explain it to her. Surely saying that my stepbrother and his girlfriend chased me through the woods and fucked me into the dirt would be a little out of pocket. Maybe I can just hide it as a trophy in the back of my closet, and she'll never be the wiser for it.

"Oh, fucktoy!" Graham calls behind me, and I realize I've paused for too long.

I pick up my skirts again and run to the left, away from the dock and further into the woods. I hope I don't get too far. I'm kind of afraid to get lost in these woods, although eventually, I'd hit water. I think.

I hear Heather's giggle behind me, and I turn, amazed to hear such a happy sound erupt from her lips. The move costs me, and Graham barrels into me, turning our bodies at the last minute so that his body breaks our fall. It still knocks the wind out of me, and I give an "oof" as he takes me to the ground.

"You're mine now, you little bitch," he growls, and I remember that I'm supposed to be fighting them, not mooning over the sounds of how cute my girlfriend is. Damnit.

I push at his arms that are banded around me. "Get the fuck off of me!" I yell, but he just laughs.

I feel his hands reach into my hair and pull my head back so his mouth can find purchase on my neck. My pussy gets wet, and I stifle a moan. He's taken his tuxedo jacket and bowtie off, but he's still in his dress shirt, so when I snap my head forward and bite into his shoulder, I get a mouthful of expensive cotton.

"Oh, what a bad girl," Heather tsks at me, and I feel her standing over the top of us, just watching for now.

"She's just asking for it, isn't she?" Graham laughs back at her, and I stifle a groan again. The way they're talking about me, like I don't even matter, like I'm an object to be used and abused, gets me so hot. I love the moments where I am truly their fucktoy, here for their pleasure. The thing I've learned about Graham and Heather, though, is that they both get off on getting me off. I'm never left unsatisfied.

"Tear her dress off her," Heather demands.

I yelp. "No! Not the dress! Please!" And as I keen out, I really do mean it. I don't want this dress ruined.

Graham rolls me to my back so that I can look up and see Heather looming above me. She's taken off her dress, and she's standing above me in her lacy pink bra and panties. Involuntarily, I open my mouth like I can beckon her pussy to my lips in a silent offering.

"What is it, pet?" She croons, and I squirm in Graham's arms.

Then I hear a loud ripping sound and look back to Graham as he tears the most expensive thing I've ever owned, from bodice to skirt. I watch in fascination as his muscles test the limits of his dress shirt and the veins in his neck pop. And for good reason. This is a thick material. I can't believe he just annihilated it. Christ, that's sexy.

"You fucking animal!" I screech at him.

He grins wickedly at me. "Now your cunt is mine, and I'm gonna fill you full of my cum."

"Fuck you!" I slap him across the face, and the spot glows bright red as his grin gets wider.

"You get me so hard when you fight me," he growls. He slaps my exposed breasts twice in quick succession and then tears my panties with another loud rip, following the complete desecration of my clothing with a slap to my clit. I jolt as a novel pleasure rips through my body. That's the first time he's slapped my clit, and I have to say: big fan. I'm already trash for him slapping my face, but the force of his blow to my most sensitive nerve is sublime. "Pretty girl, hold her down while I get my dick out."

Heather smirks, steps out of her panties, and lowers her cunt to my face as she grabs my arms and pins me to the ground. She's facing toward Graham so that my nose is tucked into her ass and prodding at her hole while my mouth is open on her cunt, tasting the delicious musk of her. I'm restrained, so I can't grab her thighs and pull her down to smother me, but as I plunge my tongue into her and start to fuck her with my tongue, she sits down more firmly on my face, and I moan.

"If you want to safe out, snap your fingers three times. Do it now so I know you've heard and understood," she commands.

Snap. Snap. Snap.

"Good girl. Keep eating me. You're doing so well, but you have to keep it up when Graham starts fucking you," she coaches.

And then I feel Graham slide into me, stretching me out. I try to pant, but my mouth just ends up with more pussy in it, so I place open-mouthed kisses on Heather's cunt as I try to breathe with a cock in one hole and a pussy on the other. I am so far gone at this point; this is absolute heaven. I lick feverishly at Heather as Graham pounds into me, his belt making a clinking sound as his hands massage into that erogenous zone at my hips, making me come around his cock.

I can't see above me, but I can hear when Heather and Graham start making out over my body. The sound of their mouths meeting over and over and their mingled moans turn me on, even as obstructed as my view is. Heather's orgasm drips into my mouth.

"I want her from behind," Graham tells Heather, and I hear them kiss again before Heather is lifting off of my face and giving me a chance to breathe.

I'm already boneless from the abuse and the orgasm, so I let them move me like a puppet. Graham pulls out of me and rolls my body over. Smacking my ass, he instructs, "Get on your hands and knees, fucktoy."

Heather positions herself under me, elbows propping

her up, legs parted so I can see her glistening pink pussy. Her hair has half come down, her tan skin is rosy and flushed, and she looks like a debauched goddess. She grabs me by the hair and pushes me down to her opening.

"Get to it. You're not done until I say you're done, little freak," she says sternly.

Then I feel Graham plunge back inside of me. He's so much deeper from the back, gloriously hitting my cervix every time he thrusts into me.

"I'm obsessed with this ass," Graham says right before he administers several spanks to said ass. I feel him gather up what he can with his hands and squeeze. "God, you're both so fucking hot. I love watching the two of you."

"I love watching the two of you, too, baby," Heather moans out.

"Where do you want me to come, Heather?" Graham asks.

"In that tight little pussy. I want to see it drip out of her," Heather responds.

"Yes, Ma'am," he tells her, and something about seeing the man who dominates me being submissive makes me clench around him.

"Use your fingers, little freak. Three of them, right on my G-spot," Heather instructs me.

I do as she asks, sliding three fingers inside of her without prep. She's so slick from her orgasm and my saliva that they go in easily. I curl my fingers inside of her and find that ribbed front wall. I press down with force as my tongue flicks over her clit, and then she's coming again, filling my palm with her juices as she cries out.

She sinks onto the forest floor and pushes my head away from her.

"God damn, little freak. You're so good at that," she compliments.

Graham takes the opportunity to slide his hands up from my hips to my breasts, grabbing them roughly and pulling me up onto my knees to a vertical position with my back pressed to his front. At some point, his shirt has been unbuttoned and we're skin to skin. He kneads my breasts and pinches my nipples.

"Say you like this," he coaxes.

I'm so out of energy, but I manage to answer him. "Never," I respond.

"Say you love my dick," he commands.

"I don't," I lie.

"Say you'll be mine forever," he demands.

I tense. I'm not sure what this game has turned into. I do like this. I do love his dick. Does he really want me to be his forever? If I say no, then am I actually admitting I will be? If I say yes, it ruins the scene.

I decide not to answer, bringing my hands up to his wrists and scoring my nails down them. He grunts and rearranges his hands, placing one on my stomach and one on my throat. I try to move the hand off my stomach, but he squeezes my throat in response.

"Stop. Every part of your body is perfect. I like your shape, I like your skin, I like these curls," he nuzzles into my hair. "Don't ever let anyone tell you differently."

I turn my face into his chest and trail my lips over his pecs, silently thanking him for the words. Too often, I've been the fat girl, or the black girl, or the girl with wild hair. And none of those things are inherently bad, but people have done a damn good job of making me feel like they are. I'm trying not to tear up in the middle of a scene, but fuck, I feel so seen.

Graham runs his hand along the curve of my stomach, and it makes me shiver. He's fucking me so roughly, his left hand is squeezing my throat, but his touch on my belly is feather soft, caressing my skin. His hand dips down to where we're joined, and he swipes up some of my cum to lubricate my clit. I drop my head back on his chest and moan audibly as he fucks into me faster and rubs me earnestly. My arms go behind me, and I sink my fingers into his hair, needing something to grab onto while my orgasm spins up. Then I'm coming, clenching hard around him and crying out.

He pushes me back to the ground and keeps me there with a hand on the middle of my back. I close my eyes and pillow my head on my crossed arms as I feel him pound into me with his other hand wrapped around my shoulder. He stills, and I feel the warmth of his cum flood me as he groans.

I feel my damp curls being moved off of my forehead.

"What a good girl you were for us," Heather coos at me, and I preen. "Such a sweet little sugar."

I'm dizzy from subspace, so it takes me a minute to realize this is the aftercare portion of the night. Heather gets into rare form and is actually nice.

"Thank you, Ma'am," I say, soaking it up.

She runs her long fingers delicately over my face, tracing my cheekbones and my lips with the pads of them. Behind me, I feel Graham relieve the pressure off my legs and begin to massage my ass and hips. I got double-teamed in a scene, and now I get double the aftercare? Holy shit, this is the tits. If this is wrong, I never want to be right.

"Can you carry her, baby?" Heather asks Graham.

"Can I carry her?" He scoffs. "What do you think this is? Of course, I can carry her. Come here, little sister." He rolls me to my back and hefts me up into his arms. He grunts as he rises from his knees to standing.

"I'm too heavy," I tell him.

"There's no such thing. If I couldn't carry you, I'd step

it up in the gym. But as it is, I can carry you just fine," he assures me.

I whimper and fling a hand out, searching for Heather.

She's putting her clothes back on and then picking up the remnants of my clothing. I wait with my hand out until she takes my hand, and I hold it as we all walk toward the house. "I'm here, I'm here," she gently tells me.

"Mmm. You're like sugar right now," I mumble against Graham's chest.

They both laugh.

"Fucktoy, are you trying to say something?" Graham tries to sound harsh, but I hear the laughter in his voice.

"Mhm. Usually, she's so mean, but she's so nice after a scene," I explain without thinking. "No- wait- I mean-"

"I know what you mean, little freak. Are you hungry? I know you like sushi after a scene, but I don't think our place is open this late. I'd have to make you something," she says.

I make some noises but even I don't know if I'm assenting or disagreeing. Then I lick Graham's nipple. It's right in my face, after all.

"You can eat Graham later if you'd like. But for now, you need some water and a snack. How about some chocolate-covered pretzels?" She offers.

"Something sweet for our sweet," Graham agrees, and I look up at him and smile. He looks down at me and smiles softly back, kissing me on the forehead. "Yes, she likes that. Do you want a bath or straight to bed?"

I make another noise. Apparently, I've gone non-verbal.

"That's fine. We can wash the sheets tomorrow," he responds. Okay, and apparently, they now understand my R2-D2 sounds.

I hum. Then I panic and look over at Heather with a

sound of alarm.

She looks up at Graham and he nods.

"I'll stay, little freak," she confirms, and I hum again, burrowing deeper into Graham's arms and clutching the hand she's given to me.

"Just a warning, though, pretty girl: little sister and I are really into somno," he warns.

I look over at her to see her smirking.

"Love that for you two. I also love that I'll get to watch if you should happen to wake me up," she says as she squeezes my hand.

We get to the house, and Heather opens up the back door so Graham can carry me through. He probably has no idea that I appreciate his understanding of me right now, but I kiss his pec in thanks anyway.

Graham takes us to his room, which is out of the ordinary because he and I usually sleep in my room. I bite his nipple and shake my head, hoping he will understand.

"Okay, your room it is," he agrees and changes direction.

Heather drops my poor dress and panties at the foot of the bed, then pulls the covers back on the bed while Graham drops to his knees so he can lay me gently on the soft sheets.

I lay expectantly as they both undress. Graham slides out of his unbuttoned shirt and unbelted pants, then he takes off his black boxer briefs. Heather slips her dress over her hips.

"Shit, Graham, her water and pretzels," Heather says.

"Fuck, you're right. You crawl into bed with her, and I'll run downstairs," he answers and turns to go.

I keen out, and he turns back around. "I'll be right back, little sister. I promise," he assures me and kisses my lips. He backs away just as fast, and I cry out again. He gives a laughing sigh, then brings his mouth back to mine. This time he gently coaxes my mouth open, licking into my mouth slowly. Then he pulls back and pecks my lips once, then each of my eyelids. I sigh happily, and he leaves.

Heather crawls into bed on the other side, facing me, and runs a hand up my thigh.

"Are you sore?" she asks.

I shake my head.

"Okay. We need to get that makeup off of you. Off both of us, but let's come down a little first, hm?" She continues to pet my thigh.

Turning toward her, I look her up and down. Her dainty peaked nipples, her slim waist and hips, her jutting collarbone. I reach out to run my fingers along said collarbone and she smiles at me. Then I tap my lips, and she smiles wider. I so rarely see her without barriers, and I wish I could tell her what it means to see it now.

I open to her as she pulls me into her body, throwing one of my legs over her hip. I feel my wet pussy push against her skin, and our breasts push together. She kisses me leisurely, dancing her tongue around mine as she runs her hands up and down my back soothingly.

The door groans open, and then I hear, "Fuuuuuuuck, that's gorgeous. Stay just like that so I can take a picture," Graham bites out.

Heather laughs against my mouth, but then she melts back into me when I grind my pussy against her hip.

The bed dips and then Graham is spooning up behind me, nipping my shoulder.

"All right, ladies, take a break. We all need water and a little carb kick," he attempts to interrupt, but I just kiss down Heather's jaw to her neck, where I begin sucking a bruise into her skin.

My head gets pulled back until I'm blinking into Heather's eyes.

"Enough," she tells me softly. "Sit up and drink some water."

I do as she says, and we all rehydrate and eat some pretzels. When I've come back to myself a little, Heather takes me into my bathroom and takes off both our faces, sitting me on the counter and wiping it away with remover and a washcloth. Then she totes me back to bed, where I promptly fall asleep feeling the safest I've ever felt in my life.

CHAPTER 29

GRAHAM

A month as an official yet private throuple passes. Heather ends up eating dinner with Pey's and my family nearly every night and no one blinks an eye. She also ends up sleeping over all of those nights. We find ourselves in different sleeping arrangements every time: sometimes I'm in the middle, sometimes Heather is in the middle, and sometimes Pey is in the middle. On the nights that Pey is in the middle, I fuck her from her slumber. When she wakes up, she finds Heather sleepily smiling at us and then adds her into the mix by making Heather come with her hand. All in all, everything is working out. Everyone is thoroughly sated, we're all together, and my heart is full. Except for the looming threat of Peyton leaving us.

And there's still the issue of us not being publicly out. When Heather resumes her traditional Friday blowies before I start, Peyton does not join her. It's one thing to arrive and depart school in the same car. Our peers are unimaginative creatures and completely settled in their heteronormativity; they could never conclude that we're all together. But Peyton coming into the locker room while Heather is giving me head probably would trip the trigger of at least some of the guys on the team, and that's still a landmine we're not ready to step on.

Friday night sees us at an away game, but Peyton is still up in the stands, bundled up in the cool winter air and splitting her attention between Heather and me according to who is doing the more exciting thing at the time. I watch her watching Heather between plays, and I feel her watching me whenever I throw a pass. I can't believe this is my life. Football and my two girls.

Except.

Except, except, except.

But every time it pops into my brain, I just fuck the pain away.

After the game, which is a win over Oakland we just eke out by the skin of our teeth,

we stay in the neighboring town of Murfreesboro in an effort to be out in public together but still maintain anonymity. We get a half-booth at Joanie's, a local haunt, and Heather and I sit on the same side just in case anyone else from our town stayed behind to grab a bite before heading home to Wickersville.

"Hi, I'm Ashlynn, and I'll be taking your order today. Can I start with a drink order for y'all?" The waitress introduces herself.

Heather takes the lead, saying, "He and I will both

have the sweet tea, but the lady will have the lavender lemonade."

Ashlynn nods and turns to Peyton. "Oh, you're gonna love it. We make the lavender syrup in-house." She makes a note on her order pad. "I'll let you look at the menu. We serve breakfast all day, so you'll be wanting to check out the made-to-order crêpes if you're a breakfast lover." She walks away, and I turn back to the table, noting Peyton's wide eyes.

"How'd you know what I wanted to drink, Heather?" Peyton asks softly, like she can barely get out what words that are important to her.

"Little freak. You're always saying you're 'trash for lavender.' Of course, that's what you'd want to drink." Heather says point-blank.

"What if I wasn't in the mood for it today?" Peyton says.

"Then you'd speak up. Obviously," Heather responds carelessly and starts perusing her menu.

Peyton is opening and closing her mouth as her eyes get glassier and glassier. Finally, she just brings her menu up to her face and hides behind it.

I smile behind my menu at how cute the two of them are and focus on what I want to eat.

"Look, pretty girl. There's a 'Swiss congeniality' patty melt. You love that movie," I say to Heather, running my hand up her leg, which is now covered in sweats after freezing all night in her cheerleading skirt.

"I saw, and I'm definitely getting that. The pun is too good to pass up," she responds and leans into my shoulder.

"'Swiss congeniality?' Like *Miss Congeniality*?" Peyton clarifies.

"Please don't say it's problematic. Gracie Lou Freebush is an icon," Heather groans out.

"Uh, no. It passes the Bechdel test on numerous

occasions. It's just old, Heather," Peyton informs her.

"Okay, but like, the early '00s were such a good time for chick-lit cinema. We've had a lack of movies like that since superhero movies came into vogue," Heather parries.

"Not wrong, but we have *Barbie*," Peyton reminds her.

"Correct, but I like the girlypop classics. Sue me," Heather tells her.

"How millennial of you," Peyton quips.

"Ew, stop, no, it is not. You like *Gone With the Wind*, and I don't call you a boomer!" Heather accuses.

"Okay, also passes the Bechdel test, and Scarlett is a total Blanche who serves cunt that whole goddamn movie!" Peyton cries.

"What's the Bechdel test?" I interrupt, and they both swing their gazes to me.

Then Peyton turns to Heather and narrows her eyes. "He's been yours for years, and you haven't trained him properly? What have you been doing? Just bullying me and fucking him? No time to get in any conversation?"

"Sometimes lessons slip through the cracks, little freak. This is one of them," Heather tells her.

"Ex-fucking-scuse me. I'm not a puppy. You don't have to train me," I glare at both of them in turn.

Heather grabs my chin and turns me toward her. She uses her other hand to run her fingers through my wind-tousled hair. "Aren't you, though?" She says in a low voice. "Aren't you my good boy?"

I swallow.

Because yes, yes, I am.

She continues. "You are my puppy. Mine to train and to protect. Mine to punish and reward."

"Yes, Ma'am," I agree in a husky voice.

Peyton giggles from her side of the table, and I look over to see her making a whipping motion at Heather.

I snap at her, and she sits up straight and looks down at the table.

"Sorry, Sir," she murmurs, and I bite my cheek so I don't laugh or smile. Looking over at Heather, I see her biting her lip, trying to accomplish the same.

The world is really missing out. Hierarchical power exchange is the most fun I've ever had in the bedroom. I Dom Pey, Heather Doms both of us. 10/10 recommend.

"Back to my," I cough, "training. What is the Bechdel test?"

"Oh. Right. It's a feminist measurement that asks three questions. One: does the media in question have at least two named women in it? Two: do those women have a conversation? Three: is the conversation about something other than a man? Most media fails. Because the bar is on the floor," Peyton explains.

"That's it?" I ask.

"Yep," Heather confirms.

"Slowly but surely, I'll make an unproblematic cishet white boy out of you," Peyton grins.

How are you going to do that when you're leaving us at the end of the summer? I think to myself, and I wish I could say it out loud. I'm so tired of keeping my frustration pent up inside of me. But Heather and I haven't even talked about this, and I'm doing my damnedest to not think about it. I also don't want to hear Peyton say that this is a fling, or that it's temporary, or anything else that would fill me with rejection and anguish.

But apparently, Heather does not feel the qualms I feel because she segues to, "I got my early decision back from UT, by the way."

"Heather…" I caution because I really don't want to have this conversation in public, in a foreign neighborhood, and before we've even gotten our food.

"Congratulations, Heather," Peyton pastes on a smile that I can easily recognize as fake at this point. I just don't know why it is.

Heather turns to me, "And you, baby boy?"

"Heather. I've had a spot on that team since Sophomore year, as you well know," I grit out.

"Great. So you're going to Rocky Top. I'm going to Rocky Top. Tell me again, Pey, where you applied?" Heather presses.

Peyton's eyes are wide and she's visibly panicking.

I sigh. "Heather, stop it," I say, trying to keep the peace. I'm trying desperately to hang on to this happiness, and Heather is determined to sabotage it before we've even run the course of things.

"No, Graham. I want to hear her say she didn't apply. I want to hear her say why. I want to know why she doesn't want to be with us the way we want to be with her," Heather raises her voice, and now I'm doubly glad we're not in Wickersville because people at the tables next to us start looking over in worry or amusement. And honestly, I cannot believe Heather alluded to a future between the three of us. This is the first time any of us have done such a thing to that degree.

The waitress takes that moment to bring our drinks and I tell her "thank you" while Peyton and Heather sit glaring at each other. I don't even think they hear her when she asks for our food order, so I just order on behalf of all three of us: the Swiss congeniality patty melt for Heather, the captain caprese crêpe for Pey, and the Nashville cluck'n hot sandwich for me.

"You're not going to say anything to me?" Heather demands, and I run a hand over my face.

"Heather, you know you shouldn't ask questions you don't want the answer to. Can you not?" I manage to get it out, sounding rational as I grab her nape and start massaging her taut neck.

But Peyton answers before Heather can back down. "Why won't I take a chance on Knoxville? I don't fucking know, Heather. Maybe it's because the two of you can't even take a real chance on me. Everything is behind closed doors. You've made it clear that your reputation is more important than building something with me. You can't come out as pan or poly. I know where I stand. I'm just some fun experiment in high school. Come college, y'all will go your way, and I'll go mine, and then you can have some other girl fill in and be your college tryst before you return to blissful heteronormative monogamy and pump out 2.5 children while Graham goes pro. You don't think I don't see exactly where this is going? I do. But I've just shut the fuck up about it because I can have you until we go to college. I'm not asking for more. So don't ask me for more, either." Her voice has raised progressively as she ranted, not stopping for a breath. At the end of her words, her face is purple, and her eyes are glassy again. She shoves up from her chair and stomps away to the bathroom, but not before I see two tears fall down her flushed cheeks.

I deflate into my seat and lay my head back on the wall.

"Fuck, Heather. Was that really necessary?" I groan.

"Yes, Graham. That really was necessary. I can't just pretend like you obviously can. Which isn't very like you, by the way. I kept waiting for you to broach the subject like you always do. I kept thinking oh, Graham will find a good way to bring this up. He's always pushing me to have the hard conversations. But you never did! And now, look. I've fucking made our girlfriend cry." She punctuates her words by slamming a hand onto the table, and the liquid in our glasses sloshes with the force of it.

"Of course, I'm not going to bring it up!" I yell and

then realize I'm causing a scene again. At this point, we're the show with dinner, so I try to lower my voice so only Heather can hear me.

"Why would she want to be with us when she could have, like, an intellectual? Someone who can analyze the plays she's in and the books she reads and take her to, like, salons or whatever smart people do?"

"Three things. One, do you even pay attention to what she reads, Graham? It's smut and pop culture. Two, I think we meet her where she's at just fine. And three, Graham Abraham: are you calling me a dumb jock?" She fake glares at me at the end of her words.

"Fuck. Pretty girl-" I start, but she cuts me off.

"I'm teasing you, but I'm also making a point. You don't think I'm worthless other than dancing, so I don't know why you think all that floats around in that head of yours are flags and downs," she tells me.

"Okay, but you're wrong about one thing. This woman reads Tolstoy and Sartre for fun," I remind her.

"And she likes to do it when she's curled up in bed with us. We don't have to have everything in common with her, Graham," she admonishes me.

"I think I'm supposed to have something in common with my girlfriend other than our kinks," I complain.

"And you do. Your values are the same. That's something." She pushes my hair off my forehead soothingly as she says it.

"Apparently, she disagrees. What gave her the idea that we want to have kids?" I pull her hand off my hair and kiss her palm.

Heather shivers. "I don't really know. I thought we were over seeing each other as the stereotypes, but here you are doing it to her, so I guess it's valid she's doing it back to us."

"Heather… I'm in love with her. I don't know how to lose her. And I don't know how to do this. I don't even remember falling in love with you; it was so long ago. One day we met, and then the next, I was convinced you would be my wife. I've never wavered on that. And you never even questioned it. It was as acceptable to you as it was to me. I don't know if I can handle Pey's rejection," I explain.

Heather nods. "Come here." She tucks herself into my side, taking the arm that she tucks under and putting it around her. Then she takes that hand and places it on her tit.

"Heather, I can't just play with your tits in public," I tell her.

"Oh, we've already made a scene. I don't think we're shocking these people now," she shrugs, and her shoulder brushes my chin. "I'm glad you finally told me. Like it was some big fucking secret. You know I knew. And you know I knew that you knew that I knew."

"Stop saying knew. It's starting to sound weird," I complain. "And I know you're in love with her too."

"Duh. That was obvious when I didn't want to murder her in cold blood when I found out she was the one you were fucking," she says succinctly.

"You were fucking her, too," I remind her.

"What does that have to do with the price of tea in China? If it had been anyone else, I would have raged. I don't know where she gets off thinking she's replaceable. I can't see myself ever sharing you with someone else." She turns her head and kisses my throat.

"It just works with us," I agree.

"It just works with us," she parrots.

"Heather… I'm ready to be out about it," I say hesitatingly.

"I know you are. I don't think I knew how important it

is to her," she sighs.

"You're more perceptive than I am. I think you mean you weren't ready to admit to yourself how important it is to her," I say delicately.

"Same, same," she huffs.

"You know it's not," I laugh.

"Okay, fine. You're right. Ugh, what am I going to do?" She moans.

"Seems like you're going to come out. That's what," I grin.

"Yeah, laugh it up, straight boy. This is way easier on you," she accuses.

"Um. I'm dating my stepsister. That's a landmine all on its own," I parry.

"Right. You forget how intimately acquainted I've gotten with Peyton's mother. Regina thinks you walk on fucking water," Heather reminds me.

"Until I tell her I've deflowered her sweet baby girl. I think all bets are off at that point. Then I'm just some entitled white boy who is a threat," I reply.

"You are just some entitled white boy." She pokes me in the side.

"Then you're just some entitled white girl," I counter.

"Ah, ah, ah. I'm a minority now. I'm a queer woman." She puffs up her chest.

"A spoiled and entitled and white queer woman," I nudge her.

"Anyway. I've upset her enough, and now she's given me things to think about. You should sit with her when she comes back. Try to coax her back into not hating me." Heather scoots away from my embrace and then gives me a little push.

"Yes, Ma'am. I'll go grab her at the bathroom and try to sweeten her up," I inform her, scooting out of the booth.

CHAPTER 30

PEYTON

When I don't think I can stay longer in the bathroom, I sigh and take one final look in the mirror. I've blotted my face, but I'm puffy and so red my dark complexion isn't covering it up. I guess it's fruitless, anyway. I'm pretty sure they saw me crying. And even if they didn't see me crying, I've spent a while in this bathroom after I was visibly upset. 2+2=4 and all that.

Opening the bathroom door, my eyes immediately meet Graham's, and I can tell I'm about to experience peak golden boy charm from him.

I cross my arms and glare at him. "I needed a fucking escort back to the table?"

He smiles that patented Graham smile that's so sweet

it puts molasses to shame. "Absolutely you do, little sister. Come here, and let me hug you first."

I want to resist, but I also want to sink into this easy familiarity where everything is happy and safe, so I go to him and let him fold me into his arms. I don't make it too easy on him, though. I just stand there with my arms down by my sides woodenly and let him work to soften me up.

"Don't be like that. She's sorry she pushed. I'm sorry I let her. We're both sorry. You are important to us, and you're certainly not replaceable," he tells me.

It's everything I want to hear. Almost. But I finally move my arms and put them around his waist. He holds me for a moment, and we stay locked together in a contented embrace.

I feel him pull back, and I panic. I don't know if I can go back to that table with Heather right now. But maybe if I have a little more comfort.

"Sir?" I mewl.

I see his mouth twitch in pleasure before he answers, "Yes, fucktoy?"

"May I have a kiss?" I say sweetly.

"Always," he smiles at me before his mouth comes down on mine.

It's exactly what I'm craving at this moment. His tongue coaxes mine, drawing me into a sweet and soft kiss of comfort. His whole body is loose and easy, from the way he's making love to my mouth to the way he's got his arms wrapped around me. For once, his body language isn't possessive. He's treading lightly, carefully opening me up to him, making me submit to him slowly and bit by bit. I've had this kiss before. It's his apology kiss. All at once, it feels familiar and like home, but also like I'm on the precipice of something new. Like if I want to change something, this is the time to let him know how I feel. So

I wait for him to finish kissing me. I enjoy his mouth on mine, and then when he pulls away, I draw my line in the sand.

"I meant what I said. I can't do this in the dark anymore," I tell him.

"We both heard you. I'm ready. She needs more time. She's fucking a woman. I'm just fucking my sister," he explains.

I hit his chest with the back of my hand. "Graham, I'm not your actual sister. What if someone heard you?"

"Then I guess they'd think we were pretty kinky," he winks.

I bury my head in my hands and laugh. "Stop trying to win me over. I'm upset."

"I will never stop trying to win you over," he grins, and I wish that he meant that word: never. "But I know you're upset. I'm not trying to diminish that."

"Do you think she will ever be ready?" I ask hopefully.

"Yeah, little sister. I think she will." He calms me by leaning down and pressing a kiss on my forehead.

I nod under his lips, but I'm not convinced. I'm just a stepping stone for these two. I can't plan for a future that includes them both. It's just like Graham said. One day, sooner than I think, I'll be at Christmas dinner staring at Graham and Heather as husband and wife across the table from me, and my best-case scenario is that I'll have a partner at my side so that I'm not completely pathetic.

We eat dinner and drive home, and the interactions consist of Graham doing all the talking and being overly charming, Heather saying nothing but looking at me longingly, and me pouting while trying to think of how I'm going to say no to sex tonight.

When we make it up to Graham and my rooms, I make to turn into mine but they start going into his.

I pause and throw myself in front of Graham's door to block it.

Heather raises an eyebrow. "We're not allowed to go to bed?"

"Not if you're not going to bed with me," I retort.

They glance at each other and then back at me.

"We thought it might be better if you had some space from us, little sister," Graham says softly.

"Is that what you think I want, or is that what you want?" I demand to know.

"Definitely not what we want. Right, pretty girl?" Graham leans forward and nuzzles into Heather's neck.

"No, little freak. It's not what we want," Heather says in a low and cautious voice.

"Then," I make an upright circle with my finger to illustrate that I want them to make a 180 and go back toward my room.

They wordlessly turn and shuffle into my room. I follow and watch them soundlessly take off their clothes and fold them into piles, placing them on the hope chest at the foot of my bed. As I make to do the same, they head into the bathroom to brush their teeth. I'm moving slowly, confusedly, so they finish brushing just as soon as I move to join them. When I come back into the bedroom after brushing, I see they've climbed into bed, Graham at center, and curled into a two-person comma.

"What is even happening?" I shriek.

They both open their eyes and look at me in confusion.

"We're going to bed," Heather says, and the duh is implied.

"Okay, but like… without sex?" I shriek again.

Graham sits up, opens his legs, and pats the space between them, encouraging me to sit. I crawl onto the bed and sit between his legs, my back to his front. He grasps my hips and pulls me closer so that our bare skin is flush from my ass to my neck. Then he leans down to my ear closest to Heather and breathes into my ear.

"There is not one single moment that I don't want you panting and whimpering under me, taking my cock in one of your sinful fucking holes. But I also heard the subtext of what you said today. It seemed like you needed to be reassured that you're not a convenient fuck for both of us. And you're not. We can spend the night in a bed together and not have it centered around sex, Peyton. That doesn't mean I don't crave you. You feel me getting hard right now, don't you? You're pressed up against me, and I want to rut into you, I want to claim you, I want to make you beg. But not at the expense of your feelings," he says with heat.

I squirm at his words.

"I want to fuck," I decide.

"Mmm. All right. Pretty girl? What do you think?" Graham asks Heather.

"Oh. I co-sign on everything Graham said," Heather agrees as she leans forward to take the closest of my nipples into her mouth.

While she laps at me, Graham gathers my curls up in a hand and tilts my head to the side, exposing my neck for him to bite down on, and my pussy floods.

"Sir... Ma'am..." I moan out, and both of them hum in pleasure. "Stop," I try to say, but it comes out as a moan.

"Stop isn't your safeword," Graham growls as he leaves open-mouthed kisses on my shoulder.

"I want you in my ass, Graham, while Heather fucks me in my pussy," I manage to moan out, and they finally stop what they're doing.

"You're sure? You haven't done anal yet," Graham hedges.

"Yes. I'm sure. I want it. Please," I whine.

"I'm not telling you no, fucktoy. I'd be hard-pressed to ever tell you no. I just want to make sure," he says, continuing. "I've fucked Heather anally before, but we're going to go slow, and you have to communicate with me while we do it, okay?"

I nod at him.

"Heather, you'll be on the bottom. I need you to pay attention to that clit so she's nice and relaxed," he instructs and leaves the bed so that we can get into position.

I stand up next to him and wait for Heather to get a purple strapless strap-on and lie in the middle of the bed.

She raises an eyebrow at me. "You're going to put it in for me, little freak," she demands, and I bite my lip to hide my smile.

I crawl over her, watching her watch me as I move. Her pupils expand into blackness as she moves her gaze from my lips to my tits, and I feel myself getting wetter at her response to me.

She thrusts her fingers into my hair and uses it as an anchor as she pushes me down to her slit. "You can apologize for dinner with your mouth on me," she tells me.

"Apologize to you?" I burst out but offer no resistance as I move down her body.

"Be a good girl, little freak," she says warningly.

I huff but drink her in as I settle between her legs. Her pink pussy is bracketed by her tan skin, and as I spread her lips apart, I can see she's glistening. Still a little salty about her implying that dinner was my fault, I lean in and blow against her clit before turning and sinking my teeth into her thigh. She yelps and tries to pull me off her by my hair, but I dig in harder. When I feel a coppery tang against my lips, I pull back and start to admire the blooming bruise but my gazing is cut short by a yank of my hair. I look up at her, blood pooling in the corners of my mouth, and she's glaring down at me. The grip on my hair tightens, and then she's leaning down to administer a smack across my cheek.

"If you're going to be a brat, this night is going to go a lot differently," she says harshly.

I swear I can feel each finger's impression on my face. It burns so sweetly.

I just stare at her blankly. I kind of want to be a brat, but I also really want double penetration, and I don't think they'll do something that takes so much care and sweetness if I need to be punished.

"Yes, Ma'am," I mutter, and I feel my hair being pulled at its roots.

"Try again," she growls.

"Yes, Ma'am," I say louder and cast my eyes downward so she can't read the mirth in them to be good.

"Better," she begins. "Continue." And then my head is being pushed back down, so I'm smothered in her pussy.

I wrap my hands around her muscular thighs, resisting the urge to press my thumb into the fresh bite and incur further wrath. I sigh internally, thinking that I simply do not get enough credit for not being as big of a brat as I really could be.

I lick a slow path from the bottom of her hole to her clit, and I feel her relax around me. The muscles in her thighs loosen, and the hand that's holding my curls goes slack. I continue to lick at her, making circles over and around her clit. She moans under me, and I briefly wonder what Graham is doing.

I pull up and look over at him. He smiles lasciviously at me and strokes a hand over his hard cock.

"Keep going, fucktoy. You two look so hot. Heather is

almost ready," he coaxes me.

I lean back down and lick at Heather's abdominal crevices. Her stomach contracts under me as my tongue traces paths over her skin. I push two fingers into her wet cunt and feel her immediately contract around my fingers, telling me she's close to coming. My fingers crook to find the ribbing of her G-spot as I move my mouth back to her clit. I lick her, applying pressure as my fingers dig into that ribbed ledge of her, and I press down with the tips of my fingers.

"Fuuuuuuuck," she yells out as I feel her cum gush around my hand.

Peppering kisses over her thigh, I reach for the toy. I pull out of her pussy and wipe her cum all over the toy. Then I slide it into her cunt, making her sigh.

"Turn it on. Then you can grind against it while you're on top of me, and it'll help get you prepped," she tells me, and I do as she's instructed.

After I've turned the toy on and she's writhing under me beautifully, I crawl on top of her. I run the toy down my slit, getting the toy wet, and then I position it so it's vibrating underneath my clit. I settle on top of Heather, our tits pressed together, peaked nipples dragging across the others. I lean down to kiss her, and she raises up on her elbows to meet me there. Grinding down harder on the toy between us, I attack her mouth. She meets my tongue thrust for thrust as her hands run down my back and over my ass, finding their destination's end as they wrap around my thighs as though to pull me closer.

I feel Graham's form dip the mattress as he comes up behind me. He massages my ass, and then I feel his thumbs pull me apart. The ring of my asshole is circled, and it makes me squirm on top of Heather. A pause, and then his wet and eager mouth is on my hole, and my brain short-circuits. I've stopped kissing Heather, and I'm just panting into her mouth.

She pulls back and grins. "Oh, she definitely likes that. What a good boy you are, baby," she croons to him, and I feel the vibration of his moan. "Do you like that, little freak? You like your ass eaten?"

I moan in response.

"Mmm. You're going to love it when you're so full of both of us. Ass and cunt, just so full." She continues in a growl, "You belong to us, little freak."

I hear the click of a lube bottle and then shiver as the cold liquid dribbles onto my skin.

"Okay, little sister. Just breathe. I'm going to start with a finger," Graham informs me, and then I feel a slippery finger enter me.

It feels foreign but in an exciting and thrilling way.

"More," I tell him.

He laughs, and then I feel the stretch of a second finger slip in.

"How's that?" He asks.

"Mmm. I felt a burn that time, and it feels like I want to push you out," I tell him.

"Go with that. It'll help adjust if your sphincter is contracting, and you'll definitely want to bear down when it's my cock that's pushing inside you," he says gently.

"More?" I ask, and he laughs.

"Not yet. I'm going to play with you a little. Get you to open up a little before I do another finger and then my cock," he tells me.

"You're doing so well, little freak," Heather praises me, and I lean down to kiss her again.

Our mouths move in the most delightful dance as Graham scissors his fingers inside of me.

After a while, Graham speaks again, "All right. Now we

try a third finger."

I pull away from Heather. "No, I want your cock. I want it to burn a little," I tell him.

"My little masochist," he laughs.

"Hold my hands?" I ask Heather.

She raises her hands from my thighs to cradle my face with both her hands. "Of course, little freak." Then she kisses my forehead and lays her hands on either side of her face.

I take them in mine and hear the click of the lube bottle again. Then I feel Graham's cock positioned at my back entrance as he braces one of his hands on my shoulder.

"Fuck, fuck, fuck, fuck," I chant as I feel him work into me. He's so big, and it burns, and it feels so wrong, and what am I even doing?

"Bear down, little sister," he reminds me, so I push against the force of him, and the burn eases a little as he pushes more of his thick cock into my ass.

A tear runs down my cheek, and Heather leans up to kiss it away.

"Use your safeword if you need to," she reminds me.

And I think about doing that, but I know how good this is supposed to feel if I just push past the initial wrongness of the whole thing. So I shake my head.

"I'm all the way in, so I'm going to give you a second before I start moving," Graham tells me.

My ass is full of cock, and the toy that's in Heather's cunt is still vibrating against my clit. I breathe from my diaphragm and begin to feel my anxiety dissipate. I flex my muscles around Graham's cock, testing out how he feels inside of me. The sensations are new, and now that my ass is fully stretched around him, it doesn't necessarily feel bad.

"Mmm," he groans. "You keep clenching around

my cock, fucktoy. Do I feel good inside you? You feel so fucking good."

"I... I think I'm ready for you to move," I tell him.

One of his hands is still on my shoulder, but the other comes to my hip and massages me. I close my eyes as he starts to slide out of me. His movements are slow and gentle as he finishes pulling out and as he pushes back into me. I sink into the motion, my pussy starting to tingle as I relax into the rhythm. Where before it felt wrong in a bad way, now it feels wrong in the most delicious of ways. I let a moan loose.

"You ready for Heather?" Graham asks.

"I'll check and make sure she's wet enough, or it's going to feel like a bad pinch if I go in before she is," Heather says. "Lean up for me, little freak."

I move to sitting on her, putting my back against Graham's front. He wraps a hand around my throat and grabs one of my tits with the other. Heather leans up and thrusts two fingers inside of me.

"Oh, I think she's fine," she declares, pulling two glistening fingers out of my cunt. "Come here, little freak. This is at your speed. Sink down on my cock whenever you're ready."

She's holding the purple vibrator erect, ready for me, and I position myself at the tip of it.

Graham kisses my temple. "You can do it, fucktoy. Be a good girl for us and take us both."

I push against the vibrator and start to take it in. And I really regret that I'm the one in control of how much of Heather's cock I'm taking in.

"I- I- it's too much!" I cry out.

Then Graham is pushing me down onto her, and I'm suddenly so full. Two of my three holes are filled, and it is incredibly overwhelming. I love being filled, but this is a whole different echelon of filled.

"Fuck!" I yell.

Heather laughs. "Good boy, Graham. She was gonna pussy out."

I glare at her, but she thrusts up into me, and I moan at the movement and the feeling of our pussy lips touching as she bottoms out into me. Then Graham starts moving inside of me at the same time and…

I feel like I'm being turned inside out.

"Bite my shoulder if you need to," Heather comforts me, and I do. I sink my teeth straight into her meaty shoulder, and she yelps but doesn't push me away, just squeezes my hands tighter.

I squirm around on top of Heather as they bring me closer to orgasm. I'm so glad I pushed through my initial discomfort to get to this point. This feeling is transcendent. I feel the most complete I've ever felt in my entire life. And I don't think it's just how well I'm getting fucked, even though that's sublime. I think it's just… the two of them.

Taking a minute to gaze at her, I watch Heather: eyes closed, mouth slack, blonde hair spread across the pillow, our contrasting hands clasped together. I'm glad she's not looking at me now, on the precipice of her orgasm.

I look back at Graham, who is also watching Heather, but then catches me looking and grins at me, leaning forward to pull me into a kiss.

When he pulls away, my face is wet with tears.

He frowns at me. "What color, Peyton?"

"Green," I sob. And I'm not lying. I am green. But I've made a critical error. I can't escape from myself anymore. I've realized, being sandwiched between Graham and Heather, that I love them both. My heart beats for them both in equal but differing ways. Do they understand how we are three parts of one whole?

Graham smacks my ass and brings me back to the scene. I turn back to Heather, and she's grinning up at me, golden and luminous from multiple O's.

She pulls one of her hands away from my grasp, pops a finger in her mouth, and then slides it between our bodies to rub my clit.

I gasp.

"There she is. You don't look nearly wrecked enough, little freak," she tells me.

She grabs my throat and pulls me into her so she can kiss me while she rubs my clit, and I go off like a bomb.

"Ugh, pretty girl, I wish you could feel how she clenches when she goes off," Graham tells Heather as he continues to pump into me.

"I feel her cum dripping down onto my cunt," Heather confirms.

"Fuuuuuuck," Graham groans as I feel him fill my ass with his cum.

He finishes coming inside of me and then slaps my ass as the conclusion. I whimper and pull off Heather, collapsing beside her on the bed.

Heather groans as she pulls the double-sided vibrator out of her body and curls up behind me, tucking a leg between my legs. She nuzzles into my neck and growls.

"You were such a good girl for us, little freak," she tells me.

Hearing her tell me I'm good never gets old. It's the praise I crave during and after a session, and makes me feel validated for giving my trust to her. But all I can think of is... how good of a girl? A good enough girl for her to really and truly commit to me?

CHAPTER 31

HEATHER

It's a Sunday afternoon after I've been forced against my will to attend church with my family as usual. I walk through the Huntington household's front door to hear a loud argument coming from somewhere in the house. I sigh when I recognize the voices that are engaged in verbal combat. I hear Peyton's high and soft voice and Graham's low baritone, and I wince.

I pass Willow carrying laundry through the entryway and grab her attention.

"Willow, how long have they been going at this?" I ask of her.

"At least thirty minutes that I know of. One of them will get frustrated and walk away, but that just ensures they find a new room to argue in. I can only imagine it's been longer than that, and they started upstairs in one of their rooms," Willow responds and continues on her path. "Good luck with all of that."

I gather my hair up in a ponytail and secure it with a hair tie from my wrist. I don't know how that's going to help me in the next few minutes, but I do feel better donning some armor.

Following the voices into the living room, I find Peyton squared off against Graham. She's only in black leggings and a purple bra, and he's only in grey sweats. I can only imagine they forgot the rest of their clothing as this argument gained steam, and now being fully clothed in the living room around their parents and their housekeeper is the last thing on their minds.

"You fucking prick!" She's yelling at him when I enter.

"And you're a pretentious cunt!" He yells back.

Neither of them has noticed my entrance, and I sit down on the couch to watch them. They're in front of the massive television, so it's like I'm watching a film unfold. Except the film has characters in it that I'm actually invested in, and I'm worried about the real-life ramifications of whatever this argument is.

They're panting at each other, and I raise an eyebrow, thinking they're about to turn one form of passion into another despite being in a position where their parents can come into the room at any time, but then Peyton turns away abruptly. Graham grabs her elbow and jerks her back around.

"I'm tired of you running from me. Stop being a coward and just admit that you're wrong," Graham growls.

"Me? Wrong? Never!" She exclaims and punctuates it by rearing her head back and spitting on his face.

"Peyton..." he warns her.

"Stop calling me Peyton!" She yells. "I want to be fucktoy

or little sister. I hate it when you call me Peyton."

"You want me to call you that when anyone can walk in?" He grits out and looks around. His gaze finally falls on me. "Pretty girl? How long have you been here?"

"Long enough to know you've both lost your marbles. What in the fuck is even going on?" I ask, darting a look between the two of them.

They both scuffle for a moment, Peyton trying to pull her elbow from Graham's grip. She slaps his arm with her unencumbered arm, and he grabs her by the throat.

Having had enough, I bring two fingers to my lips and whistle. They both jolt and, as I hoped, pull apart.

"You," I point to Peyton. "Tell me what happened. And you," I point to Graham. "Shut the fuck up until it's your turn."

Graham crosses his arms and pouts, but Peyton smirks smugly and preens.

"Graham took my new notebook," Peyton tells me. "And when I found it on his desk, he told me I was fucking insane!"

Graham opens his mouth as though to disagree, but I hold up a finger to pause his words.

I think through what she said, then wave him on to plead his case.

"She came in half-cocked and slapped me across the face before I even had a chance to tell her that it's my fucking notebook!" He argues.

"And I should slap you again, you piece of shit! I can't-" Peyton begins and raises a hand.

"Enough," I bite out.

I watch them at a standoff. Things have been at a boiling point since our argument in the diner a month ago, but we've all been ignoring reality. I thought we had more time, but I suspect the real reason Peyton and Graham are at each other's throats is that we're all unsure of where we stand. And I feel like that's mostly my fault. I haven't been able to come out, so we haven't been able to come out, which means we're all still operating in the dark. Fuck.

"Do you two think that maybe this is about more than a notebook?" I ask them.

They look at each other and then look away.

"Right. That's what I thought. Why don't we put everything on the table, shall we?" I say archly.

Peyton folds first. "It's been months that we've been together, and I feel like we're getting nowhere. I still feel like a dirty little secret."

Graham runs a hand down his face. "What's the point? You're just going to leave us when you pick some college that's far away from us," he says heatedly.

"You know, you don't fucking own me, Graham Huntington," Peyton cries out.

"Of course I fucking do. You are mine, Peyton," Graham growls.

I hear a throat clear behind me, and we all turn to see Ashton's bespectacled face standing on the living room threshold, Regina hovering behind him. "I really hope that's not true since I just sent a check for Peyton to UT for the computer engineering program."

I turn back to Peyton and gape at her, seeing Graham echoing me.

She tucks her arms behind her back, and I can see her blush from here. "Ashton, I didn't really want them to know that I was going to school with them."

I turn back to him and watch as he adjusts his glasses.

"Well, I feel like this argument might end if Graham knows you're going to be with them. And I'm really tired of this racket," Ashton explains.

"You- you know that we're together?" Peyton stutters.

"Baby girl, we're a different generation than you are, but we aren't stupid," Regina huffs.

Graham's mouth drops open. "And… you don't care that we're stepsiblings?"

"Graham! Why are you pressing your luck right now?" I admonish him.

"It's all right, Heather. It's not ideal, but it's not like you're blood relations. Just know if you break up, we are absolutely not taking sides," Regina goes on. "And if you knock Peyton up, there will be hell to pay."

"Omg, Mama, I don't even want kids. And I got the IUD, remember?" Peyton reminds her mother.

"Yes, I recall. Which, speaking of Graham, I have a bone to pick with you," Regina tries to step into the room, and I wince, readying myself for another argument.

"You know what, Reggie, why don't we leave the kids to sort out their issues alone?" Ashton guides her by the elbow out of the room. "I think our work here is done."

They walk out of the room, and I hear, "Can I at least talk about how he Doms her at the dinner table?" from Regina, but I don't hear Ashton's response. Bless it, I'm glad we were saved from that conversation.

"I guess those two knew a lot more than they let on," I say hesitatingly.

"Little sister, why would you not tell us? That you had applied? That you had gotten in? That you had decided you would go?" Graham demands.

"Why would I when you weren't even fully bought in?" She counters.

"Fuck, Peyton. I am fully bought in! I am in this! I want you for the rest of my God damn life!" Graham shouts.

Peyton blanches. "What?"

"You are forever for me. Just like Heather. I want you both. Goddammit, Peyton. How do you not know that

I'm in love with you? How do you not know that this is where we've been headed ever since I threw you in that dumpster on your first day of school? You and Heather are everything to me. Fuck, I know I'm not enough for you, but I want to be. I want to be the man who supports you as you get your degree, as you convince Dad that you deserve to be his protégé, as you take over the company." He walks over to her and drops to his knees in front of her. "I want to have a house full of you and Heather, and cats, or fish, or ferrets, or whatever the two of you want to take care of while I'm playing away games. I want the opportunity to love you until we go gray and wrinkly, and I have to take some fucking medication to get it up to be of use to the two of you so you don't fuck without me. Peyton, I want you to be my fucking wife. You're not a dirty fucking secret. I'd give up my entire future in the NFL if it meant having both of you. Did you hear me? I'll say it again." He takes her limp hand. "Peyton DeVal Stratford, I love you. You and Heather are it for me. From now until forever."

Her eyes are wide as she stares at him.

"You... love me?" She breathes wondrously.

"I love you," he confirms. "I'll say it as often as you want."

"I love you, too, Graham," Peyton says with a wobbly smile. Two tears track down her face, and I see her grip around his hand tighten.

"Say it again," he grits out.

She gets down on her knees so she's more at his level, placing a hand on his cheek. Her thumb brushes over his lips delicately.

"Graham Abraham Huntington, I love you. But maybe we can wait on the proposal until, like, maybe our frontal lobes are fully developed?" She laughs tearfully.

"We're going to be together forever regardless. So we

can do this on y'all's timetable, little sister," he grins at her.

Then he's kissing her, palming her ass with both hands, pressing both of their bodies together as they kneel on the living room floor. They finally stop and pull back.

Graham turns to me and clears his throat. Peyton looks down and away.

"Oh, for fuck's sake. Come here, little freak," I tell her as I pat my lap, beckoning her to sit on my lap.

She stands up to walk over to me, and I bite my tongue because I want to tell her to crawl, but this is absolutely not the time for such things.

She straddles me and sits down on my legs. Running my hands over her thighs, I take a minute to bask in the weight of her body on mine.

"Today I came out to my parents," I begin.

Her mouth drops open.

"And it went exactly like how I thought it would. They threatened to cut me off, and I laughed in their faces. When they saw how little I cared about their money, they backpedaled and tried to convince me that I should marry Graham." I look over to Graham. "Apparently, they think you'll somehow pull me back to the straight and narrow. I explained that we're in a relationship with Peyton, but they assured me that I was just going through a phase and that when I had gotten through college and wanted to become a good wife to you, we'd dispense with all the 'foolishness...'" I make air quotes with my fingers when I say this last.

Peyton starts to wiggle away, but I put my hands around her back and push her to stay on my lap.

"...Which is never going to happen, little freak. I agree with Graham. I think I knew that day when you ran into me in the hallway, and it scared me. Love at first sight, and it was another woman? Unthinkable." I pause to laugh, then I thread my fingers in her hair and pull her head back so that she's looking up into my eyes. "Then you were such a goddamned brat. I didn't know what else to do with my immediate obsession other than bully you and-"

"I love you, too!" She bursts and kisses me.

I lick into her mouth slowly and teasingly until I've worked her into a squirming mess.

"Great. Now we can dispense with all the cheesy bullshit," I say and nip her ear.

"I like the cheesy bullshit." She blinks up at me so innocently.

"Yeah, yeah, yeah. We love you. Blah, blah, blah. We want to be with you forever. Blah, blah, blah. We don't need to talk it to death," I tell her.

"So you won't tell me you love me whenever I want?" She bites her lip.

"Ugh. Yes, of course, I'm going to tell you as much as you want. You're a needy little bitch, and I've accepted that," I grin at her.

"Mmm. Tell me again. Tell me like Graham," she begs.

"Like Graham?" I raise an eyebrow.

"You know… middle name me and call me your wife," she says entreatingly.

I flick my eyes to Graham. "You're such a bad fucking influence," I tell him, and he laughs. Then I turn back to Peyton and stare at her in those beautiful brown eyes. "You are the love of my life, Peyton DeVal Stafford. You are my wife in all the ways that matter, and one day it will be official legally."

"If you hate romance so much, why are you so good at it, Heather?" she sing-songs to me.

I roll my eyes. "What if every time you tell me you love me, I give you a spank? Hmm? Does that sound like I like romance to you?"

"It does if you know I love to be spanked. So..." she pauses, and I ready myself. "I love you, I love you, I love you, I love you!" She throws her hands up in the air with a flourish.

Graham laughs from behind her, and I point at him. "You're next, baby boy. You just encourage this ridiculous behavior from her."

"I want to hear how you love me too," he grins mischievously.

"You two are the fucking worst." I stand, pick Peyton up under her ass and carry her over to Graham, who is still on the floor. I get to my knees in front of him, so he's the back of a Peyton sandwich. "I love you," I tell him and then kiss his nose. "And I love you," I direct at Peyton and kiss her nose. "I love you both very, very much. Now stop torturing me."

Graham puts his arms around both of us and nuzzles into my neck. "I love you, too, pretty girl."

EPILOGUE 1

9 MONTHS LATER
SEPTEMBER

HEATHER

Graham walks into our dorm room carrying the last of Peyton's and my boxes, dropping them in a huff at the foot of our extra-long twin beds, which I have pushed together in the center of the room.

"Anything else you want me to do, my queen?" He asks sarcastically.

I untangle myself from Peyton's napping body. She got too excited about today being move-in day and stayed up late reading *The Woman In Me*. When I asked her what she was doing reading about an aging pop star, she gasped and told me Britney was an icon and also that Regina raised her on Britney's music. Her taste in memoirs aside, she was beat after we checked in, and I put the sheets on the bed. She immediately collapsed onto the fresh linens. Not one to miss an opportunity to snuggle her, I tucked in next to her.

I look over at Graham with a raised eyebrow. "You want to try that again? You literally volunteered so you could feel like a big man. It's not like I can't lift this shit myself."

"I know. But then I carried all y'all's boxes for you while y'all cat-napped and looked so cute together. I still have to take my boxes to my room. Which I have to share with Adrian while you two get to be roommates," he complains.

"We've been over this, Graham. You got to live with her, and now it's my turn. You know we can't move off-campus until our Sophomore year. Then we'll all move in together. And it's not like we won't have sleepovers with you or one-on-one dates like we've been doing the entire year we've been together. You'll see us both plenty, baby boy." I reassure him.

"I know, I know. I just hate it. Even though I do like that y'all have each other. She was so broken-hearted when she found out Sam was joining the military instead of coming with us to college." Graham frowns down at her. "I almost offered to pay for Sam's college expenses myself if it would mean she would be with us."

"You know how stubborn Sam is. She wouldn't have let you," I respond.

"True enough," says an effeminately male voice behind Graham, and then Adrian's blond head is peeking into the room.

"Man, you're already done?" Graham asks with exasperation.

"I mean, I only had my boxes and you had two sets of boxes, so I don't see how I wouldn't have finished at least at the same time as you. I know I'm not a big, strapping beefcake." Adrian flutters his eyelashes. "But I do keep in shape. You know. For my lovers."

"Adrian, stop hitting on me. I'm taken by your best fucking friend. You'd think you'd know I'm off the menu by now," Graham explains.

"Oh, honey. This is just paying my respects. I'd be a lot more tactile if I were hitting on you," Adrian croons.

"It's true," Peyton sleepily says, eyes still closed and body tucked into mine. "Gay men touch first, ask questions later. Their version of a hello is a palm to the crotch."

"If the dick twitches, then there's interest there!" Adrian squeals in agreement, coming over to lie on Peyton's other side and snuggling into her.

"Hello, love," Peyton mumbles and wiggles back into him.

"Hello, poppet," Adrian responds and settles in.

"Oh, come on! Now Adrian is taking my spot?" Graham exclaims.

"I'm just keeping it warm for you, honey pie," Adrian chortles.

"Maybe I'm ready for a break; maybe I need my spot right now," Graham prods.

"Ooh, sugar. Is your stamina really that low?" Adrian looks up at me, aghast. "No wonder you two need each other to stay satisfied. You know if you find a good man, he can go for hours? You can upgrade this model and not have to go muff-diving ever again."

Graham looks ruffled and starts to open his mouth.

Peyton elbows Adrian. "Stop picking on my lovers. Graham has great stamina, and I love fucking Heather. There are literally no complaints in our relationship, you little shit-stirrer. Leave the pot alone, this recipe is perfection."

"Ugh, fine, I'll stop... if Graham agrees to be my wingman at the club," Adrian says smugly.

"What's wrong with me being your wing-woman at the club?" Peyton asks in offense.

"I'll get more takers if people think we might be together. And also think of all the men that will hit on him- I'll break the news he's straight and taken and then swoop in to dry their heartbroken little tears. It's a perfect system," Adrian explains.

"Well, you can't argue with that. You should wingman for him, Graham," I co-sign.

Graham glares at me.

"We'll all go, so we can watch you get uncomfortable. Also, so we can fantasize about you being with a man." Peyton fans herself. "Wouldn't that be hot, Heather?"

"Actually, yeah. I bet you'd be a great bottom, baby boy," I agree.

"I would absolutely not be a bottom," Graham sputters.

"Sounds like something a bottom would say," Adrian sing-songs.

"You're a bottom for me; what's the difference?" I bite the inside of my cheek to hide my grin.

"Um, you don't use your cock on me when you top me, Heather," Graham points out.

I look over at Peyton, to see her eyes have opened. We make eye contact, and I wink at her. "Yet. I haven't fucked you with my cock, yet."

She giggles.

"Absolutely fucking not!" Graham exclaims. "This is an exit only." He points at his ass.

"You should try it, honey. You have that glorious thing called a prostate. You've never felt anything like it, I promise," Adrian assures him.

"Mmm. Thanks for the upvote, but I think we do plenty in bed without introducing pegging to the mix," Graham retorts.

Peyton grumbles.

"Don't worry, little freak. We have the rest of our lives to convince him to try it. We'll get there," I assure her.

"It would be so hot," she groans.

"I agree," I say and turn to look at Graham in the eyes. "Challenge accepted, baby boy. I'll have that ass. And speaking of, shouldn't your ass be working on those boxes?"

"I could do that, or I could crawl into this cuddle puddle," he grins.

"No, Graham, there's no room for four of us on these beds," I caution.

But he's crawling in behind me anyway. I smush myself closer to Peyton, which of course, I don't mind, and wrap my arms around her waist. My hand brushes over Adrian, and I roll my eyes. I've gotten used to Adrian since I've come out. Sam and Adrian are around so much that Graham and I have become close enough to call them friends of ours, so much so that even I'm sad that we will spend the next four years without Sam. Graham, Peyton, and I are our own little family, but Sam and Adrian are definitely extensions of our family.

After coming out, my friends were more concerned about which girl I was fucking than that I was fucking a girl, but suffice to say we're not as close now as before. Those were always superficial relationships, proximity friendships, and none of them are going to be UT cheerleaders or in my dance program, so it's not like we wouldn't have drifted away regardless. It still sucks sometimes, and I'm definitely not looking forward to telling my new peers that I have a boyfriend and a girlfriend. It's definitely not like when Graham told his football buddies he was fucking two women and got high-fives all around. I'm sure the same will happen here in college and in his business program. Sigh. Men.

Later that night, Peyton is sandwiched between the two of us. I could roll my eyes about Graham refusing to leave us for a night, but I was as guilty when it was the two of them living together, so I guess I have to shut the fuck up about it. We're all fast asleep. I wake up to the sound of a whimper, and I smile and roll to my side for a good view. Pulling back the blanket that's over the top of the three of us, I watch as Graham slides his thick cock into a sleeping Peyton.

Her eyes clench shut, and her mouth twists into a little "o." Graham turns and bites his pillow, groaning into it.

I slide my hand down to rub at my clit, lubricating my finger before I apply pressure. I buck against my hand as my eyes devour my two loves. Graham is staring hotly at me, gazing at me like this is a performance he's putting on for my express enjoyment.

I scoot closer to them, wedging one of my legs between theirs, and whisper to him, "Can you multitask? Can you finger me while you're fucking Pey?"

He throws his head back in a soft moan and weaves his hand through their legs to reach my center. His fingers plunge into me, and I stifle a gasp because he immediately puts three of his meaty digits inside me.

I tuck Peyton into my body, and I feel her mouth open on my shoulder in a sleepy attempt to kiss my skin. Then

I lean over her to Graham and pull him in for soft, sleepy kisses. I whimper into his mouth and grind against his hand.

Sometimes, when I'm less in my head, his kisses still make me dizzy with want. I get overwhelmed by how much I want him and how grateful I am to have him. Right now is one of those times. His fingers are working me into a frenzy as his mouth drives me absolutely wild, and it's enough to almost have me on my knees for him.

At that thought, I draw my nails down his back in deep marks. I feel his skin split as I claw down his back, and he pants into my mouth as a reaction.

"Pretty girl," he moans as I move my mouth from his mouth to his jaw, down to his neck, where I sink my teeth into his neck. "Fuck, fuck, fuck, fuck," he whisper chants.

"You're being so quiet. What a good boy," I praise him.

He whimpers. "I'm gonna come," he tells me.

"That's right, come in our girl, baby boy," I croon to him.

I give him my shoulder, and sure enough, he bites down hard to stifle his shout as he presumably floods Peyton with his cum. His hand pauses inside me briefly, but then he's plunging into me with gusto, using his palm to grind against my clit and making me bite my lip.

"Fuck, Heather. You're so fucking hot like this, pressing against Peyton and riding my hand," he praises me, and I let go, covering my mouth as I come all over his hand. "Mmm. Beautiful."

He leans in for another kiss, and I drowsily meet him.

"I love you," he breathes. "I can't wait to love you forever."

"I love you forever, too, baby," I smile over at him and then look down at Peyton, who is still peacefully sleeping between us. "I love her forever too."

He kisses her shoulder. "Of course. It's like a cheerleading pyramid. We're the base, and she's the flyer," he smiles back at me, and his emerald eyes twinkle.

I laugh. "Our relationship is a pyramid stunt?"

"Just trying to put it in terms you can understand," he teases me.

"Yes, because I couldn't understand it otherwise. Should I start talking to you only in football metaphors?" I prod him.

"Actually, yes, I'd love that," he nods.

"I'm not going to do that," I proclaim.

"Nope, too late, you promised." He grins at me.

"I did not 'promise.'" I make air quotes.

"That's what I heard. Too bad Peyton can't back me up. I bet she would," Graham posits.

"Will you two shut the fuck up and go back to bed? I can sleep through getting fucked but I can't sleep through an argument," Peyton complains.

"No one is arguing, little freak," I assure her, pushing her hair out of her face and looking down at her.

"I don't care what you call it. It's impeding the necessary sleep I need to be peppy for Calculus tomorrow morning," she grumbles.

"Sorry, little sister," Graham tells her and kisses her exposed forehead.

"Mmm," she groans as she snuggles closer into my neck.

Graham and I share a conspiratorial look and a peck on the lips and sink back down to our pillows. I fall asleep dreaming of Graham, Peyton, and I performing a cheer routine, meaning I fall asleep with a smile on my face.

EPILOGUE 2

GRAHAM

I'm sitting at Pey's and my parent's house, at dinner with Peyton, Heather, Regina, and my dad, my ladies and me on one side of the table, and the parents on the other. I'm sandwiched between my girls, and I've just poured everyone a glass of champagne.

Dad lifts his glass and begins, "This Easter, we're thankful for Graham being drafted into the NFL. We are so proud of you, Graham, and even happier that you got drafted to play for our hometown team, the Titans. Here's to you, son. May you turn us into a championship team!"

Everyone lifts their glasses, but I clear my throat.

"Heather is also celebrating her invitation to dance with the Nashville Ballet, and in a few short months, Peyton will come to work for you full-time, Dad. This isn't just my night."

"Of course, of course. How gracious of you," Dad agrees. "We're proud of all of you for graduating next month and embarking on the next chapter of your lives."

"We actually have more news to celebrate tonight," Heather says smoothly.

"Oh, fuck. Please tell me one of you hasn't gotten knocked up. You're too young for that. You have to build your careers first!" Regina cries out.

"Mama, stop. No one is knocked up. And also, no one is getting knocked up. We've been over this. We don't want children," Peyton tells her.

"Living that TINK life," Heather agrees and reaches across me to clink glasses with Peyton. Their glasses meet in front of me.

"What is TINK?" Regina asks in confusion.

"Three incomes, no kids," Peyton explains.

"You'll eventually want kids. I'll just bide my time," Regina huffs.

"You're really not talking me into this one, Mama," Peyton asserts.

"Okay, fine. If that's not the news, then what's the news?" Regina pivots.

"I actually am not sure what Heather is talking about." Peyton turns a quizzical eye to Heather, and I look over at her myself. My mouth twists into a knowing grin and I raise my eyebrow, waiting for her to spill the tea.

"Oh, just that I've booked a venue for the wedding next summer before Graham starts training," Heather says with a twist of her lips.

"The wedding? What wedding?" Peyton looks around

her as though she could find a sign in the corner of the room answering her questions.

"Our wedding," Heather answers.

"Our wedding?" Peyton asks hesitatingly.

"Yours and Graham's and mine," Heather explains nonchalantly.

"Excuse me? When did you propose? When did I agree?" Peyton blusters.

"I don't think you want those answers at this table in front of your parents," Heather deadpans.

"Then you probably shouldn't have sprung this on me at Easter dinner!" Peyton bursts.

"Little sister," I begin, and I hear Regina grumbling like she always does when I call Peyton that. "Stop acting like you don't want to marry us."

She huffs and crosses her arms. "Okay, but who is legally getting married?"

Heather and I look at each other and then back at Peyton.

"We thought you could marry Heather, but we would all take my name," I finally jump in.

"Oh, sure, make it patriarchal," Peyton grumbles.

"Well, since I'm pretty sure Dad wants you to inherit the company, we thought it might be nice if you had the same name as the company. Don't you think?" I coax her.

"Mmm. You have a solid point," Peyton agrees.

"Sometimes I do make some good arguments," I chuckle.

"Well, like, do I get a ring?" She bats her eyelashes at me.

"Oh, fuck," Heather says, and I laugh.

"Oh, pretty girl, I couldn't miss an excuse to go out and spend money on my girls," I explain as I reach into my inner suit pocket and retrieve the double ring box. "I was hoping to make this a more romantic moment," I pause and glare at Heather. "But if you want it now, needs must."

I set the Harry Winston box on the table and open the lid. Inside are two dazzling rings. One is an emerald cut couture engagement ring with marquise diamonds making a floral arrangement around the solitaire. The other is a pear-shaped couture engagement ring with pear-shaped diamonds forming a bow on either side of the solitaire. Both center diamonds are over 5 carats.

I sit back and wait for them to claim the ring that's theirs. Surely enough, they both squeal and choose the ring I had in mind for each of them when I picked them out.

Peyton reaches into the box first, palming the pear-shaped ring and sliding it onto her finger. I look away from her as she starts gazing at it in the light.

Heather goes for her emerald ring next and slides it onto her finger. Then she takes Peyton's hand and threads their ring hands together. I hear the tiniest little clink of diamond against diamond.

"Oh my God, it's official now? Ashton, did you know about this? Oh, my baby girl is getting married! A little unconventionally, but married!" Regina cries.

"I'm just learning about this right now, Reggie. But I can't say I'm surprised," Dad responds.

"Graham, they're beautiful," Peyton looks at me with tears in her eyes.

I shrug. "What are signing bonuses for, if not to give your wives trophies to show who owns them?"

"Watch it, baby boy," Heather warns. "If anyone is owning anyone, I own your ass. Remember that shit."

"Ashton, why do we even invite them to dinner? They just act like they're the only people in the room." I faintly hear Regina complain.

"Saves me from making conversation, I suppose," Ashton responds.

Peyton leans into my ear and whispers, "I still want to be formally collared, you know. But this is a good start."

"That would be a private moment just for us, fucktoy," I tell her and kiss her forehead.

She nods and beams at me.

I sit back and watch as the girls show Regina and Dad their rings. They're both effervescent, and I smile as I take in their joy. Peyton is easy to make visibly happy, but it takes a lot for Heather to let down her barriers and be as free with her smiles, and I'm exceptionally glad that I could get her there. She may be planning our wedding like it's her goddamn job, but I was so excited to pick out the rings. If there's one thing I know, it's my girls and how to please them.

Which is how I know this is the time to give them something they've been, frankly, begging for. The thought stresses me out, but I let their glow wash over me and ease my anxiety. We all have shades of masochism, but Heather would never hurt me for real.

Later that night, when we're tucked away in our downtown Nashville penthouse apartment and getting ready to crawl into our Texas King bed- listen, that year of two twins pressed together was the roughest of my spoiled little life- I'm still contemplating my choices when Peyton flops down on the bed and yawns.

"Did someone have too much wine?" I ask her, and she nods pathetically. "Well, I guess you can go to sleep and miss all the fun."

"'S fine. I have the rest of my life to fuck you both," she says as she flashes her ring hand at me.

"You might want to be awake for this, fucktoy," I tell her.

"I'm too tired, Graham. Can we just rain check?" Heather crawls in next to Peyton and nuzzles her neck.

"You're too tired to take my ass virginity?" I ask archly.

Immediately, they both perk up as though I have shot caffeine straight into their veins.

"Let me get my strap," Heather says hastily. "Little freak, you in?"

"You fucking him while he fucks me, right? I'm in 1000%. I could not be more in. I'm the most awake of my entire fucking life right now," Peyton confirms as Heather goes to the toy chest.

Peyton gets on her hands and knees and crawls across the bed, her naked and thick body getting me hard as she bites her lip seductively. "I'm wet just thinking about Heather's cock in your ass," she tells me.

"Show me, little sister," I say as I stroke my cock leisurely.

"Mmm, I don't know. What if I'm shy?" She brats, sitting on her haunches and pressing her legs together.

I walk over to her and palm her throat, squeezing the sides. "Let me see that cunt, fucktoy," I demand.

She swallows around my hand. "Make me," she purrs.

My hand cracks across her face, and I growl out, "Show me what belongs to me."

She whimpers and then flips onto her back, spreading her legs open in a spread-eagle.

"Mmm. I think I should have a little taste," I tell her.

"Yes, Sir. Please, Sir," she keens.

Heather lays on the bed next to Peyton and turns her head to watch us. She empties her hand onto the bed, and her strap and a bottle of lube fall onto the linens. As I lean down to lick into Peyton, I see Heather start to rub at her clit.

I start at Peyton's clit and lick down her slit, thrusting my tongue into her core when I get there. I feel her hands weave into my hair as she bucks up into me. I tongue fuck her until she comes all over my face, and I groan into her center. Her earthy and sweet flavor surrounds my senses.

I pull up to see my girls kissing, Heather's strap-on harnessed to her body. I watch them, stroking my dick until they pull apart. Then Heather is sitting up, slapping my ass, and telling us to scoot up on the bed.

Peyton crawls backward onto the middle pillow, and I follow, crawling on top of her. I kiss her fervently, rubbing the tip of my dick over her clit. She moans for me, and then I'm sliding into that sinful, wet heat.

"Okay, Graham. You know how this goes. You're just on the other end of things this time," Heather coaches me.

"If ya'll can do this, I can do this, pretty girl," I defend.

She smacks my ass. "That's what I like to hear. You're going to love it, baby boy."

I hear the click of a bottle and then feel a finger slide into my ass.

"That's it? This is what I've been so afraid of?" I scoff.

"No, you've been a little bitch about taking my cock. This is just a finger," Heather laughs and strokes in and out of me. Then she hits what I can only imagine is my prostate, and I'm lighting up like Disney World's fireworks show.

"Oh, fuck, Heather. Right there. Shit. Is this what a G-spot feels like?" I pant out.

I feel more pressure, and then I'm being filled with more flesh, so I imagine I'm up to two fingers now. I start fucking into Peyton, which is fucking me back onto

Heather's fingers. I am simultaneously being filled and filling Pey, and the feeling is rapturous. I fuck into Pey, making her moan under me while Heather scissors her fingers in my ass. Then Heather pulls out, and I'm left feeling empty.

"Okay, baby. This is the moment. I'll go slow for you," Heather tells me, and I feel more lube being dribbled onto my ass.

Then I feel a big pressure, and I remember to bear down as Heather pushes her cock into my ass. I pause fucking Peyton and just try to soak in the feel of my cock inside her as Heather pushes more of her cock into my ass. When I feel her pelvis hit my back, I'm so relieved that I've actually done it.

Then she turns the vibrator on, and I groan.

I look down at Peyton, who is watching Heather wide-eyed, pupils blown out with lust. Her hands come to my ass to grab handfuls and spread my cheeks apart.

"You ready for me to move?" Heather asks.

I huff. "Don't go easy on me."

She laughs. "If you fucking say so." Then she starts pounding into me hard, ensuring my body moves inside Peyton.

My brain is absolutely scrambled. My prostate is being pegged by one of the girls I love, my cock is fucking into the other, and the sensations are short-circuiting my thought process. I'm being spun up faster than the rinse cycle on the washing machine. In the middle of all the pleasure, a thought slips by. Am I into pegging? But everything is moving too quickly for me to reach out and grasp the thought and turn it over in my hands. I'm too high for words and definitely too high to participate more than the passive amount that I'm currently performing.

Peyton must realize I'm too far gone to be of much use

because she licks a finger and slides it between our bodies so she can rub at her clit. I feel her cunt clench around me, and that, combined with the cock dragging over my P-spot, has me unraveling, filling Peyton's pussy with the most cum I've ever managed to create in one sitting. The orgasm lingers, little aftershocks that have me releasing trace amounts of cum into Peyton as Heather continues to pound into me.

Peyton squeezes my cock like a vise as she comes, and then I feel Heather's teeth sink into my shoulder as she comes too.

I collapse onto Peyton's body, cock still ensconced inside her, as Heather pulls her dick out of me.

"Safe to say that went well," I hear Heather say.

I groan in response. "Fuck, I'll never be the same again."

"So we can do that again? You took my cock so well, baby. That was the hottest you've ever been," Heather praises.

"I feel like we can save it for special occasions. God, Heather. The way you fuck is insane," I moan.

"You're not the only athlete floating around here, you know. I keep it tight," Heather preens.

"Do I get the aftercare now? I feel all floaty," I explain to them. "Not that I don't get aftercare usually. But I need bottom aftercare, not top aftercare right now."

Peyton pets my hair. "Of course, you get aftercare, Sir. Whatever you need."

"Little sister, can you just keep petting me? That feels so good," I ask of her.

"Yes, Sir," she agrees. "I agree with Heather, by the way. You looked so hot taking her."

"Mmm. I'm glad you enjoyed that, fucktoy." I nuzzle into her neck. "Now you know what to ask to put on your Christmas list."

"It's only Easter!" She argues.

"I said what I said," I parry.

"Yeah, okay. We'll see about that," Heather cuts in. "You're gonna crave it now just like little freak does. Even more than her. But you can protest your way to the bath. Let's get you settled between us, and I'll iron out some of your knots." She holds out a hand to me, and I take it, getting up from the bed and holding a hand out to Peyton.

They tote me to the bath, where I'm a Graham sandwich between the two most incredible women I've ever met in my life, and where I listen to them chat while I think about how we got here from one seemingly ill-fated brush in a high school hallway.

ACKNOWLEDGEMENTS

Thank you to my alpha reader and the other half of my soul, Catherine Jauch. I am so different now than when I was writing all those manuscripts that will never see the light of day, but the biggest thing that changed was that I had you. You were my sounding board, my reassurance, my biggest critic, my editor, my positivity, my raison d'etre. You truly get me on a cellular level. As the founding member of my fan club, I wrote this entire book for you (minus one scene that made you squirm and I'm sorry but it's for the good of the realm, Peaches).

Thank you to my beta readers, many of whom happen to be the besties. Ciara Godina, my love, my soulmate, you're truly stuck with me. I meant it that day in the barracks when I told you (grumpy, mean, sarcastic) that we would be best friends. Nearly 16 years later, several long-distance scenarios, and a couple of marriages later, we endure. I won't stop my assault on you to make you move closer to me, but I will promise to always make you a priority no matter what city we find ourselves in. Brittney Thigpen, thank you for being my smut buddy in book club and forcing me to do things like book a spontaneous trip to Paris. I can't wait to see where the years take us. R.M. Bellamy, who I was also convinced right away would be my BFF (I swear, this isn't a normal problem of mine… Okay. It is. When you know, you know!), who has been known to talk me off book-related ledges, and who made the grand gesture of flying down to Orlando to edit this book with me. Savannah Durham (but to me you will always be Toastie), who is proof that the internet can garner you some good friends. Thank you for being my hype girl. Ashley Sette, who gave me the idea for *If Not Autumn, Fragments of Sam,* and who I had faith could give me some good input on this book.

Thank you to my best friends (some who might never read this) who are always in my corner. Micayla Kiepert, my lifelong best friend but really my sister. We are as alike as we are different. You drive me ten types of crazy. And I never want to know what life feels like without you. Blake Hardin, the only man I've ever trusted point-blank. The original model for what a straight cishet man is supposed to be. They broke the mold when they made you. Jeremy Butler, my favorite Chief. I know you are always in my corner and rooting for me, and I hope you know that I am happy to be the same for you. Sean Day, who I can always count on to make me laugh in times of stress. It's your superpower even when sometimes I have to yell at you to be serious. Melissa Kramer, who is one of the safest places to land I have ever met. Lauren McDaniel, who is my favorite zoomer. I can't wait to travel the world with you. Alia DeLong, who has become one of the most important people in my life despite her dislike of Nesta (but you do love Aiden, so I'll guess we will look beyond it).

Thank you to my mama, Kimberly Susan Smith. In a parallel universe, you are my Regina. I'm so glad we got a chance to fix us and be who we are today. We are unconventional, misunderstood to many, but together we are perfect. Thank you for accepting me for who I am and growing with me.

Thank you to my therapist, Sandra Banjoko. Did you think I'd forget about you? Sandra, I could only get so far alone. But through you challenging me and encouraging me, I have managed to make a better life. When I told you I had put this book on pre-order, we talked about how in our first session I had told you that I would know I was getting better if I started writing again. And here I am, finishing a whole entire book. I didn't just "start writing again." I fulfilled a lifelong goal.

Thank you to Charly, for giving me a gorgeous cover and interior. I can't wait to work with you again!

And finally, thank you to whomever you are reading this. Thank you for taking the chance on an indie author and supporting me and this small (v smol) subgenre. I hope it made you feel something positive.

STALK ME!

Website
https://www.alexlabruyerebooks.com/

Goodreads
https://www.goodreads.com/author/show/46984137.
Alex_La_Bruyere

Instagram
https://instagram.com/
alexlabruyereauthor?igshid=OGQ5ZDc2ODk2ZA==

Facebook
https://m.facebook.com/groups/1405990146625766/

TikTok
https://www.tiktok.com/@alexlabruyereauthor?_
t=8fxvkjn4lh0&_r=1

Please leave me a review on Storygraph, Goodreads,
Amazon, etc. if you would be so kind. Indie authors
thrive off of reviews! And just a friendly reminder that
if you choose to post a negative review, I would not like
to be tagged in those reviews on socials. *I'm just a girl*
whose mental health is precarious. XOXO

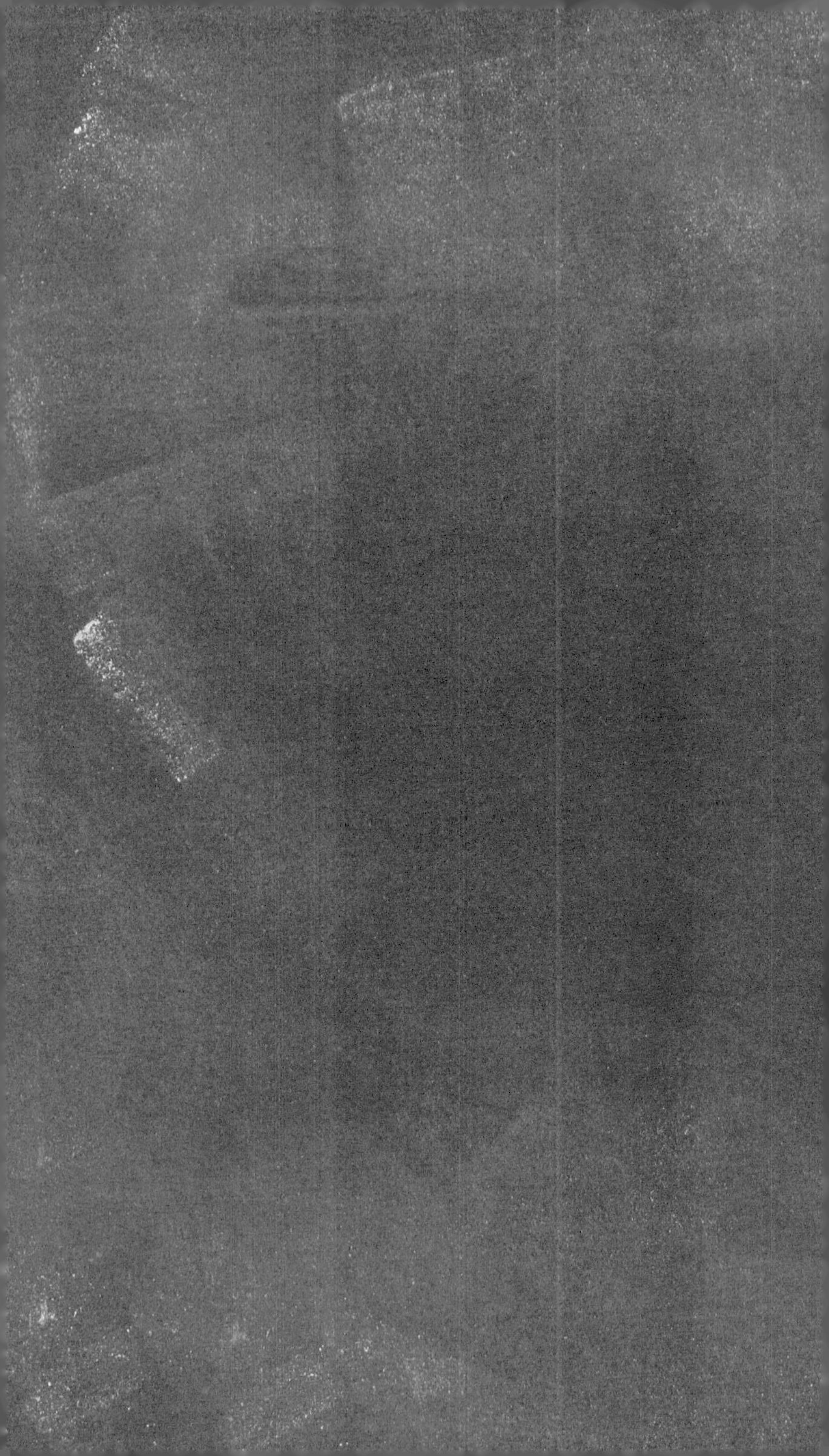

ABOUT THE AUTHOR

Alex La Bruyere is retired Navy, so if you're reading her books: Congratulations. You're officially a patriot. She's been writing ever since someone put a pencil in one hand and a book in the other. She believes in hedonism and will absolutely recommend you take the day off to read that book you've been meaning to read. Her books are poly, queer, and kinky only because she herself is poly, queer, and kinky. She wants you to live your best smutty life, whether that's through fiction or if it translates to the real world.